"McQuade, leave me alone."

Tory backed away quickly, bumped into the wall
and came to a sudden stop. McQuade loomed
over her, shutting out the world. She slowly
raised her eyes to his, dreading what she might
find there.

"Maybe I don't want to leave you alone," he
murmured, one hand going out to rest on the wall
behind her. "Maybe I want to kiss you."

She swallowed painfully, her heartbeat
accelerating. "McQuade, I have to go."

She turned to go but he reached out and took her
arm. She let herself be drawn back against the
wall, let his hand remain on her arm. She was
acutely aware of him as he moved his hand slowly
up and down her arm, creating an erotic friction
that made her pulses pound.

"What are you really afraid of, Tory?"
he murmured.

"The storm," she breathed.

"Which storm? The one outside . . . or the one
in here?"

ABOUT THE AUTHOR

Katherine Ransom loves to while away weekends at New England country inns and loves to visit Cape Cod. Her delight in the region comes through in *Come Fly With Me,* which is set in and around Nantucket. This is her debut with Harlequin American Romance, though she is no stranger to romance, having written many love stories under the name Katherine Granger. Katherine makes her home in Connecticut with her cat, Barnaby, and her dog, Samantha.

KATHERINE RANSOM

COME FLY WITH ME

Harlequin Books

TORONTO • NEW YORK • LONDON
AMSTERDAM • PARIS • SYDNEY • HAMBURG
STOCKHOLM • ATHENS • TOKYO • MILAN

This book is dedicated to John Mogerman, M.D.,
with affection and gratitude.

Published September 1991

ISBN 0-373-16408-4

COME FLY WITH ME

Chapter One

Cargo McQuade sat with his feet on his battered wooden desk, staring balefully into the future. Taking a swig of beer, he sighed and pushed his sweat-darkened baseball cap back on his head.

"Women," he muttered disgustedly. "Who needs 'em."

Looking around at his office, he groaned out loud. It was a mess. Empty doughnut boxes, opened crates and piles of old newspapers cluttered every surface. Airplane parts and greasy rags littered the floor. On his desk, a half-dozen half-empty coffee cups grew a bumper crop of mold.

Sighing, he took another swig of his beer and wiped the back of his hand over his mouth. He had blunt fingers with short nails and airplane-engine grease ground into the knuckles.

Something had to change. His office was a disaster, his business was running in the red and he was sick of trying to fly his battered plane on empty.

He'd thought if he just got a secretary, he could keep going. She would simply walk in here and straighten up his office and somehow, magically, everything would be all right. With his office in order and his books finally balanced, he'd assumed everything else in his helter-skelter life would fall into place.

Only trouble was, he couldn't find a secretary who'd stay longer than a day. They came, took one look at the mess and invariably turned on their heels and left. Just today it had happened again. That's why he was sitting here drinking beer when he should have been working.

Finishing his beer, he crumpled the can in his large hand and swiveled toward the wastebasket. Squinting, he eyed the basketball hoop hanging on the wall over the wastebasket. Taking careful aim, he threw the can toward the hoop. It hurtled through the air in a leisurely arc, twisting and turning and catching the rays of the sun in its flight so that it became not a beer can but a dazzling rocket, a missile sent on a holy mission, the vehicle of all McQuade's hopes and dreams. He watched it swish through the net and for an exultant moment felt that success had visited yet again. But when the can landed precisely in the center of the wastebasket, so did all his dreams.

"Two points," he said, shaking his head at himself. "Is that all you've got to show for yourself?"

Outside, his twenty-five-year-old plane sat on the concrete landing strip, a bull's-eye painted on one side and the words Tough Luck Airlines on the other. The plane was as bedraggled and woebegone as his office. What he really needed, he realized, was a challenge. Chartered flights required no expertise. Shipping freight was deadly boring. Ferrying an occasional passenger between Cape Cod and Nantucket or Martha's Vineyard had become mechanical and monotonous. His life was predictable, dull and boring. He needed something to liven it up.

The shrill ringing of the phone interrupted his thoughts. He stared at it, wondering what Vineyard grocer would be on the other end, trying to wheedle the lowest price to ship fresh fruit to the island. For a minute he was tempted to get up and walk out. He'd like nothing better than to get in his plane and fly out of sight, over the horizon, just fly until he'd reached the limits of space. Then he remembered the stack of bills waiting to be paid. Like it or not, responsibility had been drummed into him from childhood.

Muttering a low curse, he reached for the phone. "Tough Luck," he said. "McQuade speaking."

"Mr. McQuade?" a frail, hesitant voice said. "This is Sister Theresa. I'm calling from a convent in Brockton."

McQuade held the phone out from his ear. A nun? He'd find it easier to believe a Martian was on the other end. "What can I do for you, Sister?" His boyhood training came back to him. Suddenly he was eight years old, sitting up straight in his navy blue trousers, white shirt, bow tie and maroon jacket, in the high-ceilinged classroom at St. Pat's that had always smelled of chalk dust, orange peels and stale heated air.

"We need an angel of mercy..." the soft voice said.

He rubbed his two-day growth of beard and looked bleakly around the office. They weren't likely to find any angels around here. "What exactly do you mean, Sister?"

"Well, about a year ago we had a wonderful donation, but we haven't been able to use it..."

"Uh-huh." He took out a cigar and began to chew on it. Damned if he cared about some silly donation. He supposed they were going to hit him up for some money. Well, the laugh was on them; he didn't have enough money to pay a parking ticket.

"You see," Sister Theresa continued, "we were given an island..."

He stared at the junk on his desk. "An island," he repeated, not really paying much attention. "Is that so?"

"Yes, that's right." Sister Theresa began to giggle. "Isn't that wonderful?"

"Terrific," he said sarcastically.

"It is! And we've been trying to think of how we could use it. First we thought it would be wonderful to build a retreat house, but of course we don't have that kind of money."

Uh-oh, he thought, here it comes, the solicitation of funds.

"But then we got an even better idea..."

"You did."

"Yes. We thought it would make a wonderful place for homeless young people. You know, the ones who get in trouble and need to get off drugs and that sort of thing..."

"Uh-huh."

"But of course we don't have any way to get to and from the island. We couldn't very well ask the children to swim there, could we?"

"Why not?" he said dryly. "Might be good exercise for 'em."

Sister Theresa giggled. "Mr. McQuade, you have a wonderful sense of humor."

He rolled his eyes. How in heaven's name had they gotten his name? Was God punishing him for his mistakes?

"Anyway, Mr. McQuade, the bishop has been just wonderful. Somehow he's managed to come up with the money to renovate the old buildings, but our biggest problem remains—how to get the children there."

"Where is this island?"

"Near the Elizabeth Islands, off Woods Hole. It's just a small place, no more than a few square miles, but it's lovely in the summer. We thought we'd teach the kids to grow produce—you know, fresh tomatoes, corn, squash, green beans. And there's a wonderful young man who wants to teach them to work with leather, like repairing shoes and making leather belts and handbags. And his wife is a weaver, so she's going to teach them to weave. And we've got plans for all kinds of other classes, where they'll learn valuable skills—sewing and bricklaying and carpentry—the kinds of things they can use to support themselves with when they finally leave the island."

"Uh-huh. Sounds great." He scratched his chin and wondered when the pitch would come.

"Well, it is—unless, of course, we can't find a way to get the kids out to the island."

Then he realized why Sister Theresa had called. She didn't want money; she wanted him to fly a bunch of juvenile delinquents to her island.

As if she'd realized he'd just caught on, she started the sales pitch: "It wouldn't take much of your time, Mr. McQuade. Just a flight to the island on Saturdays to drop off a group of children and pick up the few who're ready to leave."

"How many kids?" he asked warily.

"Oh, not all that many. Maybe twenty-five at the most."

"Sister, my plane's not big enough to fly twenty-five kids at one time."

"You could always make two trips, couldn't you?" she asked shyly.

Two trips from Brockton to some godforsaken island off the Cape. Didn't she know what the fuel alone would cost, not to mention the wear and tear?

"I'd have to charge around twenty bucks per person. Could you afford that?"

There was a short silence, then Sister Theresa nervously cleared her throat. "Oh, dear, I think there's a bit of a misunderstanding..."

"A misunderstanding."

"Yes..." she said hesitantly. "You see, Mr. McQuade, we couldn't actually afford to pay. Uh...we were hoping you could donate your services..."

He would have laughed, but that wouldn't have been polite. He shook his head. "Sister, I'm in business to make money, not give it away, and right about now there isn't a way on God's green earth that I could donate anything, much less my services."

"I see..." Disappointment radiated in Sister Theresa's voice. McQuade tried to ignore it. He hated to admit it, but he had a soft spot somewhere under his tough hide.

"I'm sorry, Sister. I can't help you."

"Oh, dear. I'm so sorry to hear that. You see, when I saw the name of your airline in the yellow pages, something just drew me to it. I had this very distinct feeling—intuition, perhaps—that you were the one who was going to help us."

"Well, I'm sorry, Sister, but you were wrong."

He could almost hear her shaking her head. "No, I don't think I was. I still have this very strong sense that you're the one I was supposed to call."

Oh, Lord. Now she was invoking higher powers on him. He slid lower in his chair and chewed on his cigar. "You must have gotten your signals crossed, Sister. Right about now, I'm the one who could use the help."

"Yes," she said gently, "I can sense that, Mr. McQuade. I tell you what, I'll pray very hard for the next week or so and see if I can't get you that help you need."

He felt a strange mix of emotions well up in him—sadness and gratitude and something that felt an awful lot like love, but it couldn't have been, because he didn't believe in love. But mostly what he felt was hopelessness. Nothing was going to change in his life unless his own angel of mercy appeared from nowhere, and that wasn't very likely.

"Thanks, Sister," he said tiredly. "I can use all the prayers I can get."

"Bless you, Mr. McQuade. We'll just see what we can work out."

He almost smiled. "Good luck, Sister. I'm sure there's someone else who can help you out."

"We'll see, Mr. McQuade," she said cheerfully. "I hope to speak with you again soon."

Not likely, he thought, but he wasn't going to argue with a nun. "Goodbye, Sister."

"Good day, Mr. McQuade."

He hung up and sat staring at the phone, wondering why a fabulous blonde couldn't call requesting his services. He'd find a way of handling that kind of request.

The thought was no sooner out than the phone rang again. He yanked the receiver off its perch and snarled: "Tough Luck, McQuade here."

"Mr. McQuade? Cargo McQuade?"

The woman's voice was low and pleasant. Cultured. Not the usual dame who called McQuade all hours of the night and day.

"That's me," he said, scratching his beard. "Who wants to know?"

"Daddy said you were a miserable excuse for a man," the woman said. "It appears he was right."

"Who's Daddy?"

"General Adrian LaPorte," the woman answered. "Ring any bells?"

"Old Iron Ass?" McQuade sat up. The old man had been McQuade's commanding officer in Nam. He'd been tough, mean and ornery, but a braver man never lived. "You the general's daughter?"

"As sure as he's still Old Iron Ass."

"How is he?" McQuade asked, his husky voice softening slightly. The only time he got sentimental was about his old comrades in Nam.

She hesitated. "He's been ill recently, but he's doing fine now. He misses active duty. He predicts you do, too."

"He turn to crystal-ball gazing now that the war's over?"

She laughed, a pleasant sound, low and soft and musical, with just the slightest bit of huskiness. A shiver went along McQuade's spine, and the hairs on the back of his neck stood up. Right then he knew she'd be beautiful. A woman couldn't sound that good and not be.

"Daddy said you'd be ornery," she said. "I like that in a man. If there's one thing I can't stand, it's a pushover for a pretty face."

"And I'll bet you have a very pretty face," he said.

"So I've been told."

He slid lower in his chair. He could picture her now—tall and blond, with a face that spelled money and a body that spelled sex. But with his recent luck, she wouldn't offer him the kind of deal he was hoping for. She probably had her own charity in mind.

"All right, lady. What do *you* want me to do? Deliver Girl Scout cookies to the Eskimos?"

"Mr. McQuade, my father tells me you're in financial difficulty. If I were you, I wouldn't treat this call as if it was a joke. I'd pay well. Are you interested in listening or not?"

"I'm listening."

"Good."

"So tell me about the job."

She hesitated. "It's rather delicate, I'm afraid. I think it would be better to talk to you in person."

"Great. When's the meeting going to take place? I'm free all day. Business is slow right now."

"From what I've heard, Mr. McQuade, business is slow most of the time."

"If you know all about me, why'd you bother to call?"

"Daddy said you were the man for me. He said you were the best damn pilot in all of Vietnam. Those are words of high praise from my father. As you probably remember, he doesn't give compliments lightly."

"As I remember it," McQuade drawled, "he didn't give compliments at all." He paused. "It is Miss LaPorte?"

"No, it's Tory Britton. I was married once, when I was quite young. I kept my married name."

"Tory Britton?" He shuffled through the extraordinary clutter in his brain. For some reason, the name sounded familiar, but he couldn't put his finger on why. "What do you do?"

"I'm a free-lance photographer."

Then he remembered. Tory Britton was the name on half the photographs he had plastered on his bedroom wall at home. She specialized in nature photography, particularly on Cape Cod and the islands. There was a stark beauty about her work that reminded him of Japanese art. Most of the women photographers he knew took cutesy pictures of kids on the beach eating ice cream or sunsets over the water.

"I know you now," he said. "I always thought you were a man."

She laughed that musical laugh. "Are you disappointed to find out I'm not?"

"No, just surprised."

Her voice took on an ironic tinge. "Don't tell me you're one of those men who think women can't do anything but stay home and have babies."

He grinned. "Sorry, I'm not usually sexist."

"Uh-huh," she said knowingly. "I'll bet your wife does all the cooking, doesn't she?"

"It would be nice," McQuade said, grinning to himself as he rocked back in his chair. "But let's get back to business. Just exactly what is this job you want me to do? Maybe I won't want it."

"Daddy says you will."

"Maybe Daddy's wrong."

"He's never wrong."

"For a pretty lady, you sound awful tough."

"Comes from being Old Iron Ass's daughter."

"Mmm," he said noncommittally. "I'll bet it does."

"So? When shall we meet? Can I come to your office late this afternoon?"

He looked around and knew this wasn't the place to meet her. She might know he needed money, but she didn't have to know how much. "Why don't we meet for dinner? That okay with you?"

She seemed to be consulting her calendar. Probably filled with high-paying assignments. "That'll be fine. How about six o'clock at Blackie's? If I leave Boston before five, I can get to Hyannis by then."

He raised an eyebrow. Blackie's wasn't his usual hangout. It was top-of-the-line—low lighting, expensive food on elegant bone china, crisp white linen and a cocktail lounge with a sleek grand piano where a sexy woman in red sequins sang old Cole Porter songs.

"Don't worry, Mr. McQuade," she said into the silence. "I'll pick up the check."

He might not have a lot of money, but he didn't like it when a woman paid for his meal. "I'm not on welfare yet, Ms. Britton. Why don't we split it?"

"Good," she said, and hung up before he could speak. He slammed down the receiver and pushed out of his chair. Damn it, she might be more successful than he, but she didn't have to flaunt it. Kicking a box out of the way, he strode out of his office and headed for the tarmac. There was only one thing he wanted right now—to be up there in his plane, soaring over everything, free and alone, the temporary baron of the sky.

"WELL?" ADRIAN LAPORTE said. "What'd he say?"

Tory turned to find her father in the doorway, his once proud body stooped in his wheelchair, his face gaunt and pale. His illness never failed to startle her. In her mind, her father was still the lean, proud man with the posture of a lifelong soldier and the eyes of an eagle. This man in the wheelchair wearing a baggy, misbuttoned cardigan couldn't be her father.

But a stroke had felled him two years ago, and his once strong legs were now thin, useless under the plaid blanket that lay over them.

"He said he'd meet me."

The general let out a deep sigh. "Thank God. Now we've just got to make sure he'll go."

"Don't get your hopes up too soon, Dad," she said, swinging his chair around. "Come on, I'll take you back to your study."

"Hogwash," he said, but he didn't shake off her hand as he might have years ago. He let her take him back to the study where a fire burned in the fireplace, even on this mild June day.

When he was settled in the wheelchair in front of the fire, Tory took a seat on the ottoman at his feet.

"Well?" he said, his once powerful voice peevish. "What else did he say?"

"He said he'd meet me. I didn't tell him why I wanted to hire him."

The general looked into the fire, his eyes filled with the old certainty. Determination made his jaw jut out. He looked like a sad caricature of the man he had once been. "He'll go," he said, nodding to himself. "He'll go."

"Maybe he won't want to," Tory said gently.

The old man grunted. "He needs money. He'll go."

"Dad, everything isn't that simple. He's got a business, and that means obligations. Maybe he's married with a couple of kids. He might not be able to go."

The old man snorted. "Men like McQuade don't get married. They sleep with whoever they want, then move on." The old man darted a shrewd look at his daughter. "Now, if it's a *real* man you're looking for, McQuade's just the ticket."

"Dad, there's only one man I'm interested in—you know that."

"That pantywaist politician?" The general snorted again. "Daniel Sullivan can't hold a candle to a man like McQuade."

"Dad, we've been through this before. I know you don't care for Daniel, but I do. Let's just drop the subject."

The general's jaw jutted out farther and his eyes took on a stubborn glint. "I can't tell you how to live, Tory, but I can tell you one thing—I know men. I've worked with 'em all my life. I'll say this one time and that will be it—Daniel

Sullivan isn't worth the spit it'd take to polish him up and bring him home to meet me."

"You stubborn old man," Tory said, her voice quivering with anger. "You're determined to break up Daniel and me. It doesn't matter that I love him. Nothing matters but getting your way." Her green eyes flared. "Well, you can talk against him all you want, but you're not going to get me to change my mind about him."

"I won't tell you I approve of someone when I don't. If that's what you want from me, you'll never get it."

"I want your blessing, Dad, even if you can't give me your approval."

The old man's mouth tightened into a thin line. He sat resolutely staring into the fire. "Sometimes I can't believe you're my own daughter. How can you be taken in by that smooth line he feeds you?"

"It's not a line," she said firmly. "He loves me."

"When you meeting McQuade?" her father asked, abruptly changing the subject.

"Tonight."

The general had already forgotten Daniel. He was lost in his own thoughts, fretting over the one thing he wanted above all else. "Vietnam's only been open to travelers a couple of years. It's too dangerous for you to go alone. Dammit, we need McQuade. You can't go over there without him."

"I'll do my best, Dad, but I can't control what he does or says."

"Bull." The general's eyes were cold. In their depths were the echoes of wars, battles and carnage, when he had resolutely refused to give in to the forces that threatened to annihilate him. He leaned toward his daughter, all the old force burning in his eyes. "You will succeed, Tory. You will convince McQuade to go with you to Vietnam and bring back my son!"

She stared at her father, a welter of emotions churning inside her. All her life she'd wanted only one thing—his love—but for some unknowable reason, all she got was his disapproval, his chiding, his disappointment. She couldn't please him, no matter how hard she tried. Now he was determined that she go to Vietnam and bring back a son whose existence he'd kept a secret until just a few weeks ago.

She got up and walked to a window and stood looking out at the carefully manicured lawn. Half a world away, she had a brother. It was still difficult to accept, yet her father was pushing her to go to Vietnam and bring him back with her. How ironic life was. If she went to Vietnam and brought back the general's long-lost son, she might lose any chance of ever gaining her father's love. This Vietnamese boy had become his obsession. If she brought him back, would her father shower all his love on him? Would she remain forever in the background, forgotten and unseen by the man she loved so much?

She suppressed a sigh and turned around. Her father was dozing. She felt her heart swell with love as she gazed down at him. She would do anything for him, even if it meant she'd be replaced in his life. Up until now, she'd satisfied herself with being her father's only child. Now she didn't even have that to hold on to.

Her father woke with a start and met her gaze. "Well?" he growled. "What are you waiting for? Christmas? Dammit, I want to see my son!"

"Dad," she said resignedly, "I'll do my best."

The general's eyes darted back and forth, as if he were watching something on the screen of his mind. "You'll see McQuade tonight?"

Her heart fell. It was all he thought about, the only thing that seemed to matter to him. "Yes, Dad, I'll see him tonight."

"Good. Then you'll be leaving with him soon."

"I'll tell him what I want, but that doesn't mean he'll be willing to go back."

"He'll go," he said, twisting his hands in his lap. "He'll have to." His hands looked like two giant spiders, locked together in mortal combat. He looked around the room, as if he were lost in a place he'd never seen before. "I want to see my son, Tory," he said plaintively. "Before I die, I want to see my son!"

Her heart swelled with pain. Tears glistened in her eyes. "Then we'll bring him back for you," she whispered, her heart breaking as she watched him. "We'll bring him back to you. I swear it, Daddy."

But the general didn't hear her. He sat looking out the window, his eyes blazing once again, his chin raised defiantly. "You'll go to Vietnam," he said coldly, "and bring me back my son. Now get out and leave me alone. Dammit, Tory, you treat me like I'm a cripple!"

She almost smiled. How like him, to look at reality and refuse to face the facts. Gently she leaned down and kissed him on the cheek. "See you later, Dad."

He brushed away her words and roughly pulled a magazine off a table, flipping the pages furiously. "I'm glad you're going," he said gruffly. "Don't come back until you've got an answer from McQuade."

"Any answer?" she said flippantly. "Or just the one you want?"

"Yes is the only answer I'll accept," her father snapped.

She smiled cheerfully and closed the door behind her, then seemed to slump. All the spirit went out of her. She rested her head against the door, tears glittering in her eyes, then roused herself.

Straightening her shoulders, she wiped the tears from her eyes. Someday perhaps her father might actually see her instead of looking through her to whatever else it was that mattered more than she did. Right now, what mattered more than his daughter was his son. And because she loved him, she'd do everything she could to bring that son back to him. But once, just once, she wished he'd open his eyes and see *her*.

She raised her chin defiantly. She might not be a son, but dammit, she was every inch her father's child. Determined, she set out for Hyannis.

Chapter Two

McQuade wasn't prepared for Tory Britton. He'd envisioned a sexy dame with blond hair in a low-cut dress, but when she walked through the door of Blackie's, she wasn't what he'd expected at all. Still, she had a way of making it all seem better than he could have imagined. She had thick shoulder-length auburn hair brushed back from a face that was nothing short of spectacular. She had wide-spaced green eyes, long black lashes, and a straight no-nonsense nose. Thank goodness for that. He hated little turned-up noses.

She wore a pair of form-fitting jeans and a light jacket of buttery soft suede over a white silk shirt. She was classy, cool and sophisticated, with a girl's slim figure that looked every bit like a woman's.

He sat and watched her as she stood in the doorway of the cocktail lounge. Many women would have been uncomfortable, but not Tory Britton. She looked completely at ease, even though half a dozen men were devouring her with their eyes.

He wondered how long it would take her to figure out who he was. Probably not long. Even though he'd taken the time to shower and change, he was still the only man here in khaki pants, white shirt, and a shabby leather bomber jacket. He looked so out of place, he was surprised they'd let him in.

Evidently he didn't surprise Tory Britton. When she saw him a look came over her face that said she'd been expecting someone disreputable and he hadn't disappointed her any.

"Mr. McQuade?"

He stood up. "That's right."

She let him pull out her chair. When he sat down across from her, he got the full effect of her beauty. It was a bit like looking into the sun; she dazzled him. It wasn't all makeup, either. Her skin was as fresh as morning and her hair bounced with vitality. No doubt about it, she was a world-class beauty.

"Well," she said, looking him over, "here we are."

"Yes, ma'am."

She gazed at him a minute, as if making her mind up about him, then hailed a waitress. "I'll have a martini," she said when the waitress arrived. "Straight up. Extremely dry."

"We'll wring it out and hang it on the line, sweetie," the waitress said, looking at McQuade with a knowing smile. "And what about you, honey? Anything I can get you?" Her faded eyes seemed to know everything about him. Her smile told him she approved of him anyway.

"I could use another beer."

"For you, honey? Anything."

He smiled. It was like that a lot. For some reason, women liked him. Maybe it was the gleam in his eyes or the way his mouth was usually quirked in a half smile. Whatever it was, it worked...at least on every woman but Tory Britton. When he looked up, he found her watching him with amused eyes.

"My father said you had a way with women," she said wryly. "It appears he was right."

McQuade ignored the statement. It wasn't the kind that required an answer. "So how is the general? You said he's been ill."

Her face changed. The amusement left and she became serious. "My father had a stroke two years ago," she said. "Right after he retired from the army. He's better now, but he's permanently confined to a wheelchair." She smiled slowly, and it was like watching the sun come out from behind a cloud. "Of course, he's as cussed as ever. I doubt that'll ever change."

"It's hard to believe the general stuck in a wheelchair. He was the most vital man I've ever known. I never figured out when he slept. I never saw him sleep the whole time we were there. He was as tough as old boots." He stared at the tabletop, trying to assimilate this new knowledge.

"He still is," she said softly.

He looked up. She was smiling but her eyes were sad.

"I'm sorry," he said.

"Thanks." Her smile widened. "Just don't let him hear you feeling sorry for him. He doesn't like it. He's liable to hit you with his cane."

"His cane?"

She laughed. "He's bound and determined to get out of that wheelchair someday and walk. He had me buy him a cane. Of course, the only thing he uses it for is to pound on the floor when he wants something."

"Still demanding as ever," McQuade said, grinning.

"Moreso, I'm afraid."

"Is this why you called me? To tell me about your dad?"

"I called you because my father said you could help me."

"Help you do what?"

She hesitated. "I'd rather not go into details right now. I need to ask you a few questions first."

He shrugged. "Fire away," he said, "I've got all night."

"The job I'm thinking of offering you would require being away for at least a week, maybe longer. Is this something you could manage?"

He tilted his head and considered her. What the hell kind of job would require him to leave for a week? "Depends on how much I'd be paid."

"Then you wouldn't mind leaving the Cape for a while?"

"Leaving the Cape?" He put his elbow on the table and rubbed his chin thoughtfully. What the hell was she up to? "I suppose it would depend on where I'd have to go."

"Your business wouldn't be a problem?"

"I'm my own boss. I don't have any regularly scheduled flights. Just happens that business is slow right now." He studied her with calculating eyes. "If I wanted to, I could leave for a while."

"Do you have a wife, McQuade? Any girlfriends?"

"No girlfriends," he said. "And I never married."

"Is there anyone who'd miss you if you dropped off the face of the earth a week or two?"

He remembered Polly, the woman who'd lived with him last year, but he thrust her out of his mind. "There might be a couple who'd miss me, but none who'd have any claim on me."

"And if they haven't got any claim, they don't matter, is that it?" she asked wryly.

He bristled at the implied criticism but kept his voice level. "Something like that."

"So you're the strong, silent type who doesn't get involved?"

McQuade toyed with his beer, studying it with unreadable eyes. "What's it to you?"

"I'm just curious."

"Don't be."

"I used to be a reporter, McQuade. I can't help it if I still like to ask questions."

"Why? You thinking of doing a story on me?"

"No, I just need to know something about you if I decide to offer you the job."

"And if I decide to accept it."

"You'll accept it," she said.

"You sound damn sure of yourself."

"No, but my father is. As you may remember, my father thinks he knows everything. To him, that's all that matters."

He chuckled to himself. That was the general, all right. "So when do we get around to talking about this job of yours?"

"In a while..." She drew figures on the linen tablecloth with her perfectly manicured nail, her face a picture of concentration. She looked up at him. "Do you think we could work together?"

"Depends on the job, I guess." He smiled lazily. "You gonna tell me about it sometime soon?"

"It's not a job, really..."

He pushed back his chair and folded his arms. "Great. Just what I need—a chance to play guessing games. Can you give me a clue, or we gonna sit here all night and play Twenty Questions?"

Her green eyes flared with anger. "If my father didn't insist you were the man for the job, McQuade, I wouldn't give you a minute's consideration."

"I'm flattered. So what are we talking here, Ms. Britton? Flying you to Martha's Vineyard some weekend, or testing the stealth bomber?"

"It's not as much a job as a request...."

Exasperated, he scraped his hand through his hair. "Okay, lady, let's have it. Just what the hell do you want me to do?"

She sat and looked him straight in the eye. "I want you to go to Vietnam with me."

Stunned, he sat and stared at her. "You *what?*" Her simple statement felt like the verbal equivalent of a well-placed bomb.

"I want you to go with me to Vietnam. Daddy says you know it like the back of your hand. He says you'd be able to help me find—'' She broke off. She didn't want to tip her hand too soon.

McQuade stared at her, even as he tried to block out all thoughts of Vietnam. But he couldn't stop them. The word echoed in his ears, bringing with it the sounds of bamboo clattering in the wind, of choppers cutting the air and incoming mortars exploding in the night. Shouts and laughter and the high-pitched screams of women and children mixed together in uneasy juxtaposition.

In an instant he was back there, where the air was so muggy it smothered you, and your body was sticky with sweat and invisible bugs sucked your blood. Vietnam, a schizophrenic mixture of rock and roll, screams and gunfire, an exotic place filled with people who watched you with fear or hope or hate, where soldiers marched in weary ranks, thinking of home and longing for love.

He pushed back his chair and stood up. "I'm sorry, Ms. Britton. I'm not your man." He turned on his heel and left.

Tory flung down some money for their tab and hurried after him. She caught up with him halfway to his truck. "McQuade, give me a chance to talk to you."

"Find someone else, lady. I'm not your man."

"My father says you are."

"Your father's wrong."

"McQuade, *please...*" She put a hand on his arm. He stopped in his tracks and looked down at it, slender and soft and ghostly pale in the twilight of Cape Cod. For a minute it was another woman's hand. He felt an unfamiliar twist in his gut. A name floated back to him, through twenty years' efforts to forget... Mai.

He shook off Tory Britton's hand and yanked open the door to his dilapidated pickup. "Forget it, Ms. Britton. Find someone else."

"I'd pay well."

"You couldn't pay me enough."

"I'd pay anything you wanted."

"You can't buy me, Ms. Britton. I'm not for sale. Now, get out of my way. I'm leaving."

"McQuade, don't go."

He turned and flashed an angry look at her. "Why me, lady? What've *I* got no other man has?"

She met his gaze with unwavering eyes. "You have my father's trust."

As quickly as it had come, his anger melted. It drained out of him like sand running out of an hourglass. "I'm sorry," he said tiredly, "but I can't help you."

For a second she seemed defeated, then she rallied. "I'm going to Nantucket this weekend for a week's vacation. I had made reservations for a flight out of Boston, but there's no reason you couldn't take me, is there?"

"You're not going to give up, are you?" he asked softly. "You're going to keep bugging me till you think I'll give in and go with you."

"Look, Mr. McQuade, I need to get to Nantucket. You fly planes. Isn't it logical that I hire you to take me?"

"Not if you've already made reservations on another airline."

"Stop thinking about me and think of yourself for a change." She rubbed her fingers together. "Money, Mr. McQuade. Filthy lucre. I'd pay you double what you'd normally charge."

He kicked at a stone, then looked up at her. "Okay. On one condition."

"Name it."

"You don't even mention Vietnam."

She hesitated, then shrugged. "Okay. It's a deal." Taking out a business card, she hastily scribbled a number on the back. "I'll be at my boyfriend's place. This is his number, if you have to reach me. I'll meet you at the airstrip Friday afternoon." She tucked the card in his shirt pocket and patted it. "See you then." Turning, she headed for her car.

Watching her walk away, McQuade had a sudden intuition of what she'd feel like in his arms. Her body would be taut, her skin soft, her breath as fresh as spring. When he kissed her, her lips would be as sweet as honey. Suddenly he didn't want her to get away.

"Nice car," he called after her, eyeing the yellow Jaguar. "Yours?"

She looked back at him and nodded. "Bought and paid for."

"You didn't tell me you had a boyfriend."

"You didn't ask."

He put his hands in his trouser pockets and sauntered toward her. "Why do you want to go to Nam?"

"It doesn't matter, if you're not interested in going with me."

"What will you do now?"

She shrugged. "Go alone, I guess."

"Vietnam's no place for a woman alone."

"That's why I asked you to go with me."

"What about this boyfriend of yours? Can't he go with you?"

She shook her head. "Too busy."

"Can't love you all that much if he's too busy to go with you."

She leaned back against the sleek yellow car. "He loves me."

"You look like you'd be easy to love."

"I suppose that's your Neanderthal way of saying you find me attractive."

He grinned. "I suppose it is."

"McQuade," she said, "don't bother coming on to me, okay? I'm not interested."

He made out an imaginary checklist. Straightforward and no-nonsense both got checks. "Your father approve of this boyfriend of yours?"

She smiled. "That's really none of your business, Mr. McQuade." She opened the car door and tossed in her pocketbook. "Now, if you haven't reconsidered my offer, I'd like to leave. It's getting late and it's a long drive back to Boston."

"Is that where your boyfriend is?"

"That's right."

"Your boyfriend going with you on vacation?"

"I'm afraid not. He's a busy man, Mr. McQuade. He's in an election right now. He'll take some time off in November, but not until."

"An election?" He looked at her as if she'd just told him she had the bubonic plague. "You can't be in love with a politician!"

"Why can't I be?" she said flippantly. "There a new law I don't know about?"

"Politicians are the scum of the earth, a plague on the planet. What do you see in the guy?"

"He's going to be the next governor of the state. I see a lot in him."

He stared at her a moment, adding up the clues. It didn't take much to figure out who this boyfriend of Tory's was. There were two men running for governor in Massachusetts, and only one of them was single. "Daniel Sullivan," McQuade said flatly.

Sullivan's posters blanketed the state, staring out at passersby from every other billboard, telephone pole and street corner. Personally, McQuade didn't find him appealing. He smiled broadly, made lots of promises, but didn't seem to have anything of substance to say. But then that's the way all politicians were, or so it seemed. Frank Dickerman, Sullivan's opponent, wasn't much better. The only difference was, he included his family in his smiling posters.

"Do you know Daniel?" Tory asked.

"No, but I read the papers." His eyes swept over her. "I can't say I picture you two together."

"Oh?" she said dryly. "Just a limited imagination on your part or do you know something about Daniel I don't?"

"I picture him marrying someone who gapes at him like an adoring peon. I can't see you doing that with any man." He grinned. "Not only that, he doesn't seem to have much of a sense of humor. I have a suspicion he's not very much fun."

Tory's eyes glittered coolly. "Daniel has a terrific sense of humor," she said tightly. He didn't, but she made allowances for that. It hurt, though, when someone who didn't even know him pointed it out.

"I guess you'd know, wouldn't you?" McQuade asked softly.

She met his gaze evenly, then pushed away from the car. Opening the door, she slid in. "Goodbye, Mr. McQuade. See you Friday."

She revved the engine and slid it into gear and was gone in a spray of gravel. McQuade watched her drive away, a smile playing on his lips. Maybe he should have taken the job, just to be able to spend a week with her....

IT WAS AFTER NINE when Tory arrived at Daniel's apartment. She let herself in and turned on the stereo, then took a leisurely soak in the tub. She wanted everything perfect when Daniel arrived. This would be their last night together for over a week. She was going on vacation to Nantucket, then she had an assignment in Vermont the following week, shooting photos for a calendar for Vermont's tourism board.

Wanting the night to be special, she took special pains with herself, using a scented lotion after her bath that made her skin soft and smooth. She slid into a black satin gown held up by the slenderest of spaghetti straps and threw Daniel's purple silk robe around her shoulders. The feel of the exotic materials against her bare skin sent shivers of expectation racing through her.

Lazily she dabbed her throat and the insides of her wrists with perfume, then wandered toward the kitchen. There was a bottle of champagne chilling there, and strawberries which she'd dip in whipped cream and feed to Daniel one by one.

"Tory?"

The front door slammed and Daniel came striding into the kitchen, a wide smile on his face. "Tonight was fantastic," he said, rubbing his hands together. "I'm going to win. I know it. I smell victory in November."

"I was hoping you'd smell this hundred-dollar-an-ounce perfume," she murmured, going up on tiptoe to wind her arms around his neck.

She might just as well have bathed in bug spray for all the attention he gave her. Kissing her hurriedly, he yanked at the knot in his tie. "It was great. You should have been there. There's a feel to a political campaign when it begins to rev up, and the feel was there tonight."

"Daniel, there's only one feeling I'm interested in," she murmured, sliding her arms across his chest. She was determined to keep trying. Sooner or later he'd stop being so excited about politics and start being a little more excited about her.

"It was great!" Daniel said, shaking her off. He clapped his hands and held them toward the heavens. "I feel fantastic!"

Tory nodded wry agreement. "Yes, you do."

Daniel spied the champagne and opened it, pouring himself a glass. He paced around the room, talking a mile a minute.

"Gleason's worried, of course," he said expansively, "but then he's always worried. That's what I pay him for. And Stubby's afraid of the debate next week—which reminds me, I want you to be there."

"Daniel, you know I'm going away. We've already talked about this."

He drained his glass, then poured himself another. "You'll only be in Nantucket. Just arrange to come up to Boston for the evening. You can stay here."

Tory poured herself a glass of champagne, burying her nose in the bubbles. "Is it that important to you?"

"It's Sid's idea. He says we have to begin appearing together in public. He wants everyone to notice that you're my guest. That way, when we announce our engagement, it won't be unexpected."

"Announce our..." She stared at him in shock. "*What* engagement?"

"Oh, come on now, honey, don't be like that. Just because I didn't ask you over a romantic dinner with roses and a band playing in the background doesn't mean I don't mean it every bit as much."

"You didn't even *ask* me!" she said, staring at him as if he'd promised she'd go to hell for him. "What are you talking about?"

"Honey, Sid thinks we should get engaged. What a worrier he is! He's been at me for the past year to get engaged. He says single men look good in the race but die at the polls because everyone votes for solid, respectable married men." Daniel put his arm around Tory and drew her toward him. "Looks like we'll have to give them something to vote for."

She shook her head to clear it. Was she awake or dreaming? "Hold on a minute, Daniel. Let's slow down, okay? We haven't really talked about marriage all that much. Sure, we've mentioned it, but isn't this rather sudden?"

"What's sudden?" he asked, grinning. "Tory, you'll make a wonderful first lady of Massachusetts. I know you haven't had a chance to get used to the idea, but give it time. Things will work out just fine, you'll see."

"Daniel, wait a minute," she said. "I have a real problem here."

He stared at her. "A problem? With what? I've just asked you to marry me, Tory. What could be wrong with that?"

"But that's the point, Daniel. You didn't ask me, you *told* me. I'm sorry, but there are a few things I like to be in on, like decisions involving my future!" She gulped down her champagne, then whirled around and poured herself another glass. "I can't believe you talked about it with Sid before even mentioning it to me."

"Hey, Sid's my right arm. I tell him everything."

"Good," she snapped. "Then marry Sid."

"Are you saying you don't want to marry me?"

She hesitated. Hadn't she been secretly dreaming of this day for the past few months? Yet now that it had come, she was acting squeamish. Perhaps it was just the way Daniel had done it—she wanted a marriage where major decisions were shared. She didn't want to marry an autocrat.

She hunched her shoulders. "I'm saying I need some time to think about this, Daniel. I don't like the way you assumed I'd marry you—"

"Okay, so you want to play hard to get. Okay, so play your little games," he said sarcastically. "Meanwhile, I'm trying to do the hard work of making sure I'm the next governor of the state. I don't have time for romance, Tory. I need a woman who's going to stand next to me and *help* me, dammit, not expect me to dance attendance on her all the time."

"Who's expecting you to dance attendance?" she said, her voice rising. She swallowed a gulp of champagne and spluttered, but that didn't stop her. "I only expected you to consult with me before assuming I'd marry you, that's all!"

"Okay, look, take a couple of weeks. I'll tell Sid to put the announcement on hold—"

"What announcement?"

"Of our engagement. What'd you think?"

"I'm sorry, Daniel, but I do need some time on this. This is really major, and we're not in this together. You're in the damned rowboat unilaterally rowing to beat the band, and I'm on the shore just standing watching you!"

"So you're saying you want to row, too?"

"Yes! That's precisely what I'm saying! I'm not going to be some cute little wife who gives up her life to help you live yours, Daniel. *I* have a life, too," she said, tapping her breast with a shaking finger. "And I want to be in charge of it."

"Okay, okay, so I made a mistake. I'm sorry." He whipped off his tie and rubbed his eyes. "God, I'm beat."

Watching him, she felt her anger dissipate, replaced by anxiety. Was she being unreasonable? On what should have been their happiest night together, they were shouting at each other. Was it her fault or his? Or was anyone to blame?

"Look, Daniel, I'll come to the debate, okay?"

"That's big of you," he said sarcastically.

"I'm trying to be reasonable," she said. "Help me out here."

He let out a sigh. "Okay, so come to the debate. You're sure you won't mind? You'll have to interrupt that vacation you're dying to go on."

"I would love to be there, Daniel," she said, resting her head against his chest.

He put his arms around her. "Sid has the whole thing orchestrated. The first debate will launch our public appearances together. The papers have already begun mentioning you, so he wants to make sure nothing's out of control here."

"And what about you, Daniel?" she asked quietly. "Do you want me there, too?" If only he'd stop talking about politics and Sid Gleason, his campaign manager, and focus on them for a while...

"Of course I do. Sid's got the whole thing planned."

She felt another surge of anger. "I'm not talking about Sid Gleason," she snapped. "I'm talking about you."

Daniel raised his eyebrows. "Hey, what's going on here? You seem a little put out."

"That's putting it mildly," she said. "Since you've come in that door, the only thing you've talked about is politics. This is going to be our only night together for a week. I was hoping it would be special."

"So was I!" he said. "Dammit, Tory, I asked you to marry me tonight!"

She had an urge to turn around and walk out. Let him sleep alone tonight and see how he liked it. Then she remembered that relationships required understanding, compromise, the ability to put the other person first. It was a struggle, but it was worth it.

"Daniel, if you really want me there..."

"Of course I want you there," he said, scraping a hand through his hair. "This is important to me, Tory."

She wished he'd said *she* was important to him, but she supposed that's what he'd meant. "Then I'll be there," she promised. "I'll make plans to fly back for the night. I'll return to Nantucket the next day."

"Good," Daniel said, taking her hand and leading her toward the bedroom. "Where'd you get this sinful gown, hon? If I weren't so tired, I'd tear it off you."

"Be my guest."

He yawned and began unbuttoning his shirt. "Believe me, on any other night I would, but I'm beat. I can hardly wait to hit the bed. I feel like sleeping a century."

"But, Daniel, this is our last night together..." Disappointment flooded her. "There's strawberries and whipped cream in the kitchen. Let me get them."

"I'm too tired tonight, Tory," he said, yawning as he hit the pillow. "Maybe some other time."

She stood and watched as he burrowed into his pillow. No romantic words, no passionate lovemaking, not even a peck on the cheek! This was turning out to be quite a night together.

"What's the matter?" Daniel asked, already sliding into sleep. "You coming to bed?"

She took off her robe and got into bed, wanting Daniel to reach for her. Instead he patted her fondly on the arm. "Night, sweetie. I won't see you in the morning. I've got a strategy meeting with Stubby and Gleason. I'll be gone before you wake up."

She lay on her back and stared at the ceiling, not even bothering to answer. Was *this* what it would be like married to a politician? One long round of debates, meetings and a friendly pat on the arm every night?

She turned on her side, putting her back to him. "Maybe I just need that vacation," she said out loud, but Daniel didn't hear her. He was already asleep and had begun to snore.

Chapter Three

Low black clouds scudded across Nantucket Sound, racing ahead of the winds that whipped the ocean into a churning expanse of whitecapped waves. McQuade rubbed his eyes and took another sip of coffee. It was a day old, but heated up it wasn't too bad.

Four days had passed since Tory Britton had met him in Hyannis and he was still thinking about her, wishing she was with him right now, preferably in bed. It was ridiculous, of course. He needed to get involved with another woman about as much as he needed tooth decay. To make things worse, he was going to fly her to Nantucket in a few hours, so he was finding it impossible to stop thinking about her.

He stood in the doorway of his three-room cottage, wearing only his shorts. "Gonna be a hell of a storm, Sparky," he said to the stuffed parrot that was mounted on his wall.

The sound of his own voice seemed to snap him awake. "Great," he muttered, scratching his beard. "Guess I better shave."

Most days were like this. He pried himself out of bed, put a pot of coffee on, then stood in the doorway and stared out at the ocean. He loved this place. He'd found it years ago when he'd first come to Cape Cod and bought it with some of the money he'd saved from his years in the army. The rest of the money had gone toward buying his plane. Twenty years later, they were still the only things he had to show for himself.

Disgusted at his thoughts, he stripped off his shorts and walked into the bathroom. He turned on the shower and stepped under the cold spray, gasping at the icy needles that pummeled his back. "I'd give my eyeteeth for a warm woman in here with me."

He said that every morning, too. Trouble was, most mornings there wasn't one. If he did venture to bring one home with him, she'd begin to get ideas about fixing the place up and moving in permanently, and sooner or later he'd ask her to leave.

He was always polite about it, of course. He never stopped seeing a woman on bad terms. It was a point of honor with him. He didn't like the idea of hurting anyone, so he always made sure they left feeling good about the time they'd stayed.

Still, living like this was lonely. Polly had stayed almost a year. She'd had the habit of bringing home flowers. She'd stuff them into glasses or old wine bottles and he'd gotten to like the smell of them, competing as they did with the salty ocean air.

She'd also made curtains, but he'd taken them down after she left. Somehow the sight of them blowing in on the breeze had made him lonely. Anyway, he liked the wooden shutters on the windows. They afforded him privacy when he wanted it, and let the breezes in when he didn't.

He smiled at the memory of her. Polly. A simple name for a simple, uncomplicated woman. She'd given him more love in a few months than he'd received his entire life, but he'd finally driven her out. She'd left in sadness rather than anger, loving him, but telling him she needed him to love her, too. He hadn't been able to. She was a good woman and he had cared for her, but something was missing. He'd finally figured out it was something missing in him.

When he finished showering, he toweled off, wrapped the towel around his middle and began to shave. The windows were rattling in the wind that moaned around the eaves. Outside, the shrill cries of sea gulls coupled with the waves that crashed ashore. It would be an interesting flight to Nantucket, he figured, epecially with a woman like Tory Britton next to him . . .

MCQUADE WAS WHITTLING a piece of wood that afternoon when Tory Britton drove up. He recognized the yellow Jaguar right away. He doubted there was another like it in the entire state. The car door opened and a red umbrella appeared. No sooner had Tory opened it than the wind grabbed it and sent it tumbling across the airfield, its spokes twirling like a baton.

If he was a gentleman, he'd go out and help her. Trouble was, he wasn't a gentleman. He sat at his desk and enjoyed the view as she got out of the low-slung sports car. She was wearing faded jeans and a plain white T-shirt that the rain soaked in a matter of seconds. She bent down and ducked back in the car to get something. He whistled appreciatively. She had the shapeliest bottom this side of the Mississippi, and her long legs didn't hurt any, either. She brought out a yellow slicker and threw it over her head, then turned and raced toward his office. He wondered if she'd ask him again to go to Vietnam with her. If she did, she was going to be disappointed. He wouldn't go back to Nam if his life depended on it.

"Don't say a word, McQuade," she said when she opened the door. A gust of wind tugged the door from her hand. It banged against the wall while rain cascaded off her. She swept off the slicker in a spray of raindrops and pushed her wet hair back from her face. After slamming the door, she collapsed against it. "It's not the best day of my life," she explained.

"Can you beat that," McQuade said, idly shaving another piece of wood with his jackknife.

She ignored him. "Can you fly to Nantucket in this weather?"

"Honey, I can fly anywhere in this weather."

She took out her checkbook. "How much?"

He pointed to a sign posting rates on the wall. "Regular rates."

"I'll double them, like I promised. All I ask is that you get me there in one piece," she said, writing out a check. "I need to leave my car here, if that's okay. I'll pick it up when we come back. By the way, can you pick me up on Tuesday and fly me to Boston, then return me to Nantucket on Wednesday?"

"Sure, but if I were you I'd schedule my vacations when I didn't have any business appointments."

"It's not business," she said, handing him the check. "Daniel's first debate with Frank Dickerman is Tuesday. I promised him I'd be there."

"Okay," he said, jamming his baseball cap down over his eyes. "As long as you keep writing out the checks, I'll keep flying."

He raced to the car and began unloading her luggage. "You're able-bodied, Britton," he called to her. "Help me load this stuff on the plane."

They were soaked by the time they got the bags aboard and were seated in the cockpit. "Are you sure you can fly in this weather?" Tory asked nervously as she fastened her seat belt.

"I told you, I can fly in anything," he said, checking the fuel gauge.

"You better know what you're doing." She hated storms, and flying in them was akin to jumping off high buildings. She took a deep breath and tried to stop her heart from racing, but it wouldn't listen. It was hammering in her breast as if it were the Grand Carpenter.

"If you're that worried," McQuade said, "why don't you pray?"

"Pray?" she echoed uneasily. "I haven't prayed in years."

"Lord have mercy," McQuade said, grinning as he headed the plane directly into the wind, "we really *are* in trouble."

"Why do I get the feeling you're enjoying every minute of this?" Tory asked when they were off the ground.

"Probably because I am."

Her knuckles were white as she held on to the leather seat. Weren't these things supposed to be flotation cushions? If they ditched, she hoped the cushion was up to holding her dead weight, because she was positive she'd faint the minute they began to go down. "Most people wouldn't have taken a plane up," she said, talking to hear herself talk. Maybe then she wouldn't think. "Why did you, McQuade? You can't need the money that much."

"It's not the money. I just happen to like flying in this kind of weather. It's a challenge."

"Dad said you used to volunteer for the really dangerous missions, but you weren't a daredevil. I'm afraid I don't understand the distinction."

"Some people get a thrill out of close calls. Something about danger turns them on. Me, I just like flying when I have to really concentrate. It keeps me sharp. I don't take unecessary chances, but I don't let fear or bad weather stop me from going up. Actually, flying on a perfect day is more dangerous than in this kind of weather."

"You're crazy."

"No, you're apt to relax on a clear day, and when you're flying, to relax is the most dangerous thing you can do."

"Then why are you flying charter flights back and forth from the Cape to the islands? I should think it would get to be pretty repetitious."

"The islands need food, they need magazines and books and matches." He shrugged. "Someone's gotta do it."

"Ever think of flying for commercial airlines?"

He chuckled humorlessly. "Honey, if you think flying to Nantucket gets repetitious, try flying to L.A. the same route every time. The same airports, the exact schedules, the rotten food. I did it for a while after I left the army." He shook his head. "No, I like being my own boss, even if the work isn't all that thrilling. But enough questions about me. Why do you need a vacation so bad you'd take a flight on a day like this? It's obvious you're scared to death."

She stretched her legs out as far as they could go in the crowded cockpit. She looked totally exhausted. "This is my first vacation in over a year, McQuade. I would have parted the waters with a rod and walked to Nantucket if I had to."

"But you're leaving again on Tuesday. Not much of a rest."

She shrugged. "It's Daniel's first debate. It's important to him that I be there."

"He's worth interrupting your vacation for?"

"He's worth doing anything for."

"Yet he can't take the time off from campaigning to go places with you."

She felt a frisson of irritation at McQuade for his jibe at Daniel, but she decided to ignore it. "Sometimes it's like that in relationships, McQuade. You give a little more one time and the other person gives more the next time."

"So Daniel Sullivan has given more than you at times?"

There it was again, that sideways swipe at Daniel. She didn't say anything for a moment, then turned her head and fixed McQuade with cool eyes. "Why the big interest in Daniel?"

"Why didn't you answer my question?"

"Because I didn't think it was any of your business," she said. "I still don't."

"No need to get huffy, Tory."

"No need to get personal, McQuade."

He shrugged. "Whatever you say. You're the boss."

"I say let's be quiet." She let out a breath and sat staring at the rain that pummeled the small airplane.

McQuade glanced at her. "It usually takes about twelve minutes to fly to Nantucket. It might be a little longer today."

"Why?"

"We're heading directly into the wind. It'll probably slow us down a few minutes."

"Just as long as it doesn't sink us," she said fervently.

"I wouldn't have taken you for a worrier."

"I saw your office back there, McQuade. It didn't exactly foster confidence in you."

"What's cleanliness got to do with flying?" he asked, grinning.

"I hope nothing."

"Are you sure you're your father's daughter? I can remember Old Iron Ass reading *Time* magazine while we were being shot at in Nam."

"That's Dad, all right." She frowned. "At least, it was..."

He glanced at her. "I'm sorry, Tory. It's not easy to picture the general confined to a wheelchair."

"At least he hasn't lost his spirit. He still acts as if he's in charge of troops. If it were up to willpower alone, he would be."

"He's quite a man."

"I haven't told him you refused to go with me."

"Oh? Still hoping I'll change my mind?"

"Won't you?"

He shook his head. "When I left Nam, I left it for good. It was another life over there, a bad dream. I don't ever want to go back."

"It was a terrible war," she said quietly. "When Dad went over there, I was in my first year of high school. It was a difficult time. Most people I knew were opposed to the war, yet my own father was one of the top leaders over there.''

"Seems like everyone either hated the war or hated the protesters. There weren't a lot of people who could see the complexities.''

"Complexities?'' Tory laughed without humor. "You want complexities, I'll give you complexities. I was raised to believe in my country, to believe that we always did the right thing. When Dad went to Vietnam, he wrote me letters that were filled with noble deeds. He told me how the young men fought bravely, believing in what they died for. He said we were in an important war, one we were fighting for the safety of democracy, not only in Southeast Asia, but in the entire world.''

She sat and stared broodingly out the window. "I shared those letters with my boyfriend. He was a senior and had planned to go to college. After he read them, he dropped out of school and signed up for the war. Four months later, I was getting letters from him. Only trouble was, his letters weren't gung ho and filled with noble deeds. He was bitter and afraid—'' She turned her head so McQuade wouldn't see the tears that misted her eyes. "And then he was killed, and the letters stopped.''

"It feels like I'm not doing anything today but saying I'm sorry,'' McQuade said. "But if it's any comfort, I am sorry.''

"Thank you,'' she said, closing her eyes and resting her head against the lined leather seat. When she spoke again, her voice was tired. "Anyway, while everyone in the country was finding out our government was lying to us, I was finding out my own father was.''

The war had distanced her from her father, but this new information that her father had left a son in Vietnam had made it worse. She didn't tell McQuade about that. Sooner or later, she'd have to if she was going to convince him to go with her to Vietnam. As it was, she was still trying to digest it herself.

"Anyway," she continued, "ever since, there's been this wall between us. We talk to each other, but neither one of us can seem to hear the other. Sometimes it feels like we've got this bad long-distance connection and both of us are shouting at each other, but all we hear is static..."

McQuade frowned as he listened. Her voice was soft and low and filled with sadness. He heard the pain, the guilt, the anguish she had felt upon finding out her father wasn't the man she had thought he was.

For some reason, he suddenly remembered sitting in the back pew of the Catholic church when he was a child, listening to the mumbled sounds that came from the confessional on Saturday afternoon. The voices had all been filled with shame, guilt, remorse. Though he hadn't been able to hear their words, he knew the people who knelt in that cloaked darkness all carried some terrible secret deep in their souls, something that made them writhe in quiet agony in the dark recesses of the church on a busy street in a small Massachusetts town.

But there was as much confession today, up in this solitary silver plane flying through the rain and wind as there had been in that old church. She hadn't told him everything, but she had said enough. She loved her father, but the war had put a distance between them that felt unbridgeable.

"It was an ugly war," he said quietly. "We were all wounded over there, in one way or another. The thing is, Tory, I don't think the general ever thought he was lying to you in those letters. That's how he saw things. For him, it was a war to defend another country's right to democracy. Other people saw things differently, that's all."

"You're right, of course, but it's easier to see that twenty years later. At the time, I became so disillusioned I could barely speak to him when he came home. Now I understand better. I realize now that truth isn't absolute, that everyone sees his own particular version of the truth. But back then..." She smiled sadly. "I think as a country, we were all terribly idealistic. What none of us seemed to realize was that choices in real life are infinitely more complicated than they are in books and movies. Everyone seemed to think he alone was right. No one had the maturity or compassion, the tolerance, to allow others to believe what they wanted to." She shook her head. "But that's all water over the dam." She peered at him. "What about you, McQuade? Were you drafted, or did you go voluntarily?"

"It doesn't matter how I got there," he said. "The only thing that matters is that I did."

"You don't share much, do you?"

"Not if I can help it." He pointed toward the ground. "There it is. You can't see it real well, but that's the Gray Lady."

"You can find your way to the airfield?"

"It's a hell of a time to be asking that now."

"I can see why you're not married, McQuade," she said, smiling. "No woman in her right mind would put up with you."

"Strange," he said mildly, casting her an amused glance. "A number of them have somehow managed."

The answer left her without a response. She glanced at him and felt the stirrings of awareness in her midsection. She was suddenly conscious of the way his T-shirt molded his upper body. Well-shaped muscles rippled across his chest and down his rock-hard stomach. His tanned arms looked like a longshoreman's. She couldn't help comparing McQuade with Daniel, whose arms were milky white and sprinkled with reddish hair. Even though Daniel was younger, he looked older.

But that was because Daniel was a politician, she thought, hurriedly coming to her boyfriend's defense. He didn't do a lot of physical work, he sat at a desk and wrote policy statements and speeches. He made important decisions that affected the entire state. Now a state senator, Daniel was destined to be a statesman. That more than made up for his lack of physical fitness.

Then she realized the plane was banking, descending toward Nantucket in a slow curve. Despite the high winds and torrential rain, McQuade handled the plane as if the weather were perfect. She felt her stomach knot up and clenched her hands. She hated herself for being afraid, but she couldn't seem to do anything about it. She wished she were as calm as the proverbial cucumber, instead of the shaking wreck she really was. The only thing good she could say for herself was that she might be afraid, but at least she didn't give in to it.

"I've got to hand it to you, McQuade," she said when he'd landed and was taxiing to a stop. "You know what you're doing in a plane."

"How you getting to where you're staying? Taxi?" he asked, ignoring her compliment.

"I suppose so. I didn't plan that far ahead." She gathered up her pocketbook. "I'll see you here Tuesday afternoon about two?"

"Tuesday at two. I'll file a flight plan from here to Boston and a return flight Wednesday morning."

"Thanks, McQuade...." She was about to get out, but hesitated. "Are you flying back now?"

He narrowed his eyes and peered at the sky. Dark clouds boiled ominously overhead as rain slashed against the windows and gusts of wind shook the plane. "Actually, I might stay put. Things aren't looking too good. I'll check with the control tower before I decide anything."

"Where would you stay?"

He shrugged. "I guess I'll stay in the plane. I've slept here before. It won't kill me."

"You can't sleep in a plane!"

"I can't?" His eyes twinkled at her. "There some rule I don't know about?"

"Stop it, McQuade," she said. "There's no bed, no heat... Why, you'd die of exposure." She gave him a wry look. "Not that I'd miss you if you did."

"I've slept in a lot worse conditions than this, sweetheart."

"Look, let me give you some money," she said, rummaging in her pocketbook. "You can rent a room for the night."

"No thanks. I don't need handouts, Ms. Britton."

"Who said anything about a handout? I'd have you deduct it from my bill on Tuesday."

"Personally I'd prefer to sleep here and get the full fare on Tuesday. Right about now I need all the money I can get. I've got a stack of bills on my desk that makes Mount Washington look like an anthill."

"Then come to my place. I've got a guest room."

He shook his head. "Thanks, but I'd rather stay with the plane."

Suddenly, a loud crack of thunder splintered the sky and a brilliant flash of lightning lit up the sky. They caught sight of two men in yellow slickers racing toward a small plane, ropes in hand.

"They're going to tie the plane down. Looks like we made it just in time," McQuade said mildly. "I doubt I'll get clearance to leave today. May as well settle in for a long night."

"That does it," Tory said. "You're coming home with me and I won't hear any arguments. You'll be doing me a favor. I'm scared to death of storms. I need someone to keep me company, or I'll hide under the bed all night."

"Scared of storms? A big girl like you? What do you do when you're taking photographs and a storm blows up?"

"I hide. Now stop giving me a hard time and let's find a taxi. I just want to get home."

"I don't have any clean clothes with me," he protested.

"You won't need any clothes," she said sarcastically. "This is Nantucket, not Boston. I wasn't planning on taking you to the symphony."

"Testy little thing, aren't you?"

She ignored him as she eyed the sky. "This is the one thing I don't like about Nantucket. When there's a storm out here, it feels like the devil himself is after me."

"Maybe you should have thought of this before you got the urge to fly over in this weather."

"I don't need a lecture, McQuade. I need company. Are you coming with me or not?"

He rubbed his jaw and pondered the weather. It was abysmal. He'd slept in the plane before, but he always paid for it the next day with cramped muscles and a surly temper. Sighing, he looked at Tory. "Yeah," he said, "I'm coming with you."

On a good day, the empty fields of Nantucket resembled the English moors. Desolate, windblown and seemingly limitless, they extended into the distance, merging with the blue sky and bluer ocean until they faded from sight. With the wind and rain tearing at them, they lost the softness that sunlight gave them and became threatening. As the taxi left civilization behind, McQuade began to understand why Tory wanted company. She lived on the outermost edge of the island, in an area that remained mostly unpopulated.

Twenty-five minutes after leaving the small airport, the taxi pulled up at the end of a muddy lane. "That's it, folks," Harry Gordon, the driver, said. "I try to pull in there and I'll be stuck till next weekend."

"Great," Tory muttered under her breath. "That's the last time I take Harry's taxi."

"Where the hell is this cottage?" McQuade asked, peering out the window and seeing only a blowing curtain of rain, illuminated occasionally by a flash of lightning. Thunder rumbled ominously in the background.

"It's at the end of this lane," she said, stuffing money into the driver's outstretched hand. "Around that curve."

"If you were much farther out, you'd be in England."

"Can it, McQuade," she said, struggling into her slicker as the taxi drove away. "Not another word or you'll sleep outside."

"Wouldn't be the first time," he said mildly.

"Good, then I can put you up in the dog run and not feel guilty at all." She looked at the pile of luggage Harry had dumped on the ground and muttered a low curse. "I wonder whatever happened to the idea of service? Harry Gordon's made a ton of money off me the past five years, the least he could do is drive us all the way to the cottage."

McQuade picked up the two heaviest suitcases. "Quit complaining. Pick up that wicker thing and let's get going."

They set off with their heads bent into the rain, the wind driving into them, flinging their slickers out behind them like yellow flags.

"Great day for a walk," McQuade shouted above the elements.

"Just shut up," Tory said from between clenched teeth. "Your help I need. Your sarcasm I can do without."

"Got any food in this romantic little hideaway of yours?"

"A freezer full of the stuff," she said. "And a microwave and a fireplace and central heat. All the pleasures of home. Trust me, you're gonna love it."

Yeah, he thought to himself, just like Marie Antoinette had loved the French Revolution.

When they rounded the curve, Tory's summer home came into sight. Even to McQuade's jaded eye, the scene was spectacular. The cottage sat on a promontory above the ocean, surrounded on three sides by rolling fields of beach grass and wildflowers. The flowers' pink, yellow, blue and lavender colors melted into one another under the deluge of rain, giving the scene the appearance of a water-soaked impressionist painting. Beach plum and lilac bushes shrouded most of the house from sight, but it looked like a typical Nantucket cottage, with gray shingles that had faded to silver and a number of ells that had been added over the years. The rain prevented McQuade from seeing much, and to be honest, he didn't much feel like looking. Right about now he wanted a hot shower and a cold beer. Any other amenity was superfluous.

"You choose this place because you like to be miles from the nearest person, or because you're just plain cussed?" he asked as they trudged the last few muddy steps.

"What's the matter, McQuade? A little rain and you start getting surly."

"Last I knew, you hired me to fly you here, not tote your entire belongings through monsoon and mud to the ends of the earth. You want a safari, Ms. Britton, I recommend Africa. At least it's drier there."

"You surprise me, Mr. McQuade," she said airily. "An old foot soldier like you shouldn't mind a little one-mile hike."

"I left the army because of conditions like these, and I wasn't a foot soldier."

"Ah, that's right," she said sarcastically, "you were one of those brave flyboys who dropped napalm on the Vietnamese."

He hadn't dropped napalm, but her careless words struck him harder than a blow from a closed fist. It was as if they had been aimed at some invisible wound that festered somewhere deep inside him, suppurating and unhealed. They caused a spasm of pain that made his face twist in agony, and he saw it all again, the orange-yellow fire from the sky, the straw-roofed conical huts that went up in flame, the women, the children, the old men running, their mouths open in silent screams that no one could hear above the world-gone-mad sounds of automatic weapons, planes, choppers and bombs.

He tried to shake the memories loose but they refused to leave, and suddenly he saw her—the one person he had tried the hardest never to remember... Mai.

He saw her as he had last seen her, staring in horror at her burning village, turning to look at him, her young face so beautiful it made him catch his breath. But her eyes were wide with fear and she turned from him and ran, crying in anguish, screaming to her mother, her father, her little brother...

"No!" she had screamed. "No! NO!"

The word seemed to split the air, growing louder and louder until there was no more gunfire, no mortars or grenades exploding, no orders, no friends, no foes, just the word hanging in the air, reverberating and echoing, like a million explosions in a tiny room...

"*Noooooooooooooooooooo....*"

But it wasn't Mai crying out now, it was him and the world was a mad place, crazy, insane, and his head was splitting and he had to hold it together because it felt as if it were going to crack in two....

Chapter Four

"We're here, McQuade."

Tory's voice interrupted the memory, and he came back with a start, standing dumb in the Nantucket rain, staring out toward the angry sea, his face dripping with rain and tears.

Tory was unlocking the door, taking off her dripping slicker, directing him to put the bags in the bedrooms upstairs. He stood outside and stared at the ocean, letting the wind blow into his face while the rain washed it clean. He breathed in the salty air, taking it into his lungs with gratitude. There was no smell of carnage on this air, no lingering scent of death. Here all was clean and fresh, as new as on that first innocent day when this strange, terrible world had been created.

"McQuade! You're dripping wet! Are you coming in or are you going to stand there like a zombie?"

He turned and looked at her, and for a moment he didn't know who she was. All was strange, unearthly, dreamlike. He was not here, she was a ghost, the world was filled with tears.

Mentally he shook himself and forced himself to walk inside. He closed the door. It was a kitchen, clean and white and filled with light. Green plants hung in white pots in front of the windows and gleaming brass pots and pans were suspended from a white-painted ladder mounted horizontally overhead. Two wing chairs upholstered in a cheerful flowered material sat on either side of a fireplace where birch logs waited on the soot-blackened hearth.

He adjusted quickly, pushing the memories back into their hole and seizing on his customary wry demeanor. Humor was a good shield; it held questions at bay and made people think all was well.

"No wonder you wanted to get here," he said, looking around. "Looks like the inside of some fancy decorating magazine."

"And what do you know about fancy decorating magazines?" Tory asked, putting on a kettle of water and taking big white mugs down from a shelf.

"Every once in a while I fly a bunch of editors and photographers from some of those magazines in New York to the Cape or the islands. I usually stick around while they photograph the places, then fly them back." He looked around the room. "They'd love this place. I can hear them now, oohing and ahhing over it."

Tory smiled. "Coffee?"

"Beer, if you've got it. But first I want a shower." He glanced at her. "You wouldn't happen to have a clothes dryer around, would you? Since this is all I've got with me, I'd like them to dry before next week."

"Not only a dryer, but a washer. The guest room's this way," she said over her shoulder, leading him down a narrow hall and up the steep stairs to another tiny hallway. At the end, there were three doors. She opened the one on the left. "This is the guest room. You'll stay here." He caught a glimpse of a small room with an old bed covered in a quilt, hunting prints on deep forest-green walls and white-painted woodwork.

She opened the middle door. "This is the guest bathroom. Just undress and throw your clothes out here. I'll pick them up and do a quick wash."

"And meanwhile what do I do? Stand in the shower for two hours until the wash is done?"

"McQuade, for a generally resourceful man, you display a severe lack of imagination." She opened a door. "This is the linen closet. There are towels in here, and if they're not big enough to cover that muscular frame of yours, there are quilts and blankets in the guest room. If you're lucky, you might even find some old clothes of Daniel's in the closet. Use your head, McQuade, just don't parade around in the buff. I might not be able to resist you."

"Well, if it gets too tough," he said, dumping her suitcases in front of the other door, "think of Daniel. I doubt I could ever compete with the future governor of Massachusetts."

"I imagine you're right." She smiled sweetly. "Thanks for being so understanding."

He watched her walk down the narrow hall, then turned and went into the bathroom. It was a small room with an old-fashioned claw-foot tub, a wood-framed mirror over the pedestal sink, a narrow-paned window overlooking the ocean and a skylight overhead. The rain slashed against the panes, and thunder continued to rumble in the distance. Occasional flashes of lightning illuminated the room.

He turned on the hot water. He'd better shower fast, or he'd be stuck with no water at all if the electricity decided to go out.

TORY CARRIED her suitcases into her room. In the guest bathroom, the shower was still running. She doubted she'd see McQuade anytime soon, so she headed for her own bathroom. After a quick shower, she changed into clean jeans and a heavy Irish-knit sweater, tied her damp hair back with a red bow, and descended to the living room.

McQuade was standing at the French doors that stretched across the entire front of the room overlooking the ocean. He was wearing an old pair of baggy jeans that Daniel had left behind the previous month. His chest was bare, though, and she felt her stomach wobble at the sight of him, half-naked and gloriously male, standing outlined against the light from the windows.

She told herself it was normal for a woman to be attracted to a beautiful male body, but she wasn't sure she believed it. Hurriedly she looked away, focusing her attention on the living room, but it reminded her of Daniel. He hated the cottage, though he admitted it was decorated nicely.

Plush couches and chairs were upholstered in bright pink flowered chintz. A pink-and-white dhurrie rug covered the pickled oak floors. A tall stripped-pine armoire hid a television and stereo system, and a long pine trestle table sat in front of a large bay window. On it were stacks of decorating and gardening books and wicker baskets containing magazines and paperback mysteries. A pink-and-white plaid wing chair sat in front of the table.

McQuade turned to look at her. "One thing I can't figure out about you."

"Oh?"

"With a weekend place like this, how do you ever leave to go back to work?"

She smiled as she turned on a lamp. A warm pool of light fell across the couch, making the room even more cheerful.

"I love my work, McQuade. I didn't use to, not when I worked as a newspaper reporter. I felt like a leech then, living off of people's pain. Now I take pictures of the ocean, trees, rivers..." She wandered to the French doors and stood watching the fury of the storm outside. "I never get tired of nature. People tire me, but not the ocean, the sky..."

"How does Mr. Sullivan feel about your career?"

She hesitated. Daniel had mentioned that she would probably want to quit her job and be a full-time housewife if they married. It was something she couldn't contemplate—being without work she loved. "We haven't really talked about it all that much,'' she said. Least said, soonest mended.

She pasted a bright smile on her face and headed for the kitchen. ''Enough idle chatter, McQuade. I'm starving. Let me show you how a not-so-famous photographer puts a meal on the table in under thirty minutes.''

''VOILÀ,'' Tory said twenty minutes later, whisking a cover off an ironstone platter and revealing two perfect omelets surrounded by slices of crisp bacon and sausage links. ''And there're English muffins, blueberry muffins and just plain toast,'' she added, pointing toward a wicker basket heaped with goodies. ''Take your pick.''

McQuade reached for a miniature blueberry muffin. He popped it in his mouth just as a brilliant flash of lightning lit up the sky. Seconds later there was a crashing boom of thunder. The lights flickered a moment, then died.

''Uh-oh,'' he said. ''We got trouble.''

''Right here in River City,'' responded Tory nervously. Storms were the one aspect of nature she feared. It was strange that she wasn't able to make peace with thunder and lightning, but that was the case, nonetheless.

''Well, at least we've got hot food to eat,'' McQuade said cheerfully. ''And a candlelight dinner never hurt anyone.'' He stood up. ''Where are they?''

''Where are what?'' Tory flinched as another flash of lightning was followed quickly by a tremendous crack of thunder.

''The candles.''

''Bottom drawer,'' Tory said, gesturing nervously toward a pine dresser. ''Right-hand side.''

''Good thing it's still light out,'' McQuade said, retrieving a pair of candles and putting them in the pewter candlesticks on the table.

''It won't be for long,'' Tory said, glancing anxiously out the window. Flashes of lightning kept the sky lit up almost continuously while thunder shook the floor, making the candles quiver in their holders.

"Eat up, Tory," McQuade said gently. "Your meal's getting cold."

Tory threw him a worried glance. "I don't feel much like eating right now."

"What do you feel like doing?"

"Hiding," she breathed, her heartbeat catching as a particularly loud clap of thunder shook the foundations of the cottage.

"Never would have taken you for a coward," McQuade said equably, helping himself to another muffin.

"I'm *not* a coward," Tory snapped, then literally jumped out of her chair when the lights came on and the refrigerator motor started. "Thank God," she said, slumping back in her chair. "I wasn't looking forward to a night without electricity."

"It gets inconvenient," McQuade allowed. "But, then, if you're sleeping, you don't really need electricity, do you?"

"I do," Tory said fervently. "When I can't sleep, I read, and when there's a storm, I'm up all night."

"Well, stack up the books," McQuade said cheerfully, then shrugged when the lights went out again. He looked at Tory, whose face showed clear signs of the strain she was under. "Ever tried braille?"

"This is not a time for jokes, McQuade," she said. "Dammit, we're totally isolated here. It could take days for the electricity to come back on."

"Days?" He shook his head, his eyes twinkling with amusement. "I'd speak to the electric company if I were you. Shake 'em up a little. Threaten to sue or something."

"McQuade, I don't need humor right now."

"What do you need?"

She didn't respond. She folded her arms and sat huddled in her chair, trying to act as if she weren't afraid. The act wasn't working.

Watching her, McQuade realized she was right—she didn't need humor. She needed something he didn't have a right to give her—a strong shoulder and loving arms.

"Too bad Daniel's not here," he said softly. "I'll bet he could take away those jitters of yours."

"Not likely," she said without thinking. "Daniel has no patience with me when I get scared. He tells me to grow up." Her eyes flashed as she glanced at McQuade. "I suppose that's what you're thinking, too."

"No," he said slowly, "that's not what I'm thinking at all."

Her face grew red. She'd let the cat out of the bag. Now McQuade knew that Daniel wasn't always the thoughtful, considerate guy she wished he was. She looked away, miserable and fearful at the same time. It had been like this since she was a child, except then it had been her father who had laughed scornfully when she begged him to hold her.

"*Hold* you?" he'd echoed one time when she was seven years old. "What for? You wearin' diapers? Grow up, Tory. You're not a baby, you know."

But she had remained a child in this one area—storms frightened her silly. She knew it was irrational, but since when did knowing something make it any easier to deal with? She flung down her napkin and pushed away from the table. She just wanted to get away from McQuade. If he wanted to tease her and make fun, let him do it when she wasn't around.

"Tory?"

She ignored McQuade and kept walking. All she wanted was to reach her room, lock the door and spend the rest of the storm hiding under her blankets. Blindly she ran up the creaking stairs. She was almost at the top when her foot slipped and she felt herself begin to fall.

Screaming, she fell backward. In her mind, she saw what was going to happen—saw her body tumbling backward down the narrow staircase, her mouth opened in a wide scream of terror, saw the blood, heard the bones snap into pieces— But suddenly she wasn't falling. Instead, she was rescued by a pair of muscular arms that caught her before she could fall, then she was clutched against a strong chest, cradled in a man's incredible warmth. She smelled the moist heat of McQuade's body, felt the tingling brush of the hair on his chest against her cheek, heard the soothing murmur of his voice. A surge of heat went through her and she had to fight the urge to wrap her arms around his neck. He smelled so clean and felt so strong she wanted to melt into his arms. For a moment, she rested her head against his chest and gave herself up to the sweetness of being held.

"It's all right, Tory," he said gently, picking her up and climbing the stairs toward the second floor. "It's okay to be afraid."

But what she was suddenly afraid of wasn't the storm. She steeled herself to ignore her body's urgent new promptings. "You can put me down, McQuade," she said, her voice quivering despite her efforts to appear unshaken. "I know how to walk."

"Didn't look like it just then. If I hadn't been right behind you, you would have taken a nasty crash."

"My head's hard," she said, pushing out of his arms when they reached the landing. "I'd have lived."

"Yeah, but with more brain damage than you could afford," he said, grinning at her efforts to recover her aplomb.

She stared at him a moment, trying to ignore her response to his nearness, shaken by the sudden knowledge that Cargo McQuade was extremely attractive. How could she have ignored his hypnotic eyes when she first met him? Why hadn't she noticed his build, the strength of his hands and arms, the flat stomach, rippling muscles? How could she have been so blind?

And what the hell was she doing alone in her cottage with a man this lethal?

Aware that she needed to get away from McQuade, she
turned and ran, heading straight for the safety of her bedroom. But McQuade was right behind, misinterpreting her
fear.

"Tory, wait!"

His strong hand came out and gripped her arm. He swung
her around to face him. She backed up, wanting only to put
as much space between them as she could, but she bumped
into the wall. McQuade was so close she could feel his breath
on her face, so solicitous she might have laughed at the humor of the situation if she hadn't been so dangerously attracted to the man.

"Tory, fear is nothing to be ashamed of. You don't have
to run away from me."

She didn't miss the irony, but she tried damn hard to ignore it. "I'm fine."

"Then why is your voice quivering? Why are your pupils
dilated like that? My God, woman, you're shaking all over."

She was shaking because some sort of bonfire had erupted
in her body, a wild yearning that made her want to reach out
and touch his bare skin. But before she knew what was
happening, McQuade scooped her up in his arms and was
striding down the dark, narrow hallway.

"What are you doing?"

"I'm taking you to your bedroom."

Alarms went off all over Tory's receptive body. Vainly she
pushed against him. "Put me down."

His voice was low and deep and sensual. "Sweetheart,
stop fighting me."

She stiffened. She had to fight him, but not the way he
was thinking. She took a deep breath, then immediately re-
gretted it. She had inhaled the dusky male scent of Mc-
Quade. Her pulses began to pound. Weakly she clung to
him, wishing she could stop her senses from responding to
his nearness.

It was no use. Her body was healthy and young and filled with hormones. She was a woman, and here was the most beautiful man she'd stumbled on in ages. She felt a faint throbbing response deep inside herself and knew she had to fight it. She loved Daniel. This couldn't be happening to her. It *shouldn't* be happening.

"McQuade," she breathed, "leave me alone."

She was shaking inside, even while a wild, sweet urgency filled her. Her breath grew shallow. She closed her eyes and let her hand move over McQuade's wide shoulders. An immediate response erupted in her midsection as awareness of him filled her senses. His skin was like satin beneath her palm, smooth and clear and filled with a man's heat. She inhaled again, losing herself in the clean scent of McQuade, feeling the heat spreading through her body, setting her aflame with desires she hadn't known existed.

McQuade put her down and she backed away quickly, trying to put as much space between them as she could. She bumped into the wall and came to a sudden stop. McQuade loomed over her, shutting out the world. She raised her eyes to his slowly, dreading what she might find there.

"Maybe I don't want to leave you alone," he murmured, one hand going out to rest on the wall behind her. His head dipped toward her, but his lips stayed away. "Maybe I want to kiss you."

She swallowed painfully, her heartbeat accelerating. "McQuade, I have to go."

She turned to go but he reached out and took her arm. She let herself be drawn back against the wall, let his hand remain on her arm. She was acutely aware of him, her senses as finely tuned as the most precious scientific instruments. He moved his hand slowly up and down her arm, creating an erotic friction that made her pulses pound.

"What are you really afraid of, Tory?" he murmured, his breath brushing the hair back from her ear.

"The storm," she breathed.

"Which storm? The one outside... or the one in here?"

His words left her no room for escape. She couldn't pretend nothing was happening, yet she knew that was her only hope. She focused on Daniel, knowing that if she kept thinking of him, she'd be able to resist this sudden attraction that was flaring between her and McQuade.

"I have to go, McQuade. I promised Dad I'd call when I got here."

"Took you a long enough time to get around to it, didn't it?"

"I promised I'd call after five." She glanced at her watch and saw it was well past six. "I had to unpack and make us dinner," she added lamely.

McQuade was so close he almost touched her, then he drew a long breath and stepped back. "By all means," he said. "Call your Dad. Tell him I gave him my best."

"Thanks," she said. "I will."

She pushed away from the wall, but McQuade stood unmoving. She came to an abrupt halt.

"Well?" she asked, lifting her chin defiantly. "Aren't you going to move?"

"Do you really want me to?"

She had to look at him then. She met his eyes and saw the knowledge in them. He had been aware of her response to him, had felt the attraction himself, was even now daring her to act on her desires rather than run away. She knew her only hope was in pretense. She had to make him think it was the storm she feared, that she hadn't felt anything for him when he had held her.

"McQuade, I appreciate your willingness to stay with me, but I'm a grown woman now, not a child. I have to learn to face my fears. Storms won't kill me—" She flinched as a particularly loud clap of thunder shook the cottage. "At least, I don't think they will." Nervously she backed toward her bedroom door. "Right now I just want to call Dad."

Once inside her room, with the door safely closed and locked, she leaned back against the wall and began to shake. A tumult of emotions possessed her—fear and desire and confusion. All melted together, fusing from the heat of their intensity. She pushed away from the wall and began unpacking.

Finally she dialed her father's house.

"Hello?" Her father's frail voice was reassuring on the other end of the line.

"Dad, it's me."

"You talk to McQuade the other night?"

Why was that the first thing out of his mouth? Lately he lived for nothing more than this son in Vietnam. Why hadn't he thought of him years before if he was so important? "Yes, Dad," she said, pushing the thoughts aside. "I talked to him."

"Well? What'd he say? He going?"

"Not yet," she said. "I mean, he hasn't agreed to go yet." She didn't want to tell him that McQuade was here with her now. Her father would never understand, and she didn't want to explain things anyway.

"Damn it, Tory, when are you gonna *get* him to agree? Next year sometime?"

"Maybe I'll see him this week," she answered finally. "I have to go back to Boston on Tuesday for Daniel's first debate."

"Daniel," her father scoffed. "When are you going to wake up and see he's not nearly enough man for you?"

"Dad, we've been through this before—"

"Yes, and we'll continue to go through it until you wise up!"

"Or until you do!" she snapped.

Her father began to cough, making her immediately feel guilty. "Dad, calm down. Let's not get all riled up about Daniel."

"No," the old man said grudgingly, "he's not worth it."

"Dad," she said tiredly. "Please."

"So about McQuade," her father said, his voice rising with hope. "You'll see him sometime this week?"

"I...I'll try to." For some reason, she couldn't bring herself to admit that he was right here under the same roof with her.

"Agh, don't even bother. You coming to Boston on Tuesday? Fine. Afterward, come see me and bring McQuade with you. I'll talk him into going to Nam with you."

"What if he won't come with me?"

"He'll come," the general said brusquely. "And, Tory? Take a good look at McQuade while you're at it. What you see just may open your eyes a little, show you what a real man is."

"Good night, Dad," she said, and hung up hard. Dammit, she didn't need her father telling her to look at McQuade. Her own body was already doing a great job on its own....

McQUADE ROSE AT DAWN, found his clothing in the dryer downstairs, dressed, drank some orange juice and ate a cold blueberry muffin, then set out to walk back to Nantucket town.

At dawn, the moors of Nantucket were starkly beautiful. A morning mist shrouded them, turning them into a vast, still place of whispering grass that echoed with the sound of the thundering surf. On the eastern horizon the sun was a perfect globe, like a faint golden disk suspended in silver. The hoarse, haunting cry of a lone sea gull wafted eerily through the hushed morning air.

But McQuade didn't notice his surroundings. He walked with the long, loose stride of a soldier, eating up the miles between Tory's cottage and the airfield, his head bent as he pondered what had happened the night before.

He'd been around women too long not to recognize physical attraction when it struck. He'd felt it for Tory and he'd bet his livelihood she'd felt it, too. She'd been smarter than him, though—she'd pretended nothing had happened. Given even a nod from her, he would have taken her to bed and made love to her all night. Thank God, she'd been more sensible. He didn't need to get involved with another woman. He'd done enough damage to the women who had cared for him.

Striding along the empty roads of Nantucket, he tried not to remember the past, but for some reason, it wouldn't be pushed away. He walked faster, filled with sudden anxiety. The memories were coming back and he couldn't seem to stop them. They tumbled from the depths of his being, like old photographs spilling out of a faded album. He wanted to run, but where could he go? The moors were empty, a vast sweeping place that might have been the edge of the world.

He came to a stop and stared at the moors, but he didn't see them. Suddenly he was back in Saigon, a bustling street filled with sidewalk vendors. The alien sound of the Vietnamese language filled his ears. People hurried by, bumping into him, reaching out to him. "You buy whiskey? You buy smokes? You buy soap, soldier?" The faces swam around him, swirled like insistent ghosts, smiling, shouting, pushing against him, crowding him into the past, forcing him to return.

From out of the Nantucket mists, a young boy appeared, smiling, swimming up to him, pushing his grinning face into McQuade's. "You buy *ma tuy?*" he asked. "Mary Jane?" His face wavered, disintegrated, reappeared, his grin wider, his eyes filled with some strange, dark knowledge. "You buy pot, soldier? Grass? *Ma tuy?*"

The crowds pressed in on him, suffocating him, demanding, pleading, offering, begging. Hands stretched out to him, leading him back to the past. The smells of the marketplace came back to him, the smoky scent of meat cooking on sidewalk fires, the acrid odor of fresh fruit beginning to rot, the perfume on the women in short skirts and high heels. "You want *bum bum,* soldier?" they asked, giggling, smiling, touching him. *"Bum bum,* soldier?" Their voices came back, high and strange and filled with deadly promise.

McQuade shook off the image, only to have another appear in its place. A young girl, small, petite, so beautiful she took his breath away. He came to a stop and stared at her, fighting to see her through the tears that suddenly filled his eyes. He struggled to see her, to find her in the mist. He stood and forced himself to find the memory, to search through the thousands of images and find the only one that had ever mattered.

As if carried on a gentle breeze, her name floated back to him through the rubble of the past, rising out of his consciousness through the pain and sorrow, the ugliness and shame, past the guilt and remorse, the anger and the rage: *Mai.*

And then she came to him, as he had first seen her, a young girl in the teeming marketplace of Saigon, appearing out of the noise and confusion like a vision, exquisitely fresh and untainted, rising out of the ugliness and filth. Her name had been Mai, but he had called her Lavender in the beginning, because she was holding a piece of lavender silk when he first saw her at that sidewalk market.

He saw her as he had seen her then—her blue-black hair, long and fine and very straight, the thin, lithe line of her back, the slightly rounded shape of her figure beneath the baggy black pants and white shirt she wore, the innocence in her eyes coupled with a playfulness that took his breath away.

"What is your name?" he had asked.

She had dropped her gaze shyly and had smiled. Then she had done an astonishing thing. Against the custom of the Vietnamese with strangers, she had lifted those large liquid brown eyes and looked him in the eyes. "I cannot speak with you," she said softly.

Her voice was low and musical, so gentle on his ears he felt as if he were falling into a kind of trance.

"But I want to know your name..."

Her eyes remained on his. "I am sorry. My mother would be very angry."

Later, he found out she had come to Saigon with her mother to buy food in the market. That day, though, her fierce mother had spied her talking with him and had snatched away the lavender silk, tugging at Mai while she shouted in Vietnamese. Watching her being dragged away by her protective mother, he had no idea he would see her again. That first time, she had been just a beautiful girl in a strange, exotic city filled with foreign sounds and indistinguishable words.

McQuade inhaled the fresh scent of salt air and felt a strange beauty well up inside him. Tears spilled from his eyes, coursing unnoticed down his face. The sweet memory of her mixed with terrible pain and produced some strange new feeling he had never before experienced. He was crying and his heart was breaking but an almost holy beauty filled him, and he suspected it was the ghost of his youth come back to haunt him, forcing him to look back at everything he had lost—his innocence, his hopes, his dreams, all shattered now and lying on the ground of a burned-out village in an overgrown and long-forgotten jungle in a foreign land called Vietnam.

He raised his eyes to the heavens and saw in them the only hope he had. Up there, alone and free, he soared with angels and communed with God. Up there, in the limitless blue sky, memory left him and he was whole again, lifted up from all earthly cares and suspended in an unnamed country where all was peaceful, tranquil and serene. Up there, he found the strength to go on living.

He raised his hand and dashed the unwanted tears from his eyes. No sense thinking about it; there was no solution to his problem, no medication for his pain. He turned and began to walk toward town. When he got there, he'd get a big breakfast of bacon and eggs and he'd wash it down with three cups of the blackest coffee he could find. Then he'd get in his plane and fly back to Hyannis. On Tuesday he'd pick up Tory, fly her to Boston, get a room for the night in some cheap hotel, bring her back on Wednesday, and then he'd fly out of her life forever, free again, totally and eternally free.

Chapter Five

On Tuesday afternoon at two minutes before two in the afternoon, McQuade taxied the plane as close to the hangar as he could. He watched as Tory walked toward the plane. She wore a flowery summer dress with a wide white collar and no sleeves. The skirt billowed out behind her as she walked, making her look as fresh as the morning dew. She carried a small overnight bag, a pocketbook and a wide-brimmed straw hat with white ribbons floating behind it. She looked scrumptious, like a million bucks in the safest bank in the country. In that instant, all his previous plans to forget her were forgotten. Suddenly the past did not exist. Only Tory did.

He jumped down from the plane and went to meet her. "You're right on time," he said, taking her bag from her.

"Career girls have to be," she said, flouncing past him without so much as a hello.

He raised an eyebrow. "Nice to see you, too."

She ignored him and climbed into the plane. He stowed her baggage and climbed up beside her. "The plans are still on for Boston, aren't they?"

"Of course they are. Why do you even ask?"

"You're in such a snippy mood, I wondered if Daniel and you broke up."

"You only wish."

He chuckled as he taxied the small plane toward the runway. "Uh-huh, I guess I do at that."

"I haven't thought about you once since I discovered you gone Saturday morning," she lied. "I've thought of Daniel almost constantly."

"I'm glad to hear that. Wouldn't want any broken-hearted woman crying up a storm in my plane."

"Dream on, McQuade." She gave him a sidelong glance. She had to approach him about seeing her father. Maybe she'd better bite the bullet right now. "My father wants to talk to you."

"What about?"

"Some business he'd like to transact with you."

"No way, Tory, not if it's about Vietnam."

"Look, if you want to refuse after he's talked to you, fine, but at least have the courtesy to hear him out."

He checked the instruments, spoke to the control tower, and headed the plane straight down the runway. When they were in the air and Cape Cod was visible on the horizon, he said, "Okay, but don't expect me to agree to go with you. Vietnam's not in the plans, sweetheart."

"Maybe the reason you don't have much of a life now, McQuade, is because you haven't come to terms with the past."

"What do you mean I haven't got much of a life? I've got a great life!"

"Yeah, right. Flying a broken-down airplane, in hock up to your neck, no family, nothing but a rusted-out pickup truck and a plane that's ready for the garbage heap. Some life."

"I didn't say you had to approve of it," he said shortly.

She dropped her gaze. "I'm sorry. I don't have a right to criticize your life-style."

"That's right, you don't. Now, if you don't mind, I've got some concentrating to do. It's busy as hell up here today and I don't want you to miss your boyfriend's big night."

"What's the matter, McQuade?" she taunted. "I hit too close to home? Have you been looking at yourself in the mirror lately and not seeing what you like?"

"Honey, it's no worse when I look in the mirror than when you do. In fact, it might be a lot easier. At least I don't lie when I'm feeling horny."

"What's that supposed to mean?"

"You know damn well what it means, hotshot."

"I'm afraid I don't."

"Tory, admit it. The other night you wanted to kiss me so bad you almost fainted."

She stared at him, then felt a faint blush infuse her face. "That's absurd!"

"Okay, it's absurd," he said. "You staying at Daniel's tonight?"

"Of course. Where else would I stay?"

McQuade shrugged. "Your own place?"

"I want to be with Daniel. Anyway, his apartment is right downtown. Mine's farther out." She glanced at McQuade. "And where are you staying?"

"The cheapest place I can find."

"Go with me to Vietnam and you'll be staying at the Ritz every weekend."

"You sure are hot on Vietnam. You want to do a photo shoot on it and sell it to a big magazine?"

"It doesn't have anything to do with work."

"Good, because I'm not going."

"You need money, McQuade. You'll go."

"Like hell."

She glanced at him. "You never did say where you're staying tonight."

"I said the cheapest place I can find. If that's a gutter, so be it."

"Well, for crying out loud, McQuade, if you're so hard up, stay at my place."

"It's nice of you to offer, Tory, but I'll find a flop-house."

"McQuade," she said, exasperation ringing in her voice, "you really are the most stubborn man. Here." She pushed her key into his hand and wrote down her address. "Just make sure you turn off all the lights when you leave and lock the door."

"Sweetheart, I don't take charity."

"Good, because I don't offer it. Just take the key, will you? You'll be doing me a favor, anyway. I think I forgot to water my plants."

He shrugged. "Okay," he said, pocketing the key along with her address. Sometimes he couldn't understand women. They were unique on all the earth, puzzles made by God to punish man for his sins.

THE BOSTON WOMEN'S VOTERS' League had rented the biggest auditorium in Boston for a series of debates between Daniel Sullivan and Frank Dickerman. By seven-thirty, the auditorium was only half-filled. Daniel paced back and forth behind the stage, nervously glancing at his watch and sneaking looks at the audience. Tory sat on a pile of packing crates, filing her nails. She was more than a little put out. Since she'd appeared an hour ago, Daniel hadn't said more than two words to her. He was too busy listening to some little blond floozy who batted her eyelashes at him and kept brushing imaginary lint off his impeccable jacket.

"Dammit, Sid," Daniel said, adjusting his tie. "It doesn't look good. Where is everybody?"

"Danny," Sid Gleason assured him, "you worry too much. Go back to studying your notes and leave the worryin' to me."

Stubby O'Brien hurried up to Daniel, his arms loaded with white paper bags filled with coffee and doughnuts. "Here, boss. Thought you'd like a bite to eat."

"Take that food outta his sight!" Sid Gleason shouted, racing up and pushing Stubby away. "You know he's got a weight problem! What's the matter with you? You lost what little brain you got?"

"Boys, boys," Daniel said, sarcasm oozing from every pore. "Let's not get excited. It's only the major event of my political career..." he loosened his tie as his face grew red and his voice rose "...and no one's *here!*" He threw down his notes. "Damn it all! Why isn't anyone here yet?"

"Calm down," Sid Gleason said, giving his arm a fraternal pat. "I promise you, they'll be here."

"Yeah? When? Next year?"

Sid smiled reassuringly. "Next year you'll be sittin' in the governor's chair. Don't worry, Danny." He picked up the notes and smoothed them with his freckled hand. "Here, study these some more. I hear Dickerman's gonna announce a tax cut. Be prepared. You know our response. We'll accuse him of rhetoric, mumble some stuff about pulling Massachusetts out of the deepest economic hole in its history, shoot off some firecrackers and wave the state flag. I tell you, Danny, you're a shoo-in."

"That's right, Dan," the little blonde said, patting his arm as if she owned him. "Relax, you'll win hands down."

From the sidelines, Tory watched with surprise. She'd never seen Daniel lose his cool. She didn't much like the way he looked when his face was mottled with red and his hands were shaking from nerves. She also didn't like the way Blondie was acting so possessive. Who was she, anyway? Someone they'd picked up in a political gutter?

For some reason, Tory thought of McQuade and she found herself smiling. She couldn't envision McQuade losing his cool. He wasn't the type. He might yell at somebody, but only to whip them into shape. He was the kind of man she'd like on a sinking ship. He might not get out, but everyone else would....

A high-school band started warming up at the bottom of the stage. Tory wished she had earplugs. Why couldn't they ever find a band that could play together? This one sounded like sixteen different groups, all competing against each other.

"Tory," Sid Gleason said, sidling up to her, "you look great. Nice dress." He raised an eyebrow as she went on filing her nails. "But tonight, Tory, you think you could look more interested than you usually do?"

She stopped filing her nails and stared at him. "What do you mean, look interested? I'm always interested in what Daniel says."

"Yeah, well, we know that, but not everybody does. There was an item in the paper today..." He shoved a folded-up paper at her. Three lines of gossip were underlined in red. Her eyebrow rose as she read the words:

Snappy free-lance photographer Tory Britton might like politicians, but she didn't look too interested in politics at a local rally last week. She was spied in the company of gubernatorial candidate Daniel Sullivan, yawning from boredom and glancing at her watch repeatedly. Hey, Sully, maybe she's trying to tell you something...?

She looked at Sid. "This is sheer junk."

Sid shrugged. "Yeah, but it's negative, you know? Danny wasn't too pleased."

"How would you know?" she asked. She'd never really liked Sid Gleason. Spending more time in his company wasn't changing her mind any, either.

"Hey! I'm his number-one man, you know?" Gleason brushed some crumbs off his polyester jacket. "He tells me everything."

"Yeah? He tell you to hire that little blond floozy over there to keep him company when I'm not around? My God, look at her, she looks like she's slept with every man in Boston."

"Good grief!" Sid exclaimed, his face going beet-red as he looked around, hoping she hadn't been overheard. "Keep your voice down, Tory! A rumor like that get started, Danny'd be dead in twenty-four hours."

Tory sighed. "I was only joking, Sid." Actually, she did think Blondie looked like she slept around, but she didn't think Daniel was one of the men. He was the epitome of Mr. Middle Class America, straight as an arrow. Daniel Sullivan wouldn't have an affair if his life depended on it.

She allowed herself to briefly ponder the thought of Cargo McQuade in bed, then banished the thought, horrified that she had even wondered.

"Tory?" Daniel called to her, surrounded by his minions. He didn't bother to look for her as he spoke with first one adviser, then another. "Tory?" He glanced at her impatiently and realized she was seated on the crates. "Good grief, Tory, you might rip your dress!"

She stared at Daniel, wondering why she had always made excuses for him. He had absolutely no sense of humor whatsoever. How had she stood it the past year?

"Sweetheart," she reassured him, "I won't rip my dress. I promise."

Daniel sighed in exasperation and said something to Stubby O'Brien. Stubby glanced at Tory and whispered something to Daniel. Daniel threw down his notes. "Damn it, Stubby, just do it!"

Stubby advanced slowly toward Tory. "Tory?"

"Yes, Stubby?"

"Daniel doesn't like the hat."

"What hat?"

Stubby ran a thick finger around his shirt collar, looking like he'd rather be anywhere but here. "Your hat, Tory."

"And he told you to come over and tell me?"

"Of course. That's what I'm for. I do what Daniel tells me."

Tory felt incipient anger rippling under her skin. "Dammit, Stubby, what's my hat got to do with anything?"

"It's the image, Tory, the picture he wants to present. The hat's a bit flighty, you know? It might make people think you're not serious or somethin'."

"Serious? Well, who cares if I'm serious! I'm not the candidate, Daniel is!"

"Yeah, but in politics, the candidate's wife is the invisible running mate."

"I'm not his wife," she snapped. "Not yet, anyway."

"Well, if you want to be married to the governor of the state, you gotta start takin' these things seriously, Tory."

"Thanks, Stubby," she said. "I'll remember that." She tossed her head in the direction of the little blonde. "By the way, where'd you dig her up?"

"Francie?" Stubby smiled. "Hey, she's a little trooper, ya know? She gets us coffee, irons our shirts, types up news releases . . . Hell, Danny couldn't function without her."

"Well, she's news to me. I've never seen her before."

"Yeah, name's Francine Lyman. Came on the campaign about a month ago. Started out as a volunteer and kinda made herself indispensable."

Indeed, Tory thought darkly, watching as Francine smoothed Daniel's shirt collar and looked up at him adoringly.

"Thanks for the information, Stubby," she said, then went to find her seat in the auditorium.

She sat on the sidelines in the front row, remembering how a famous first lady had made a career for herself by looking at her husband adoringly. She knew Stubby had coached her to smile and clap madly when Daniel scored a point in the debate, but her face felt like cement. More and more it felt as if she was just one of the political props in Daniel Sullivan's race for the governorship. Angrily she wondered if he would ever have asked her to marry him if he hadn't announced his bid for office.

Shocked at her thoughts, she tried to concentrate on the debate, but her mind kept wandering. She was so immersed in her private doubts about her and Daniel's relationship that she was surprised when the high-school band struck up and applause erupted. The debate was over and she hadn't heard a thing.

Feeling guilty, she went to Daniel and kissed his cheek warmly.

Daniel put his arm around her shoulder while waving to the crowd. "Smile, Tory," he said out of one side of his mouth while he continued smiling and waving. "Smile, kiddo, this is just the start for us both."

Tory felt her smile falter, but she hurriedly pasted it back on as politicians and friends slapped Daniel on the back, pumped her hand up and down in exuberant handshakes, and kissed her right and left. Frazzled, blinking at the flashbulbs that erupted in her face, hustled off the stage and into a waiting car, Tory felt as if she'd fallen into an ocean and was being carried away by a surging tide.

Press corps, photographers, reporters and hangers-on all waved signs and shouted. That ridiculous band played on, obviously ignorant of all musical theory, but making up for it with their youthful exuberance.

When at last she and Daniel were alone in the limousine and they were gliding toward the hall where Daniel would meet with his campaign workers, she expected Daniel to take her in his arms and kiss her wildly.

Instead he lit up a cigarette and turned to her. "Dammit, Tory," he said angrily, "why in heaven's name did you wear that ridiculous hat?"

Green sparks crackled in Tory's eyes. "What is this fixation you have with my hat?"

Daniel blew out smoke, looking like a bull on a rampage. "I don't know about you anymore, Tory. You just don't seem to understand what I need."

Daniel's criticism cut through Tory's heart, but she was determined not to show it. "Well, it's a good thing you've got a little cutie like Francine around to boost your spirits, isn't it?"

"What's that supposed to mean?"

"I saw her drooling all over you, Daniel. I happen to be your girlfriend, but you didn't even have time to come over and say hello. I sat there for an hour cooling my heels while little Blondie simpered around you like she thought you were the second coming of Christ."

"You're jealous!"

"Of course I'm jealous! What did you expect? That I'd sit back and enjoy watching another woman fall all over you?"

"She doesn't fall all over me, Tory. She's a bright, creative young woman who loves politics and instinctively understands me."

"Daniel, you are not very bright."

"What?" He looked as if she'd slapped him.

"You'd think any woman on earth who cast adoring eyes on you was intelligent. She just makes you feel good about yourself."

"What's wrong with that?"

Stumped, Tory sat and wondered what was wrong with that. It was becoming more and more obvious that she didn't know how to give Daniel what he wanted, just as he didn't seem to know or care about Tory's needs.

Sighing, Tory slid down in the seat. "Daniel, why did you ask me to marry you?"

"Because I love you!"

She rolled her head on the back seat so she was looking at him. "Do you?"

"Of course I do! What's this nonsense you're spouting, Tory?"

"If I don't know how to make you happy, how can I be right for you?"

"Tory, you are the woman I want to be my wife. I don't want to hear you talk this way. It scares me."

Her heart softened when she heard his words. "Daniel, I don't understand what's happening between us. I only know that when you admit you're scared, I really care for you."

"Tory." Daniel gathered her in his arms. "I'm sorry. I was so nervous about the debate, I guess I didn't even see you."

"It's okay, honey," she said, but the small ache in her heart wouldn't dissipate. Was it too much to expect that the man who loved her would *want* her with him, would notice when she was absent or present? She wondered what love really was. With Daniel, it sometimes seemed more like obligation than joy, more duty than spontaneity. Was it possible to love someone but not be right for him? Or was she simply expecting love to be without problems, mistakenly expecting things always to be easy?

Her questions nagged her during Daniel's after-the-debate celebration. She watched him closely, keeping to the sidelines, seeing his joy as he circulated the room, clasping hands, hugging, talking, laughing. He loved this life, was made for it. Oddly, she had never been very interested in politics. Could two people with such differing interests really be right for each other?

Then her gaze fell on Francine Lyman and she felt anger ripple through her. The woman was a gold digger, or she'd miss her guess. She wore a tight skirt and three-inch high heels, a low-cut sweater, and carried a glass of wine as she hung on first one man's arm, then another's. Her laugh was loud and had an earthy quality to it that seemed to promise easy sex to any man who wanted it. Tory looked at Daniel and wondered if he wanted it. . . .

Her body tensed when she saw Francine spy Daniel.
Francine opened her arms and went running to him, hugging him and gushing all over him. Tory felt repulsion ripple through her. Was *this* what Daniel found enticing, this
cheap blonde with the fake laugh who threw herself at every
man and ran her fingers possessively over him?

Tory stood and watched as Francine hung on Daniel's
arm, feeling anger rumbling inside like distant thunder. The
little witch was making a play for Daniel. Tory wondered
why she didn't walk over and slap her across the face. But
something prevented her, something she couldn't understand but was wise enough to heed. Somewhere deep inside
was the knowledge that Daniel had the right to make his
own decisions and live his own life. If those decisions and
that life took him farther and farther from Tory, then they
had a problem. And if there was a problem between her and
Daniel, they didn't need to mask it by fighting over Francine Lyman.

Inching her way through the crowd, Tory at last escaped
into the night air. She could signal a cab and have it take her
to Daniel's place, or she could go home. She had the begin-
nings of a barracuda of a headache and knew she wasn't in
the mood for more fighting with Daniel. On a whim, she
hailed a cab and gave the driver her home address.

McQuade was there, of course, and that could be a problem, but she didn't think it would be as big a problem as the
one she faced right now with Daniel.

When she got to her place, she realized she'd given
McQuade her key. She stood outside on the steps of her
town house and rang the doorbell repeatedly, then pounded
on the door.

"McQuade? Open up."

At last the door opened. McQuade stood there, his chest
bare, wearing only a pair of navy blue bikini jockey shorts.
He blinked and rubbed his face. She'd obviously awakened
him.

Tory felt a wave of awareness wash over her. He had the body of Adonis. How was she going to fight the attraction that flared between them when he looked so good she wanted to throw herself at him?

"Good grief, McQuade," she said, pushing past him. "The least you could do is get dressed."

"I didn't know I was having company," he said, closing the door and following her into the living room. "What happened? You and Daniel have a fight?"

"No, but we would have. In this case, I thought discretion was the better part of valor."

"What would you have fought about?"

Tory pressed the heels of her hands to her eyes. "Not now, McQuade, my head is killing me."

"Does aspirin work?"

"Generally. There's some in the medicine cabinet in my bathroom. Would you get me a couple?"

"Done."

She flopped into a chair gratefully, remembering that Daniel always grumbled when she asked him to do something for her. A minute later, McQuade was back with two aspirin and a glass of cold water.

"Thanks," she said, managing a wobbly smile. "You're a good man, Cargo McQuade."

"I try to be," he said.

She noticed thankfully that he'd pulled on a pair of jeans. Now she just had to contend with the most beautifully developed arms and chest she'd ever seen in her life.

"You want to talk about it?" McQuade asked, settling on the couch across from her.

She shook her head. "Wouldn't do any good. I'm still hazy about everything, anyway."

"Hazy?"

She hesitated. "I'm not quite sure what's happening between Daniel and me, but it doesn't feel good." She remembered the way he'd held her in the limousine and she felt her heart soften. "I feel as if I care for him, but something's not right between us."

"Maybe he doesn't love you," McQuade suggested gently.

"He says he does. He says he wants to marry me..." She trailed off, frowning as she stared into space. "I don't know, McQuade. A month ago, if you'd asked me if I had any doubts about Daniel and me, I'd have said none. Today...?" She shrugged. "I'm not so sure."

"Maybe you need to cool it a while. This vacation will give you a chance to be away from him a while. Sort things out."

"I need more than a week," she said, then turned to look at McQuade. "Which reminds me. We'll have at least a week in Vietnam."

"No dice," he said, holding his palms up as if to ward her off.

"McQuade—"

"No." He stood up and gave her a warning glance. "I mean it, Tory. Not tonight. You've got a headache and I don't want one. I'll see your father tomorrow, but I can tell you now, I'm not going with you."

"You haven't heard what it's about! How can you say you won't go?"

McQuade shook his head. Lately he was remembering too much. For twenty years he'd succeeded in keeping Vietnam locked away in a black box in his mind. Now the lock had been shattered and he was having a devil of a time keeping the memories from spilling all over the place, destroying the peace he'd worked so hard to find.

"Tory," he said quietly, "I make my own decisions."

She stared at him, feeling her heart soften. His quiet stand touched her in a way she'd never been touched before. She was used to men like her father, who demanded rights for themselves while walking all over hers.

"Okay, McQuade," she said quietly, "but at least talk with my father tomorrow."

"Fine." McQuade looked around. "Shall I sleep on the couch?"

"If you wouldn't mind."

"I mind, but for you I'll do it."

"You're such a gentleman under that scruffy surface of yours."

He stood looking at her, his dark eyes burning into hers. "Daniel better watch out. When he's not looking, someone just might come along and scoop you up."

She looked into his eyes and felt a thrill go through her. For a moment she was tempted to reach out and touch him, but she stopped herself. First things first: settle things with Daniel.

"Go to bed, Tory," McQuade said. "I'll talk with your father tomorrow."

"Good night, Cargo McQuade."

"Good night, Tory."

She headed for her bedroom, then stopped and turned back to him. "What's your real name?"

"That's my real name."

"Cargo?"

His face closed up. "I flew cargo planes in the army. That's how I got the name. No one's called me by my real name in over twenty years."

"But you do have one?"

"Somewhere," he said. "But I wouldn't answer to it if anyone used it."

"Someday I want to find out all about you, McQuade. I want to know where you were born, and what your real name was, not that nickname someone hung on you because you flew a cargo plane."

"You want a lot. More than I could probably ever give."

She studied his face. "You're right," she said slowly. "I do want a lot."

She turned and walked toward her bedroom, shaking inside. She had a hunch that Cargo McQuade was going to become a lot more than just a travel companion to Vietnam.

Chapter Six

"Rise and shine, Tory!"

Tory groaned and pulled her pillow over her head, trying to shut out the voice of McQuade outside her bedroom door.

"Tory?"

"Go away," she grumbled. Rolling over, she squinted at the sunlight that streamed in her windows.

McQuade tried the door and found it unlocked. He pushed it open and leaned against the doorjamb, his arms folded. "You getting up today?"

"Sometime," she said.

"I'm going to make us breakfast."

"Don't bother for me. I'm not hungry."

"Tory, a good breakfast is the foundation of a good day."

"Two eggs, then," she said, and rolled over on her stomach and pulled the pillow over her head. "In bed. On a silver tray, with a rose in a bud vase."

McQuade grinned. "Anything else?"

"A bottle of imported champagne. The morning paper." She rolled over and sat up. "Oh yeah, and a five-pound box of chocolates guaranteed not to put any weight on me."

"Is that how you celebrate out in that romantic little hideaway of yours?"

She flopped back down in bed, stretching luxuriously. "Don't I wish."

"What else do you want?"

She drew the sheet up to her chin and looked around the room, letting her imagination roam. "Um . . . let's see . . ." Her eyes fell on McQuade. "I want this tall, dark, handsome stranger to kidnap me and take me to an exotic island and make mad, passionate love to me."

"What about Daniel?"

Her smile evaporated. "Oh, hell, McQuade. You had to spoil it, didn't you?"

"Interesting," he said, grinning. "I mention Daniel's name and suddenly you're not happy anymore. It bears thinking about, my dear."

"I'll ponder it all day," she said, casting him a sour look.

"I'll have those eggs ready in a jiffy," McQuade said, closing the door.

Tory sat in bed and stared at the closed door, then flopped down and let out a huge sigh of satisfaction. Just being with McQuade was ten times more fun than being with Daniel.

"SO TELL ME MORE about your dreams," McQuade suggested when Tory sat down to breakfast.

She heard his question but was so busy looking at the food she couldn't answer him. Somehow he had managed to put together a veritable feast in just a few minutes. She eyed the scrambled eggs, sausage and biscuits hungrily.

"Hey!" she said delightedly. "Where'd you learn to cook?"

"I live alone," he said, taking a forkful of fluffy eggs. "One learns in order to survive."

"Daniel lives alone, too," she sniffed, "but he can't cook to save his life."

"Perhaps I'm better than Mr. Sullivan in certain areas."

She slanted him a wry glance. "Perhaps." Privately, she was beginning to suspect that McQuade was better than Daniel in *most* areas.

McQuade poured two cups of freshly brewed coffee. "Are you alarmed that Daniel didn't call last night?"

Her spoon paused halfway to the coffee cup. "Should I be?"

He shrugged. "I would be if I'd almost had a fight with my girl and left her and she didn't call."

"Mmm." Tory scratched her knee. "I see your point."

"It's even more alarming that you're not mooning all over the house about him."

"Oh?" She glanced at McQuade nervously. What was he getting at?

"When one is in love, I'm told, one thinks of the loved one all the time."

"You're *told?* What's the matter, McQuade? No first-hand experience?"

McQuade stirred his coffee idly. "That's right. I don't believe in the emotion."

"Don't believe in it, or don't indulge in it?"

"Neither."

"What do you indulge in? Casual sex with no commitments?"

He looked at her over the rim of his coffee cup. "Can sex ever be casual?"

"Isn't it? I mean, when there's no attachment, no...no caring involved?"

"I wouldn't know. I've never had sex with a woman where there wasn't caring involved."

"But you said you didn't believe in love."

"I don't."

She shook her head. "Solve the problem for me, McQuade. Tell me what the hell you're talking about."

"It's simple, Tory. Love doesn't exist, whereas caring is a genuine connection between two people who matter to each other."

"But you've just defined love," she protested.

"No way. I told you, love doesn't exist."

She stared at McQuade, fascinated. "I have often thought that men and women speak two separate and distinct emotional languages. This proves it."

"How?"

"What I see as love, you call caring. You refuse to use the word love. Why, McQuade? Because you're afraid it's unmanly?"

"No, Tory, because I see it as a lie. When people speak of love they usually mean 'love me,' not 'I love you.' They want to be protected, taken care of like children in a relationship that is meant to involve two adults."

"Let's say love did exist, McQuade, just for the sake of argument. How would you define it?"

He shook his head. "I'm not good with words. I can't define it."

She felt her curiosity change to compassion. "Have you ever experienced it?" she asked gently.

He sat and stared broodingly into space. "Once. A long time ago."

"What happened?"

"She died."

"I see." She dropped her gaze. Suddenly things had gotten serious. "How did it happen?"

"Falling in love or her dying?"

Tory shrugged slightly. "Both, I guess."

Again he shook his head. "I really can't talk about it, Tory."

She felt her heart go out to him. "Often the pain inside us goes away only when we talk about it," she said softly. "When we put it in words. Talking about it is cathartic."

A faint smile hovered on his mouth. "Your words right now, spoken so gently, feel like salve on an open wound. I like to listen to you when your voice is gentle, Tory. Is this what you sound like when you're with a man you love?"

Her eyes widened slightly. Was it? Even more important, was she with a man she loved? A man she *could* love? A feeling of warmth permeated her midsection and began to spread outward into her entire body. She was enveloped in it, bathed in a kind of holy heat that made her feel enormously loving, capable of genuine caring. Her hand, as if of its own will, reached out to McQuade.

"I'm not sure anymore if I know what love is," she said quietly. "I used to think you met someone and fell in love and lived happily ever after. I'm beginning to suspect it's infinitely more complicated than that."

He took her hand and held it, squeezed it and said, "I hope you find it one day."

She nodded, her eyes misted with tears, but not sad tears, happy ones, tears that signaled her joy, that seemed to radiate from the warmth that was spreading throughout her body. She felt as if she was filled with light, and she had never felt so beautiful. Not beautiful in her face or her body but in her spirit, deep inside where the warmth shimmered, bathing her in golden light.

"Tory," he said.

"Yes?"

"Nothing. Just Tory."

There had never been a more perfect morning.

Until the phone rang.

It was Daniel, irate, demanding to know where she had gone last night.

"I came home, Daniel," she said patiently. "Where'd you think I went? Timbuktu?"

"That's where you might as well be for all the good you're doing my campaign. Did you read the paper this morning?"

She felt herself grow cool. "No. Why? Banner headlines declaring you the next governor?"

"Page six," Daniel said. "Column two. Quote: *Daniel Sullivan has been seen squiring free-lance photographer Tory Britton around the past few months. Last night she was noticeably missing at his campaign headquarters after the debate. Trouble brewing...? Not if...'* Oh, it doesn't matter about the rest. What matters is that you left last night and can't seem to understand that as a candidate's wife you have to *be* there, Tory, all the time. No matter if you're in a good mood or not, you paste on a smile. Can't you understand that? Dammit, it's elementary."

"I guess I haven't understood it, Daniel," she said quietly. She opened the paper and turned to page six. "Let's see. Oh, yes, here it is..." She read along, then her eyes widened and her temper snapped to attention. "How cagey of you, Mr. Sullivan! Edit the damn article when you read it. Why not read the rest?" She began reading from the point where he had left off: *'Trouble brewing? Not if it's true what they're saying all over town. Tory Britton's got competition, in the form of a neat five-foot-five campaign volunteer who seems to know how to catch a candidate's eye...'"*

A photograph of Francine Lyman looking adoringly into Daniel's eyes stared up at Tory.

"You lowlife," Tory said, her voice quivering. "You dare to attack *me* when you're being paraded all over the page with that little floozy hanging all over you?"

"She is not a floozy."

"All right—a tramp, then. Call her what you will, the meaning's the same."

"I will not have you talk about her that way!"

Astounded, Tory blinked. "Oh? And do you have any instructions for dear little Francine about the way *she* can talk about *me?*"

"She never mentions you."

"She's too busy making a play for you, that's why."

"Oh, for God's sake, Tory. Francine is just a co-worker. We're nothing more than friends."

"Well, I tell you what. Until you can decide who you want to be friendly with, why don't we call it quits?"

"What do you mean, call it quits? Sid wants to write a press release today about our engagement. Now's a fine time to call everything off!"

"A press—" She stared at the phone. They couldn't go on this way. They needed to talk. "Daniel," she said, "I'm coming over to your place right now. We have to talk."

"Tory, I haven't got time."

"Well, you better find some," she said. "I'll be over in half an hour." She hung up and looked at McQuade. "I'll meet you at the airport in a couple hours. I have to talk with Daniel."

"Trouble?"

"We just need to talk, that's all."

"Maybe everything will work out," he said gently.

"Yes, maybe so," she said, but privately she doubted it.

TORY LET HERSELF INTO Daniel's apartment using her key. His suit jacket was lying on the floor, marking a trail to his room which included his tie, shirt and shoes. He'd obviously been so exhausted last night when he left campaign headquarters that he'd started taking off his clothes the minute he hit the door, making a beeline for his room.

A strange feeling of sadness welled up inside her. A few months ago, she would have smiled at the way he'd left his clothes all over the place. Now, she had an odd premonition that she was looking at them for the last time.

"Daniel?"

She dropped her pocketbook in a chair and walked toward the bedroom. Inching open the door she saw that the bed was empty, but the door to the bathroom was ajar. Crossing the room, she came to a stop just outside the bathroom. Daniel was standing at the sink, a towel wrapped around his waist as he shaved.

"Hi," Tory said softly.

Daniel went on shaving, not even bothering to look at her. "Did you come back to return the keys to my apartment?"

Any hopes for a reconciliation plummeted. "I thought we needed to talk."

He sighed, rinsing the shaving lather off his razor. "I suppose we do."

"Sorry to be such a bother," she said ironically. "It's odd, but I seem to remember your asking me to marry you a few days ago. What happened? Having second thoughts?"

He went to his closet and took out a pair of slacks and pulled them on. "Aren't you? What other explanation is there for the way you walked out on me last night?"

"Daniel, you didn't even notice me once we got to your campaign headquarters."

"Is that what you think I should be doing, Tory? Paying attention to you all night?"

She turned her head away. His words felt like a knife, slicing her heart into pieces. She wondered how they had ever gotten as far as talking about marriage. They were each trying to win the other's attention, yet were focused only on their own needs. She felt a terrible sense of bewilderment, as if she were in a foreign country and didn't understand the language. She couldn't talk to Daniel anymore. They were at cross-purposes.

"Daniel, we have big problems."

He let out a breath. "Perhaps we do." He kept his eyes on himself in the mirror while he knotted his tie. "I made a mistake asking you to marry me, Tory. We should wait to announce the engagement until much later. The timing's off. I need to give the time to my campaign. Sid will know when we should announce our engagement."

A yawning pit seemed to open in front of Tory. She sat on the edge of Daniel's bed and wondered how they had so suddenly gone from being lovers to being such complete strangers. She felt disoriented, as if she'd gone to sleep in one room and awakened in another. Sid Gleason had Daniel's attention and trust more than she did.

"Daniel," she said softly, focusing confused eyes on him, "please come sit next to me." She patted the bed. "We need to talk, Daniel, not just say a bunch of words at each other."

"Dammit, Tory, I've got work to do. There's a press conference in two hours. I don't have time to talk."

"And that's precisely what's wrong with us, Daniel," she said. "You don't have time for us."

"What do you want from me?" he asked. "I am the gubernatorial candidate for the state, Tory, not some hotrodder who thinks only about the woman he's dating."

"That's funny, I thought I was the woman you wanted to marry."

"You're always twisting things, Tory. I only meant that I've got more important things to do than cater to your every whim. Dammit, Tory, I'm running for governor! What the hell do you want from me?"

"Your attention," she snapped, rising from the bed. "I'm sorry, Daniel, but I happen to think a relationship is a hell of a lot more important than you seem to. The only thing that matters to you is your work. What about us, Daniel? What about *me?*"

"My work is the most important thing in the world to me, Tory. Nothing comes before it—not you, not my family, nothing." His eyes glinted with determination. "If you can't accept that, then maybe we better call everything off."

She felt as if she'd been waiting for the other shoe to drop, and now it had. Where she'd been shaking with anger only moments ago, she now felt calm. It was over. Maybe there'd be some emotional fallout, but the end was here and had to be faced.

"I think maybe we should," she said quietly.

Startled, he stared at her. "Oh, come on, Tory. You don't mean that."

"I do mean it, Daniel. I need a man who loves me, one who cares about me and pays attention to me. I won't take a backseat to any job, I don't care what it is—the governorship or the presidency."

"But that's just it, Tory," he said, excitement throbbing in his voice, "someday it could be the presidency. And you could go with me every step of the way, easing my path, behind me, urging me on. Tory, I need you. We look great together, honey." He picked up a copy of *Boston* magazine and shook it at her. "Haven't you seen how good we look together? Look at this picture, Tory. Look at it. Don't throw this away. Take some time, cool down a little. We could have it all, Tory. Everything."

She watched him with something very close to horror. The man she'd thought she knew was showing a side of himself she hadn't known existed. It was like watching a movie in which a character turns into someone else entirely. She felt sick, bereft, comfortless. She turned away from him and walked dumbly to the window and stood staring out at the early summer day with unseeing eyes.

Behind her, Daniel put his hands on her shoulders. "I know it's hard now, Tory, but it'll get easier. After the election, after we're married."

"Daniel . . ." She turned around to look at him with pain and confusion in her eyes, not knowing what to say. She knew she'd never be able to marry this man. Now she just had to tell him.

"What's wrong, Tory? Still having doubts?"

She nodded dumbly, feeling her throat close up. "Big doubts," she managed to whisper.

He took a deep breath and glanced at his watch. "I haven't got much time, Tory. Maybe we better talk about this later."

She shook her head. "There's not going to be a later, Daniel. I'm leaving for Vietnam soon."

"I've never understood this thing about Vietnam," he said. "Why is your father so insistent that you go?"

She almost smiled. Daniel had never even taken the time to listen to her when she'd told him her father's reasons a few weeks ago. It was as if Daniel couldn't hear her. Nothing seemed to matter to him but his politics—not her, not her interests, nothing but himself and his own life. She had wanted him to love her, and so in her mind she had made it so.

She wondered now if life consisted of a series of blows that ripped away one's illusions one by one. At the end of life, did you look back and see a reason for everything? Did you finally begin to understand, or did you die as confused and disappointed as she was right now?

With a mist of tears in her eyes she picked up her pocketbook and rummaged through it, pulled out his key. "Here's your key, Daniel." She held it out to him.

He didn't move to take it. "Are you sure, Tory? We could wait until you come back from Vietnam and talk about things a little more."

She shook her head and put the key on a table near the door. "I don't think so, Daniel. I think it's better this way."

He nodded. She looked at him and for the first time saw him for what he was, not for what she wanted him to be. In that instant, she realized that was the essence of love—letting others be who they were, not imposing one's desires on them.

She walked outside and stood on the sidewalk, looking at the world with fresh eyes. She had never realized until this moment that she didn't know the first thing about loving someone. She had thought love was a rush of emotions, compounded of passion, excitement and not being able to live without each other. She saw now it was infinitely more complex. Love had nothing to do with one's self, and everything to do with the other. When one loved another person, one wanted for him what he wanted for himself. Had she loved Daniel, his concentration on politics wouldn't have bothered her. She would have thrown herself into his work wholeheartedly, not stood back resenting it because it took him from her.

But she was being hard on herself. Love worked both ways. If Daniel had loved her, he would have tried to meet her needs also.

She took a deep breath and raised her hand to hail a cab. She wondered how long it would take to come to terms with the truths she had stumbled on today. She felt suddenly older, but only a trifle wiser.

Chapter Seven

At the airport, Tory found McQuade waiting for her. She didn't say a word to him, just climbed into the plane and fastened her seat belt.

McQuade climbed in after her. "Hello to you, too," he said pleasantly.

She turned her head and looked out the window. "Just fly, McQuade. I don't feel like talking."

"Maybe we better establish the ground rules right now. Do you want complete silence or can I sing? Can I whistle? Cough? Will you crack me one if I ask a question now and then?"

She didn't say a word.

He sighed and put a hand on her arm. "Tory? Are you sure you don't want to talk about it?"

"I'm sure," she said, but her voice cracked. She cleared her throat and glanced at McQuade. "I'm sorry, I guess I am being a poop."

McQuade grinned. "I guess you can be a poop every other year or so."

She sighed and pushed her hair back. "We broke up."

McQuade nodded. "I figured as much."

"My father will be thrilled."

"I gather he didn't like Daniel."

"Hated him," she said. She looked at McQuade. "You ready to meet the general?"

"Why wouldn't I be? He won't be asking me to lead an armed patrol back to Nam, will he?"

She smiled. "No armed patrols, but he can be pretty determined, McQuade. He won't want to take no for an answer."

"I can be pretty determined, too." He glanced at her. "You're on his side, aren't you?"

She looked down at her hands knotted in her lap. "Yes, I am. He's pretty impossible sometimes, but I love him, and he wants..." She trailed off, not wanting to tell McQuade too much. "Well, I'll let him tell you what he wants. I guess because he wants it so bad, I want it, too."

McQuade didn't say anything, just glanced down at his instruments, then out at the limitless horizon. It might be easy to refuse the general, but it'd be damned hard to refuse his daughter.

"FIFTY THOUSAND DOLLARS?" McQuade stared at the retired Gen. Adrian LaPorte, shaking his head at the amount the general had just offered him to go to Vietnam. "What the hell is over there, General? The fountain of youth?"

"You don't need to know what's there. You just need to help my daughter find someone."

McQuade got up and walked toward the doors that opened onto a terrace. He surveyed the impeccably manicured lawn, the perfectly pruned shrubs, the flowers that looked as if they had been grown in a hothouse and transplanted outside just hours before. The house itself was enormous, built of red brick that had faded to pink, with white-painted window trim and a slate roof. McQuade wondered how Old Iron Ass had acquired the wealth to buy such a splendid place, nestled on forty acres of wooded property close to the New Hampshire border. He supposed lifetime army generals made a lot more than bush pilots.

Turning back into the room, McQuade studied the general. He was twenty years older and about fifty pounds lighter, and though the fierce light that had once burned in his pale blue eyes had faded, it wasn't gone. Somewhere inside the general, a steely resolve still reigned. McQuade wondered who or what could be so important to the general that he was willing to pay so much money to get it.

"Well, McQuade," the general said, "will you go?"

"I need to think about it. Fifty thousand is a lot of money."

"Enough to get you back on your feet," the general said. "I did some checking. I know you're having financial troubles."

"Is that why you chose me, general? Because you thought you could buy me?"

"No," the general said, his shrewd eyes fastened on McQuade. "I chose you because I thought I could trust you."

McQuade looked unmoved. "Uh-huh."

The general's face went red. "Un-huh? That's all you have to say?" The general made a sound deep in his throat, like an old dog strangling on a bone. "You damned pup! You know what it means to have my trust?" The general banged his cane on the floor. "It means everything, damn it. Everything!" He banged his cane again so hard that a brass candlestick on a nearby Chippendale table toppled over.

Tory stood the candlestick up. "Dad," she cautioned, "watch your blood pressure."

"The hell with my blood pressure!" the general roared. "Dammit, McQuade, what's the matter with you? You got no ambition in that body of yours? No yen to make something of yourself?" When McQuade didn't respond, the general shook his head. "That damn war didn't teach you diddly."

"You're wrong, General," McQuade said. "It taught me that a lot of good men died for no reason. We had no business being there. You'll have to go a long way to convince me I'd have any more business going over there now."

"Well, at least you're talking now," the general said. "Though what you're saying is damn idealistic twaddle. Here, have a cigar."

Tory winced. She doubted that McQuade would stand for much more of her father's tongue-lashing. It might have worked when McQuade was a soldier twenty-odd years ago. She doubted it would work now. "Dad, why don't you just tell McQuade what this is all about, so he can make up his own mind?"

The general turned his head and fastened steely eyes on his daughter. "You be quiet. I don't need instructions, thank you."

Tory raised her chin, staring down her father. "You do need manners, though," she said quietly. "You're not ordering troops around anymore, Dad. I'm your daughter, in case you've forgotten."

The general glared at his daughter, as if what she'd said wasn't important. He pointed his unlit cigar at McQuade. "Know why what you just said is idealistic claptrap?"

"Why, General?" McQuade said, lighting his cigar. He glanced at Tory from under his lashes, wondering why she stood for the kind of treatment her father handed out. He had to give her credit, though. She didn't let the general's bad temper bother her. She looked as unruffled as the queen of England.

"We went to Vietnam," the general said, "because we didn't have any choice *but* to be over there. History dealt us the cards; we had to play them." He went into a long-winded, yet impassioned explanation, and when it was over he sat and stared with bleak eyes into the past. In Nam, soldiers had called that look the thousand-yard stare. Once a man got used to killing, he looked like that, older than his years with tired eyes that had seen too much.

The general shook his head. "We were there because we'd been there, holding together alliances, for over twenty years." The general sighed. His voice had gradually lost its robustness. Now he sounded like what he was—old and tired. "Hell, we were caught in an invisible net, damned if we stayed, damned if we didn't."

"Yet you never seemed to question anything, Dad," Tory said.

"It wasn't my job to question, Tory," the general responded, his voice quiet now and filled with resignation. "I grew up in a time when obedience was everything. You didn't talk back to your parents, your God or your country. You did what was expected of you and took great pride in that duty. There were rules then, standards you obeyed. Right was very clear and so was wrong. Things were black or white. I'm not saying the old days were better. I'm just saying it was different when I grew up. My world made me what I am, just as your world has made you what you are."

Then the general rallied. "But enough talk. What'll it be, McQuade? You going?"

McQuade shook his head. "General, even fifty thousand dollars isn't enough to make me go back. I'm sorry, sir, but the answer's no."

The general stared at McQuade, his eyes flinty, his face hard. He might have been carved from granite, so unyielding did he appear. "All right," he said. "How much would it take?"

"Sir, you couldn't pay me enough."

"Every man has his price, McQuade. Even you."

"What's over there that you want so bad, General?"

"What do you care?" the general said. "My money's good. I'd pay you half before you go and the other half when you return."

"General, when I left Nam I intended to never look back, much less go back. Now you're asking me to return." He shook his head. "I'd have to have one hell of a reason to go back."

The general's jaw jutted out, the cigar clenched in his teeth, his eyes filled with gritty determination. "Okay, fifty thousand dollars and the chance at a lot more. And all expenses paid, right down to getting your shoes shined. When you came back from Nam, you'd have fifty thousand free and clear, and if you were lucky, a whole lot more. No questions asked."

McQuade was getting tired of the general and his demands. It came out in the form of sarcasm. "What do you mean, a chance at a lot more? What'll you do? Buy me a lottery ticket?"

The general puffed on his cigar, then began to cough. Irritably he crushed the cigar out in an ashtray, then lifted hard eyes to McQuade. "You remember the story that circulated in Nam about the French legionnaire who smuggled a hoard of diamonds out of Germany and brought them to Indochina after World War II?"

"Vaguely." He glanced at Tory, who looked at him questioningly. "There was this story about a French soldier who served in Vietnam after the Second World War," he explained to her. "Supposedly he'd hidden a cache of diamonds somewhere in Saigon. By the time I went to Nam, the story was more of a legend than reality." He looked back at the general, as if he were an adult who still believed in Santa Claus. "Why? You can't really believe that bunk."

"I know someone who's seen the diamonds. She said it wasn't just a story. They're real, and they're still over there, hidden somewhere where no one's been able to find them."

McQuade looked doubtful. "If she knows they exist, why hasn't she taken them for herself?"

"She has," the general said, smiling coldly. "At least some of them."

"Come on, General, be real."

"I'm as real as they get, soldier," the general said, and suddenly his voice was as strong and strident as it had been twenty years earlier, when he barked out orders that made soldiers tremble. His blue eyes glinted coldly. "You remember Mme Tran?"

McQuade thought back. The name was vaguely familiar, then it all came back to him. Mme Tran had run the most exclusive restaurant in Saigon, in a magnificent house built years before by a wealthy French landowner. It was rumored she also ran an extensive black-market business, but there was no proof of it. She was half-Vietnamese, half-French and extremely beautiful. She was exotically oriental—petite and fragile-boned, with the skin of a lotus and hair like woven black silk, dark secretive eyes and an enigmatic smile. It had been impossible to tell her age. In her knowledge of the world, she seemed ancient, yet there was a dark sensuality about her that made younger women seem uninteresting and childish.

"How do you think she got started?" the general said, a knowing smile on his face. "She was the Frenchman's mistress. He gave her some of the diamonds. She told me she'd seen them all, actually held them in her hands. She said there were dozens of them, gem-quality, as beautiful as you'd ever want to see."

"And you believed her?" McQuade asked.

"I had no reason not to," the general said heavily. His face changed. It was like watching a curtain be drawn back to expose what was hidden behind it. Suddenly he was old and his eyes were filled with pain. "She was the mother of my son."

"Your son?" In his wildest dreams, McQuade wouldn't have expected that. He looked at Tory, wondering how she felt about this, but her face was averted. He wished he could see her expression, though her body language was eloquent. Sitting stiffly upright, with her face averted, she

looked as stoic as a soldier who has just seen his best friend
shot. She didn't like it, but accepted the reality.

The general sighed. "Mme Tran and I had a child together. A boy. She wanted to marry me, but that was out of
the question. I gave her money, of course, but I had a wife
and daughter at home—" He glanced at Tory, who sat unmoving, her face turned away. He frowned, as if suddenly
aware that she might find this difficult to hear. He sat for a
moment looking at her, then forced himself to go on:
"Anyway, she wanted more from me than I was prepared to
give, so she broke off with me and refused to let me see the
child. While I was over there, it didn't bother me. I was just
glad she didn't cause any trouble. But when I left Nam and
was back stateside, I began to dream about the baby."

The general moved in his wheelchair. Suddenly he was no
longer the determined man who would step over anyone to
get what he wanted. In a matter of moments, the general
had been replaced by a frail, tormented man.

He put a feeble hand over his eyes as if to shut out the
truth, but at last he spoke again. "I began to wake up at
night hearing a baby crying. Of course, when I woke up I'd
realize there wasn't a baby in the house and I'd go back to
sleep, but after a while..."

The general sat staring into space, his face tormented. "I
couldn't sleep," he whispered. "I'd hear it crying and I'd
wake up and my heart would be hammering inside me and
I'd sit up and Lily—that was my wife, Tory's mother—"
The general's face crumpled. For a moment it looked like he
would cry, but he struggled to compose himself.

Tory got up and went to him, taking his hand. "It's all
right, Dad," she said gently, her face filled with anguish.
"It's all right."

He nodded, wiping his eyes with a shaking hand. "Lily
thought it was the war. She thought I was remembering
battles, death..." He shook his head. "But it was the baby.
At first it was just the crying, then I began to dream about

a baby holding out its arms to me and crying, wailing, and its little eyes were so dark and filled with such sorrow, as if he was accusing me..."

The general took a deep breath, willing himself to go on. "I finally went to a psychiatrist. I had to. I couldn't stand it anymore. After I talked about it, the dreams began to go away. After a year or so, they stopped completely, but—" The general cocked his head, staring into the past. Thin and frail, he looked like a tiny bird, querulous, uncertain, dazed by the events of his life. "The dreams started again after I had the stroke. That's when I knew I had to find out about my son." He lifted haunted eyes to McQuade. "You have to bring him back to me, McQuade. I've got to see him before I die."

McQuade sat staring at his cigar. He didn't trust himself to speak. There was a lump in his throat the size of a boulder. He felt he'd choke if he tried to say a word. He wished he could just get up and walk out of the house. He didn't want to hear the general's pain. He didn't want to get involved. He wanted to be left alone.

"Well?" the general said. "Will you go?"

McQuade refused to look at Tory. She was watching him with anxious eyes, pleading with him silently. He couldn't stand to see her sitting there, begging him with eloquent eyes. "Look, General," McQuade said, clearing his throat, "I've got my own problems."

"I know that," the general said. "I'm offering you a way out of them."

"I don't mean just the money. It's—" He ran a hand through his hair and stood up, walking to the doors that led to the terrace outside. He stood with his back to the general and Tory, staring outside, trying to work everything out in his mind. If he was smart, he'd refuse to go. He didn't owe the general anything. But he had heard the general's story, been a witness to his pain, and somehow had been drawn into it.

And then there was Tory. She was as tormented as her father, torn apart by his pain, sitting by him, holding his hand, her face tortured as she had listened to the old man. He had seen the helplessness in her face, had instinctively guessed at the private anguish she felt at not being able to ease her father's guilt. He knew her, knew she would go alone if she had to, and he knew he couldn't let her do that.

Damn it. Why had this had to happen to him?

He had spent half a lifetime trying to keep the nightmares from Vietnam at bay. They were asking him to do something that was as painful for him as it was for them. But who would see and hear his pain? Who could he reach out to for comfort? They expected him to help them, but who would help him? Didn't they know that he carried his own demons, demons so powerful he couldn't even talk about them? The general had somehow found the way to talk about his pain. McQuade couldn't. It was locked up inside him, like a grieving child wailing in the night.

Taking a slow, deep breath, he turned around. "I'm sorry, General, but I need to think about this a little more."

"For God's sake, McQuade, what's to think about?" the general demanded. The old man was gone, replaced once more by the harsh military presence.

"Considerably more than you know," McQuade answered. He opened the doors that led to the patio. "I'm going for a walk. I need to clear my head."

Outside, McQuade sucked the fresh air into his lungs as if he'd been suffocating. Indeed, it often felt that way, when others placed demands on him. He had never wondered where his need for freedom had taken root, but he suspected it started in childhood, when he had lived in mortal fear of an autocratic father and a mother who seemed to care only about what the neighbors might think. He had escaped from that home as much as he could, hanging out at a local airfield where a pilot had taken him under his wing. By the time he was thirteen, McQuade was flying solo.

When he was fourteen he learned to fly helicopters. At fifteen he could take a plane apart and put it together again. He ate, breathed and slept planes. At sixteen, he dropped out of high school and joined the army. His flying expertise enabled him to become a pilot, then he had been shipped to Vietnam.

Remembering now, McQuade felt a sweeping sense of loss. He'd been running all his life and what had he achieved? Tory had been right yesterday—he had a broken-down truck, a twenty-five-year-old plane and a business that was always on the edge of financial disaster. His life was a disaster.

He surveyed the dense undergrowth that bordered the general's perfect lawn and knew he had to do something about his life. But what? All he knew was flying. It was in his blood, his heart and his soul. He turned back to look at the house and felt an unfamiliar twisting in his gut. He knew he needed to make changes in his life, but didn't have the slightest idea what those changes might be. The general was offering him a chance at good money, yet he instinctively knew that all the money in the world wouldn't ease the emptiness in his life. He needed something he cared about, the way he'd once cared about Mai.

The name struck him like a fist in his gut. He stood at the edge of the lawn and felt as if a vast gulf had opened before him, taking him in, devouring him. His heart ached and he felt sorrow rise up in him like a dark, unwelcome specter. All the pain and rage and guilt and remorse welled up inside him and he was taken by it, as a log is swept up by a flooding river, and tumbled headlong into looking at his past. He had spent a lifetime running away from it. If he returned to Vietnam to find the general's son, he would be faced with it, the smells and sounds and sights. They would be there again, real, not imagined, and he wouldn't be able to turn away any longer. Returning to Vietnam would be a chance to forever lay to rest the ghosts that had haunted the fringes

of his consciousness these past twenty years. But could he
do it? Could he stand still and face the past, not try to run
from it as he'd done these past twenty years?

He took a deep breath. He couldn't run anymore. Running hadn't worked. It was even more painful than standing and facing the past. He stared into the distance and knew
he had to try. He didn't think he had much of a chance to
make things better, but he knew he had to try. His mind
made up, he walked back into the house.

"Well, General," McQuade said without preamble, "it
looks like you've found your man."

The general bowed his head. "Thank God," he said.
"Thank God."

Tory let out a breath she'd been holding without knowing it. "Thank you," she said. Until this moment, she
hadn't realized just how much she had wanted him to go.

McQuade met her eyes over the general's head. He wished
he could tell her what he was feeling, wished he could share
the misgivings he felt, but she needed him and he couldn't
let her down. He realized then he was doing this for her as
much as for himself. He pitied the general and his torment,
but Tory's anguish, her sense of helplessness at not being
able to allay her father's pain, melted him. He couldn't resist her pleading eyes.

"Good," the general said, moving his wheelchair toward
the low table that served as a bar. "I think we should celebrate." He poured whiskey into three glasses. "To my son,"
he said, holding up his glass so it caught the light.

Tory looked away. Her face was blank, all emotion carefully controlled. McQuade had a sudden intuition that she
was struggling with special pain of her own. What must it
be like to find out she had a brother half a world away?
What must it feel like to know her father was fixated on this
child while barely giving her the time of day?

McQuade caught her eyes and lifted his glass to her. "To
love," he said. "Wherever we find it."

Tory drank the whiskey quickly, shuddering as it traced a fiery path into her stomach. It didn't strike her until much later that McQuade had made a toast to love, when only that morning he'd claimed it didn't exist.

"YOU'LL HAVE TO MAKE plane reservations," the general said over lunch in the formal dining room. "See a doctor about shots, get your visas updated, that sort of thing. McQuade, I'll give you a letter telling you as much as I know about the diamonds. It's up to you if you want to pursue them."

He looked at Tory pointedly. "Obviously you have a lot to do and you won't get it all done overnight. And you'll be going in the rainy season. It won't be a lot of fun. There's malaria to contend with, not to mention geckos."

"What, pray tell, are geckos?" she asked.

"Lizards," McQuade responded. "They won't hurt you, but it's rather disconcerting to wake up at night and find a couple of them hovering on the wall above your bed."

"They sound lovely," she said ironically.

"Not lovely at all," her father said, "but certainly useful." At Tory's inquiring look, he explained: "They eat mosquitoes."

"Now you tell me about all the good stuff," Tory said. "Why didn't you mention these things earlier?"

"Simple—you wouldn't have gone," the general said.

"With a fortune in diamonds waiting for us?" Tory said. "We'd have gone." She eyed McQuade curiously. At least she figured that was why he was going. No man could resist that much money. He'd told her repeatedly he wouldn't go with her to Vietnam, but he'd sure changed his mind fast enough when he heard what he'd find if he was successful.

She was vaguely disappointed in McQuade for turning out to be so easily swayed by money, but she decided to give him the benefit of the doubt.

"So," the general said after pushing his plate away, "how are you and this Sullivan fellow doing? Still going out, are you?"

Tory toyed with her food. Her father would be ecstatic if she told him she and Daniel had broken up. She pushed her meat aside and shrugged. "I went to his first debate last night, didn't I?"

"Well, anybody could go to his debates," the general said. "I want to know if you still think you love him." He snorted contemptuously. "How you could ever fall for a creep like him is beyond me."

"What I can't figure out is how you've come to the conclusion he's a creep, when you've never even met him," Tory said.

"I've seen him on television," the general said. "That was enough."

"How can you sit there and claim that seeing someone on television gives you the ability to judge him?"

"We judge people on television every day without meeting them, Tory—talk-show hosts, the local newscaster, the weather gal, the stars of the latest sitcoms." The general shook his head. "Fact is, most people today never see their local politicians in person. Everybody relies on television now. Why shouldn't I?"

"You are close-minded, stubborn and opinionated," Tory said, pushing her plate away. "If you met Daniel even once you'd see you've been wrong about him." She felt a little twinge of guilt—she knew better now than he that Daniel had plenty of shortcomings, but she couldn't admit them to her father; he'd only use the knowledge against her.

The general snorted, then turned to McQuade. "What about you, McQuade?" the general said. "What do you think of Daniel? Ever met him?"

"No, sir."

"Know who he is?"

"Yes, sir."

The general almost smiled. "Closemouthed, aren't you?"

"Guess I am at that," McQuade acknowledged.

"Well, you must have some opinion of Daniel Sullivan," the general said.

"I'm not impressed with any politician." He glanced at Tory. "But I'll reserve judgment until I meet him."

"I doubt you'll ever get the chance," Tory said. She knew she had to tell her father sometime. Now was as good as later. "We broke up this morning," she said without preamble.

The general hooted. "Hallelujah! What happened? What made you finally come to your senses?"

"Certainly not you," she said coolly. "If anything, your constant picking at Daniel kept me defending him."

The general fell silent. Watching him was almost tiring. He almost seemed to be two people—the forceful general one minute, and an old and tired man the next. Now he sat and stared at his plate, his forehead wrinkled in thought. "I bet Daniel Sullivan would be horrified to find out your father had left a bastard child in Vietnam," he said quietly. He lifted weary eyes to his daughter. "Is that what happened? Did he drop you when you told him?"

"No," she said, placing her napkin on the table. "I told him and he never even heard me. He was always too busy thinking about his campaign." She forced a cheerful smile. "But I'll bet you're happy, aren't you, Dad? You never did like him. It didn't matter what I ever wanted. Good old Dad, always looking out after himself and riding roughshod over anyone who doesn't agree with him."

The general stared at Tory, his face filled with confusion. He seemed to see her as if for the first time. "I only want what's best for you, Tory."

"Then let me figure that out for myself, all right?" she said. "Stop trying to interfere all the time."

"I haven't interfered!" the general protested.

"Not technically," Tory said. "But you act as if I'm incompetent. If I am, let me make my own mistakes. Butt out, Dad," she said, pushing back her chair. She stood looking at the hurt mirrored in her father's face, wishing it didn't have to be like this between them, then turned and walked from the room. If her father wouldn't let go of the apron strings, she'd cut them once and for all.

"YOU WERE KIND OF ROUGH on him back there," Mc-Quade said when they had taken off from the open meadow in front of the general's home.

"I didn't mean to be," Tory said, staring dully out the side window of the plane. "It's just that he won't step out of my life. He's constantly interfering, telling me what to do, who to see, what to say. I just get tired of it."

"So you go ahead and bullheadedly do anything you can to frustrate him."

"Maybe sooner or later he'll get the idea and quit bugging me."

"Tory, he's your father. He obviously loves you. I'm sure he only wants what's best for you."

"McQuade, I know that, and in quiet moments I can even accept it. But he gets to me. He has the knack of knowing exactly what to say to get a rise out of me. Sometimes I think he actually baits me." She shook her head. "I'm not going to let him rule my life. Sooner or later he's got to realize that I'm my own person, not his daughter, but *me*—separate, unique and distinct."

"So you were determined to marry Daniel Sullivan just to spite your father."

"No, I was determined to go out with whomever I wanted to, despite what Dad told me to do."

"But going out with someone and marrying him are pretty far apart, Tory."

"McQuade, do you have something against Daniel Sullivan?"

"No, I—"

"Then leave it alone, okay? Leave *me* alone. You're as bad as my father, thinking you know what's better for me than I do."

"Okay, Tory," McQuade said. "Whatever you say."

"The magic words are 'butt out.' For both you and my father."

"Butt out," McQuade repeated. "Okay, if that's the way you want it..."

"It's the way I want it."

"Fine," McQuade said shortly. But it wasn't fine. Dammit, he was going to Vietnam with her. Was this all the thanks he was going to get?

Tory glanced at McQuade. "I'm sorry. I didn't mean to snap at you."

McQuade shrugged. "It's okay."

She turned her head and stared out the window, watching the landscape below. Up ahead was Boston, the buildings looking like plastic toys spread out on a multicolored carpet. The Charles River was a slender blue rope winding among them toward the ocean. She felt as if the plane was taking her away from everything she'd ever known. In a matter of days, she and McQuade would fly to Vietnam, but the reality of the trip hadn't yet hit her.

All that seemed to matter now was the realization that her life was changing, taking directions she'd never imagined it could take. Only a month ago, she'd assumed she'd marry Daniel some day. Now Daniel was gone from her life. Two months ago, she hadn't known she had a half brother in Vietnam. It felt as if her orderly life was being tugged and pulled apart by forces over which she had no control. She felt confused, uncertain, even a little frightened. Was there nothing she could count on in this life, nothing she could trust? Was there no certainty, no stability, nothing firm, unyielding, stable?

She glanced at McQuade and felt an immediate sense of relief. McQuade could be counted on. She knew that, with a certainty that came with no doubts. Despite his often disheveled appearance and the apparent failure of his business, she knew he was solid, as stable and unmoving as a rock.

Yet there was something about him that worried her. He seemed to have a one-way ticket to Failure. His business was almost bankrupt and he seemed incapable of pulling it or himself out of the path toward destruction. It was as if something made him *want* to fail.

She studied him discreetly, wondering what demons he had brought back from Vietnam. She sensed that his time over there had been the seminal experience of his life, the cause of all his present problems. Like a shadow, Vietnam seemed to hover over him so that he was never free of it. The past, she suspected, was not over but still very much in the present.

She frowned, wondering if she and her father weren't being terribly selfish. What right did they have to badger McQuade into returning to a place that had obviously caused him so much pain? Tiredly she sat and massaged her aching temples, wondering if life would ever be as carefree as it had seemed only weeks ago.

"You'll be all right, won't you?" McQuade asked when they had landed and he had lowered her bag to the ground.

"Sure," she said carelessly, "I'll be fine."

McQuade studied her. "You sure?"

"Of course!" She forced a laugh. "I told you. I'm fine."

He put a hand on the side of the plane and stood looking over his arm in the opposite direction. "So." A silence fell over them. "Have a good vacation," he finally said.

"Thanks." She couldn't look at him. She was suddenly too aware of him. Now that she had broken up with Daniel, everything had changed. Being alone with McQuade was suddenly almost threatening.

"How you getting back to Boston?" McQuade asked after another few seconds of uncomfortable silence.

"I'll take a direct flight," she said.

He nodded, and kicked at a stone. "Well . . . I'll see you around."

She felt like a tire deflating. He was going to leave and she only realized just now that she didn't want him to. "I'll start making the arrangements for the flight to Vietnam."

"Good. My shots are up to date. I'm all set."

"You have a passport?"

He nodded. "Ready and waiting."

"That's good." She wished she could think of something to say; anything would be better than this stilted conversation.

"You sure you're all right?" he asked again.

"Sure," she said with forced gaiety.

"Look, Tory," he said, sounding almost angry. "Daniel is a certified ass. Just put him out of your mind. Don't think about him."

She nodded but she didn't know why. She wasn't thinking about Daniel, she was focused on McQuade. She didn't want him to leave. She wanted to lean against his body, feel the warmth and strength of it, take sustenance from him. She wanted to not think anymore. She wanted simply to be, within the soothing shelter of McQuade's arms.

But that was a dream, and she was faced with reality. Rallying, she smiled and said, "I'll be fine." And she really would be, she realized. She just hated to see McQuade go.

"Yeah," McQuade said. "I know you will."

She held out her hand. "Thanks for everything."

"Don't mention it."

He didn't take her hand. She looked down at the ground. He kicked another stone. She let her hand drop to her side.

"See you around, McQuade," she said softly.

"Yeah," he said, climbing into the plane. "See you around." He didn't even bother to look at her.

Chapter Eight

McQuade woke up the next day, pulled on a clean pair of jogging shorts and walked outside to the beach. The sun was dazzling in the sky. The air was filled with the razor-sharp sting of salt. The ocean crashed ashore, splintered into crystalline light, foamed onto the beach, like lace thrown across a young girl's shoulders. A gull swooped and dived for food, disappearing for a dazzling instant in the ocean only to surface again in a flash, soaring into the sky, victorious.

He smiled. He thought he knew what the gull felt like when it flew, thought he recognized the exultation that must course through its body, that incredible sense of mastery, the exhilaration that built and built and reached a dizzying peak as it headed into the sun. And then the long, slow cruise back toward earth, gliding in a lazy slide on the rays of the sun, down and down and down toward the earth, spread out below like a miniature patchwork of patterns, colors, shapes.

He set out east and walked fast, broke into an easy jog, pacing off the miles, filling his lungs with fresh, clean air, breaking a sweat, cleansing himself of everything—all memory, all pain, all feeling, save the ecstasy of muscles, sinew, ligaments working together in one fluid motion, feet slapping the hard-packed sand, legs pumping, arms moving, chest rising and falling in harmonious rhythm as he inhaled, exhaled, ran, a perfect zero, no past, no future, no thoughts, no feelings, no memories, no desires. Clean. Alone. Anonymous.

He jogged back to his cottage, took a shower, dressed in clean faded jeans and a white T-shirt, then stood staring down at the coffee that had grown cold in his mug. A fly was floating serenely in the muck. He vaguely remembered the old joke, the one about the customer asking the waiter what that fly was doing in his soup.

"The backstroke," the waiter answered.

McQuade didn't smile. He stood and stared down at the fly and felt an inescapable sense of impending doom. He felt as if he were suffocating, as if the walls were closing in on him. A nervous frisson suffused his body. He wanted to run, but didn't know what he was running from.

Turning, he made for his truck. He'd take the plane up. Up in the air, in the limitless blue of the sky, he'd find the peace that always eluded him on earth.

TORY WIPED THE SWEAT OFF her face and gazed at the flower bed with satisfaction. She was almost finished planting over fifty pink geraniums, and their cinnamon scent mingled with the salty air and her tanning lotion in a pleasant aroma. A small plane buzzed in the distance, sunlight glinting off its silver wings. Tory shielded her eyes and looked up at the plane, then went back to her plants.

Overhead the small engine fluttered and then died, and the air was suddenly silent. She looked up and saw the plane gliding soundlessly, then heard its small engine cough to life. It began a steep ascent, climbing straight up, heading into the sun. The light shimmered on it, catching on the windshield, the wings, the propeller, glinting and sparkling and winking, momentarily blinding her.

Suddenly the plane turned and with a racing engine, seemed to dive straight toward earth. Heart in her mouth, she stood up, holding her breath, watching as it plummeted toward the ocean. At the last moment, the pilot straightened it out and the plane skimmed the ocean's surface, flying maybe twenty feet over the rolling surf, kicking up waves in its wake before ascending again, arcing upward in wide circles until it was just a silver dot in the sky.

It was McQuade, of course. It had to be him, flying stunts he probably thought would impress her, like a little kid showing off in the school yard. She felt her heart soar at the knowledge that he was flying over her place. She had thought he'd disappear completely. Men like him usually did. If only there was some way to signal him to land. She stood staring up at the silver dot, willing him to land, but he continued flying in crazy patterns, forming boxes in the sky, then circles, then triangles. Then he was gone, out of sight, not even the sound of the engine left to comfort her.

She forced herself to return to her task, to revel in the feel of the hot sun on her skin, the smell of the damp earth, and the beauty of the deep green scalloped leaves of the geraniums with their generous sprouting of pink flowers. Ten minutes later, she realized the plane was back, buzzing overhead, diving and circling and soaring upward. She stood up and walked toward the hill that overlooked the beach. The damn fool. He was going to land the plane in the field behind her cottage.

Smiling, she stood and watched as the small plane came in for a perfect landing. Sure enough, it was McQuade. The target emblazoned on the side of his plane showed plainly. Just knowing McQuade was here felt like the sun coming out on a rainy day.

He opened the door and stepped out on the wing, then jumped down. He wore faded jeans and a white T-shirt. His dark hair was rumpled. He looked like the happiest man in the world as he advanced across the field toward her, a grin on his tanned face.

"I knew it was you," she said when he got within shouting distance. "You're the only man I know fool enough to try to kill yourself to impress a woman."

His dark eyes glinted at her. "Hell, I wasn't trying to impress you. That's the way I always fly."

"No wonder you're in danger of going bankrupt. No one in their right mind would trust their shipments to you."

He grinned that quirky grin and tilted his head consideringly. His gaze ran lightly down her body. "You look great."

She smiled. She was wearing white tennis shorts and a skimpy navy blue halter top that did little to cover her breasts and left her midriff bare. Her hair was held back with a white terry cloth headband. She was hot and sweaty and smelled of dirt and suntan lotion, but she felt good and knew she probably looked just fine.

"You look pretty good yourself," she said.

McQuade looked past her to the cottage. "Sunning yourself?"

"Planting geraniums," she said. "Want to help?"

"No way."

She ignored him, walking back toward the cottage where she handed him a trowel. "Here. Dig where I tell you to."

"You're a pushy woman, aren't you?"

"Very." She knelt by the plants and looked up at him. "Well? You going to help or just stand there?"

He hunkered down next to her and looked into her eyes. "I guess I'll help," he said.

She felt something ripple across her skin, like a breeze blowing over water. She looked away quickly, her hands suddenly shaking. He was too close. She could smell the fresh, clean scent of his body and felt a spasm of awareness in her stomach. He seemed to have the ability to throw a switch deep inside her, turning on some kind of internal circuit over which she had no control.

"Just dig," she said, overcoming the urge to lean forward and kiss him.

"I like a woman who's a little bossy," McQuade said softly.

His voice came from much too close. She could feel his breath on her face. She turned and he was there, so close she could only see his mouth. She stared at it, feeling attraction blossom inside her, wanting to melt toward him, knowing she shouldn't.

She stood up abruptly. "It's hot out here. Want some iced tea?"

He didn't say a word, just shook his head.

She tilted her head and looked at him. "Sure you don't want anything?"

He stood up and looked out at the ocean. Shrugging carelessly, he said, "I guess I'll have a beer, if you've got one."

"I've got one," she said, frowning at his back. Why had he come here today? Why did he act hot one minute and cold the next? She never knew where she stood with McQuade. Being around him was like watching a weather vane swing back and forth in an erratic wind. That first time he'd come here to her cottage, he'd acted as if he wanted to make love to her. Now he was alone with her again and he'd turned his back on her. What was the matter with him? Or worse, what was the matter with her, that she couldn't seem to attract him?

"Something wrong?"

Startled, she realized he was watching her. She swallowed quickly, feeling an intense flush of heat spread through her entire body. She wondered if he could read her mind, if he knew what she'd just been thinking.

"No," she said quickly. "Just enjoying the cool breeze." She wiped her forehead with her arm. "It's hot out here."

When he didn't answer, she turned and went inside the house. The door had no sooner slammed shut behind her than she heard it open again. She looked up. McQuade stood in the doorway, outlined against the light. She felt an electric shock of awareness shoot through her. Hurriedly she got a can of beer from the refrigerator. "Would you like anything else?"

He shook his head, just standing there, watching her. She began to tremble. The room fairly shimmered with sexual heat. She felt it arc across the room between them, like a flash of intense electricity spitting fire across the room. He advanced slowly toward her, his eyes fixed on hers. He stopped just in front of her, so close they almost touched. He reached out and took the beer, his fingers brushing hers. Her eyes trailed down his chest. She stood unmoving, unable to speak, caught in the dark web of his slumbering sensuality.

She felt a dusky heat growing inside her, was vaguely aware of a throbbing pulse deep in her body. She felt slow, languid, as if everything she did was weighed down by the intense sexuality she felt. A bead of sweat rolled down her neck and descended toward her breasts. The clock above the stove ticked steadily. Outside some gulls squawked, oblivious to the drama inside the house.

McQuade reached out and caught the bead of sweat on the tip of his finger. She felt herself grow dizzy, felt the heat flash inside her like a fire taking spark. He moved his finger lightly across her collarbone, then tucked a piece of hair behind her ear.

She could feel the heat coming from his body, could sense the throbbing in his blood. He stood so close he almost touched her. The pulse deep inside her ached for his touch. Lightly his hand skimmed down her arm, barely touching the skin, floating just above the surface, pausing at her wrist, touching her fingers lightly one by one. Her breathing grew shallow. She waited, excruciatingly aware of the dangerous heat that shimmered inside him.

"Maybe we better go outside," he said.

His voice shattered the mood. She stepped back, unable to meet his eyes. "Yes, I...I need to finish my gardening..."

He followed her, a few paces behind. She was achingly aware of him, but now that the moment had passed she realized she was glad nothing had happened between them.

He popped the top of the beer can and took a long swig, then wiped his hand across his mouth. "Tastes good."

She let out a breath she hadn't realized she was holding. Throwing him a sardonic look, she knelt in front of the geraniums. "You're a born freeloader, McQuade. I'll bet you'll even try to wiggle out of helping me with my gardening."

He sat down on the ground and leaned back on one elbow. "After you've sowed wild oats, geraniums are a little tame, but thanks all the same."

She went pink, but was grateful he had defused the sexual heat between them, changing it to mere flirtation. "You're a big talker, McQuade. Remind me not to believe anything you say."

He put an arm behind his head and rested his head on it, watching her with steady eyes. "You feeling better today?"

She went still. "What do you mean?"

"You and Daniel just broke up. I'd be surprised if you were happy about it."

She kept her eyes on the geranium she was transplanting. "Daniel and I weren't right for each other. I should have realized it sooner."

"Your father had been saying that all along. What made you suddenly change your mind about him?"

She patted the dirt around the geranium, wondering what to tell McQuade. She didn't know what had happened. How could she explain her sudden shift of feelings? She didn't like what it said about her—that she was incapable of clear judgment, that she was shallow, immature, taken in by appearances.

She sat back on her heels and brushed her hair back from her forehead, leaving a streak of muddy dirt on her face. McQuade reached out and gently wiped the dirt away.

"What?" she said.

"You got dirt on your forehead."

"Oh." She felt suddenly nervous. She looked out over the ocean, wishing she could find an explanation for herself in its depths. "Remember yesterday, when we were talking about love?"

McQuade nodded. "At breakfast at your place."

"Yes." She turned her head and met his even gaze. "You said love doesn't exist, but it does, McQuade. It's just that it's awfully hard to do it right. It's hard to love someone for who they are—we see people for what we want them to be." She looked down, feeling confused and chastened. "Yesterday with Daniel, I realized that. It was a sudden thing, like a flash of lightning in a dark room. I wanted him to be everything I needed in a man. Then I saw him for who he was, and realized I'd fallen in love with a dream, not the real Daniel." She frowned and dug her fingers into the damp soil. "I'm feeling very stupid, McQuade, and very afraid."

He watched her, feeling something gentle deep inside. She looked so vulnerable, was struggling so hard to speak honestly with him. "What are you afraid of?" he asked quietly.

"Mostly I'm afraid of being alone. I'm thirty-four years old. Most of my friends are already married. They have homes, children, they're stable, their lives are secure..." She looked out over the ocean, the waves flashing silver in the sun. "They tell me how much they envy me—my freedom, the fun I have." She smiled wistfully. "But I envy them. Sometimes freedom is as much a prison as marriage."

McQuade stared at Tory's profile, startled by her perception. He knew freedom's prison, understood it intimately. He wouldn't have ever thought that Tory understood it, though. She had always appeared so bright, so sure of herself, so certain.

He looked away, searching the empty horizon. "Sometimes I wonder if anyone is ever really happy," he said quietly. "Sometimes I think the whole world is searching for something. Like we've all got this deep hole in ourselves, empty, searching, trying to fill up our lives with bigger cars and flashier houses and racing up the corporate ladder."

She picked up the garden spade and began to dig in the flower bed. "Do you ever feel like you'll be alone forever?"

McQuade examined the flat horizon. "Yeah," he said quietly. "Sometimes I feel that way..."

"Don't you want to do something about it?" she asked, searching his face. "Don't you ever wish you had someone to talk to, to spend your time with, share things with?"

"I've been alone all my life, Tory." He looked back at her, his face grave. "It's too late to change now."

She reached out to touch him. "It's never too late, McQuade."

He withdrew his hand from hers. "I'm afraid it is," he said. "Sometimes people can't change, Tory."

"Who said anything about changing?" she said, gazing at him intently. "Maybe you're fine just the way you are."

He shook his head. "I'm not the kind of man for any woman to get involved with, Tory."

She looked at him and knew deep in her heart that he was the man she wanted to be involved with. Daniel no longer mattered, but McQuade did. She knew she had to take a chance with McQuade, knew it would be difficult, but he was worth it.

"Have you ever tried to be the kind of man you want to be?" she asked quietly. "Maybe you're being too hard on yourself, McQuade. In the kitchen just now, when you touched me, I wanted to be involved with you very much."

A breeze blew through the bushes, rippling over the leaves, rustling them. He turned his head and looked into her eyes. "That was sex, Tory, plain and simple. It's been flaring up between us ever since we met. Is that all you want? Someone to sleep with a few weeks? If that's what you want, I can do that for you, but that's all I'm good for, Tory—something temporary."

"Is that all it was?" she asked softly. "Just sex?"

He looked away, not wanting to see the need in her eyes. He wouldn't be able to resist her if he looked into her eyes. "You don't know anything about me, Tory. I wouldn't be any good for you. Believe me."

"I am so sick of men who claim they know what I need," she said with a shaking voice. "Let me decide what I need."

"It wouldn't work, Tory."

"Stop being the martyred hero, McQuade. Take a chance and see if it would."

He shook his head. "No, Tory."

Frustration rose up inside her. How could she reach him? What did she have to say to make him listen? She decided there was only one way—by telling him the truth. "I think I knew I didn't love Daniel the first day I met you," she said quietly. "You made me feel so alive. When I woke up that morning after the storm and you were gone, I missed you so much, McQuade. The place was empty without you. I never used to feel that way when Daniel left."

Her words were like balm on a festering wound. He was torn by a powerful desire to take her in his arms and hold her and an equally strong desire to get away as quickly as he could. It was as if the promise of love was a temptation that lured him toward disaster, as the sirens had lured unsuspecting sailors to their deaths.

"Tory—" He shook his head, his gaze filled with sadness as he looked into her eyes. "I can't, Tory."

She searched his eyes. "Can't?" She reached up and gently touched his face. "Or won't?"

His eyes were filled with pain. "I can make love, Tory, but there's a world of difference between the physical act and loving someone." He looked away, fixing his eyes on the horizon. "Something happened to me in Nam, Tory. Something inside me got destroyed. I can't love anyone anymore. I can't reach out, can't trust, can't get involved. I could sleep with you for a while, but after a while I'd leave you, and that would hurt you and I don't want to do that."

"What happened over there, McQuade?" she asked softly.

"Nothing any different from a hundred thousand other men. Maybe the exact circumstances differ, but in the end it doesn't really matter. We're all in the same shape. Screwed up." He stood up, shading his eyes as he looked out over the ocean. "I don't want to talk about it, Tory."

"Maybe you have to, McQuade."

He shook his head. "It wouldn't do any good."

She rubbed her arms, feeling as if a chill wind had suddenly blown in. There was a distance between them that she felt she'd never be able to bridge.

He nodded toward the rest of the geraniums. "You gonna plant them suckers?"

She forced a smile. "Of course. You going to help?"

He shook his head. "I've got to get going."

"McQuade," she said quietly, "what's going on between us? First you're hot, then you're cold, but you can't deny you're attracted to me."

He kept his head turned away from her, looking into the distance. "I won't deny it, Tory. I'm attracted to you. I feel like there's a tug-of-war going on inside me. Part of me wants to take you in my arms, but the other part knows that's only a temporary solution."

He wished he could tell her what he really felt. He wished he could turn to her and spill out his deepest fears, his most poignant dreams. He wished he could say: *I feel trapped, Tory. I'm caught in some kind of prison, locked up inside myself with so much misery and loneliness and unhappiness, I don't know how I get up some days and put one foot in front of the other. I want so much to have a normal life, the kind of life that most men take for granted, with a wife and kids, a home to come back to.*

"I wouldn't be any good for you, Tory," he said tiredly. "No good at all." He turned to go, but she reached out and touched his arm.

"I think you'd be very good for me, McQuade. We'd be good for each other."

"No, we wouldn't. We'd hurt each other, Tory. It's better to just be friends. You've just broken up with Daniel. Wait a while. You'll mend soon, and you won't have any regrets about sleeping with me."

"Who says I'd have regrets?" she asked softly.

He stared at her, pulled toward her like a magnet. He wanted to take her in his arms, to hold her and bury his head in her hair, to inhale the scent of her, feel her skin against his, take solace in her nearness. He wished he was a normal man, the kind who met a woman and fell in love and settled down.

But he had gone to Vietnam and fought in a war that had destroyed all hope, dashed all dreams. He had seen and done things that human beings should never do or see. And he had to live with himself. That seemingly simple task was almost more than he could manage. To love someone, to have a normal life—they were not possible for him. The rage he felt at his fate was only surpassed by the sadness that held him in its grip.

"Goodbye, Tory," he said. Turning, he walked to his plane.

HE FLEW HIS PLANE as if it were his last resort, his only salvation. He drove it straight up into the sky, soaring over the outstretched island of Nantucket, out over the sparkling blue ocean past the Vineyard, flying without a destination, wanting only to find the peace he'd always found up in the sky.

But today it didn't come, brought instead a kind of frantic anxiety, a startling new knowledge that being alone in the sky was no longer a safe harbor but instead just another form of prison. He turned the plane in a long, slow arc and looked ahead at the crooked arm of Cape Cod, slumbering now in the late afternoon sun. How beautiful it all seemed up here, how peaceful and remote and clean. It was only when you landed that you saw everything so much more clearly.

Feeling empty inside, he took the plane down, slicing through the sunlit air toward the dot of gray concrete that was his. When he had landed, he did all the necessary chores—refueled and checked gauges and lines and examined the entire plane for possible problems, then he walked slowly back to his office.

Once inside he tried to get some paperwork done, but unwanted images kept intruding. Tory's face became Mai's. Mai's touch became Tory's. Faces floated up to him from the past, like bodies rising to the surface of a pond. Finally, unable to concentrate, he got up. Raking a hand through his hair, he kicked the wastebasket out of the way. "Stop thinking, dammit."

But he couldn't. He paced his office, pausing now and then to stand at the window and stare out at his plane, his mind focused not on it but on the jumbled images and impulses that fought for his attention. Thoughts of Tory gave way to memories of Mai. He didn't want to think about her, but he couldn't help it. She was there, like a ghost in the night, preying on him. Mai, the Vietnamese girl who had died in his arms...

Memories he had held at bay for almost twenty years clamored for his attention. He stood rooted to the floor, unable to move as the images exploded in his mind. Blood and thunder and shouted obscenities competed with the memory of Mai's hand on his arm, of soft oriental music and the wind off the South China Sea whispering in the chimes on a balcony in Nhatrang. The streets teemed with pedestrians, bicycles, motorbikes, with pushcarts and food vendors. Small boys scampered in and out, begging money, offering beer, girls, movies, drugs. Heat shimmered, mosquitoes swarmed, their buzzing magnified in the soft tropical night. Rain dripped off the dense jungle vegetation. Somewhere in the dark, a footstep. An explosion of light and noise. Laughter. Card games. Beer. Girls. The creak of ancient bedsprings in the night. Rice fields, miles and miles of them, afloat in water. Scrawny cattle. Chickens squawking, shrieking, flying out of the way of U.S. Army jeeps. Choppers. Casualties. Soldiers crying, clinging to the shredded remnants of a Bible, a rosary, a girlfriend's picture. Letters home: *"We regret to inform you, Army Sergeant Alonzo Gomez...Pfc Homer Ridley...Infantryman Lyle Jennings... died honorably in battle..."*

In the early days he had lived in a dream world that consisted only of Mai. She had soothed him, loved him, laughed, flirted, caressed, talked with him, sweet words and even sweeter looks. Sighs and whispers and a touch that had driven him mad with need. He could never get enough of her. She was water in a thirsty land, food where the cupboards were empty. She had been his salvation, his hope, his joy, and ultimately his deepest, darkest sorrow. He had begun with her a boy, had ended a man. He had lost his innocence, his faith, his illusions, and she had taken them all, casting him forever into a kind of unending hell.

McQuade shook himself and loosened the hold of the memories. A gnawing uneasiness ate at him, like some dark avenging angel that had taken up residence in his soul. He began to pace again, remembering Tory. Or was it Mai? Had he made the mistake of mixing up the two? One's body had been softer than any woman's could be...and yet the other, this one, Tory...she too was incredibly soft...

He frowned and felt the familiar torment in his loins, the dark desire, the need to lose himself in the arms of a woman, to sink into the feminine softness and hence forget, not think, to temporarily erase the hell of remembered pain, the punishment of loneliness.

He grabbed his baseball cap, jamming it low on his head as he headed across the tarmac to his truck.

He drove without direction, thinking of Polly, the woman who had lived with him the previous year. Somehow she had managed to erase all memory for three entire months. Older than he was, with a raspy voice and generous arms, she had soothed him in the cradle of her loving embrace.

In the end, he had pushed her away. Something happened to him when a woman began to get possessive. Something tightened in him like a coiled spring, made him itchy and restless and vaguely anxious, made him need to stay away longer and longer until one day he turned his back and never returned. Only this time it had been Polly who had walked out.

He thought of Tory and knew he couldn't allow himself to get involved with her. Vulnerable, having just broken up with Daniel, she needed someone who could give her a future. She hadn't admitted it, but he knew she'd been hurt by Daniel Sullivan, but she would mend. She was young, taut, still resilient. She needed a man now who would help her recover, give her back her confidence, not sleep with her a while, then leave, as he himself would.

Grinding his teeth, he tried not to think about her, the smell of her, feel of her, touch of her. Tried not to imagine the way she would respond to his kisses, the sound of her, the small moans, whispers, the sweet sighs that tokened the aftermath of love.

He drove aimlessly along the main street of Hyannis. It looked faintly unkempt, like a field the day after a carnival had packed up and left. Soon hordes of summer tourists would blanket the street and it would come alive, bursting with color and noise.

He took a right turn and drove down to Lewis Bay. He parked his truck and stared at the fishing boats, the ferry, the private boats bobbing on the swelling water. After a while he started the truck up again.

He cruised slowly along the darkening streets. Blackie's was over there, where he'd met Tory only days before. Strange how so much had seemed to change, yet nothing really had. Still restless, still aimless, still a prisoner of the past. Things would never change for him; they couldn't change, because he himself couldn't.

He drove until he came upon the small bar where Polly worked as a waitress. On a whim, he stopped the truck and got out. The sun was setting, the air growing cooler. Sea gulls drifted overhead, their hoarse cries competing with the sound of traffic, kids shouting at each other on the way home from baseball practice, housewives calling out from station wagons.

It was all so settled, so serene. Everyone seemed to have a purpose, a reason for hurrying, somewhere to go where they were wanted, needed, loved. He had nothing. There was no one who needed him, no one who wanted him, no one to care if he lived or died. He had wanted it this way, had purposely kept his distance from others, feigning disdain for the intimacies of domestic life, claiming a need for solitude.

He almost laughed, remembering Greta Garbo's famous words: "I vant to be alone...." But it wasn't amusing, and if he laughed his laughter had an edge to it, sardonic, bitter, cynical, perhaps. Laughing at himself, not the film star. Knowing himself, knowing who and what he was, wondering if he fooled anyone else.

He stepped inside the bar and heard the immediate soothing strains of an old Billie Holliday tune. The blues, sung by an aging blonde with a throaty voice. He took a seat at the bar and ordered a beer. Sat with his hands wrapped around the bottle, head bent, sinking into the welcome quiet of the bar, where the piano and singer formed a pleasant backdrop to the ache in his heart.

"Hello, McQuade." He looked up. Polly stood there, smiling, her eyes filled with something that looked like sadness.

"Hello, Polly. It's been a long time."

"Almost a year," she said, her voice husky from years of smoking cigarettes. "Care if I join you?"

He knew he should get up and walk out. He'd already hurt Polly once. He didn't need to again. He struggled with himself only a moment, then succumbed. "I'd like that. Buy you a drink?"

"Thanks." She ordered a beer and they found a booth in the back of the bar. They sat down together, and were immediately swallowed up by the high backs of the booth. They were in an island of their own, lost in a world of smoke and laughter and the lonely sound of the blues. They talked and laughed, and after another beer somehow McQuade's hand drifted toward hers, brushed against her arm. He felt her sway closer, smelled the familiar scent of her perfume, the powder she had always used in the morning, the underlying hint of cigarettes that hung around her like morning haze on the beach. Memories swept back, like the tide rushing in on a deserted beach. Maybe he could forget Tory if he turned to Polly...

"You look sad, McQuade," she said.

He sat staring at his beer, watching the beads of moisture dripping down the glass. He nodded. He was sad. There was no sense in denying it. "Yeah," he said, taking a swig of beer, "I guess I am..."

She smiled, a smile as ancient as the wind, as knowing as the sky. She touched his hand. "You know what you need, McQuade?"

He shook his head. "What?"

"You need to fall in love," Polly said, exhaling a thin stream of smoke.

He sat and watched the smoke dissipate in the air, then looked at Polly. "I almost loved you, Polly."

She had the saddest smile in the world. "Almost isn't good enough," she said.

"Maybe it would be different this time," he said, letting his fingers trail across the smooth skin of her arm. "Maybe we could try again."

She shook her head. "No, McQuade."

He felt desperation well up inside him. "Polly, I need you."

She shrugged. "You need someone, that's for sure, but it's not me."

He inhaled her perfume and felt his senses stir. "It could be. Come back to my place. Let's try again, Polly. Maybe I could learn to love you."

Polly blew a thin stream of smoke up into the air, her face unreadable. "You know, McQuade, if I were any other woman I'd slug you."

"Slug me? For saying you're desirable?"

Polly turned to him, eyes quietly angry. "You lousy bastard. Do you always treat women the way you treat me?"

Stunned, he stared at her. Here came the sky, it looked like, tumbling right down on top of him. "I'm sorry?"

"You should be sorry," she said, her voice filled with anger. She looked like a little terrier facing a bull. "How do you think I feel? Have you ever bothered to put yourself in my shoes and wonder what it must feel like to know you've come back after almost a year to use me for sex?"

He stared at her, awkward and off-balance. "I—"

She plowed on before he could say anything. "I don't have any illusions, McQuade. I knew it wouldn't be more than a one-night stand, maybe two if I got lucky. Do you know how that makes me feel, McQuade?" Her face began to crumple. Her chin wobbled and tears sprang into her eyes. "Dammit, you could have treated me like I'm a human being and not some whore." Her face collapsed completely and she began to cry.

Remorse rose up inside him, thick and pungent, like smoke from a fire started with damp logs. In that instant, he truly despised himself.

He reached out to take her in his arms, but she pushed him away, struggling to regain control, her chin raised proudly. He realized then he had fallen even lower than he'd thought possible.

"I'm sorry," he said, trying to find the words to explain himself. "I'm lonely, Polly. I couldn't stand it any longer, and I remembered you."

"Have you ever once thought of anyone but yourself, McQuade?" she asked in a low, angry voice. "Damn you, have you ever wondered what the other person might be feeling?"

She searched for a tissue in the pocket of her waitress's uniform. Finding one, she dabbed at her eyes. "Damn," she said in a shaky voice, "I must look horrible. I have to go back to work pretty soon, too."

"Polly..."

"I know I'm no beauty." She glanced at him, busy rubbing mascara off her face. "It must have been quite a shock waking up next to me last year." Tears sprang into her eyes again, but she blinked them away.

"Polly," he said gently. "Don't." She couldn't meet his eyes. She looked terribly vulnerable, as if she might break in two if he said the wrong thing. His heart went out to her. "Polly, I feel only gratitude toward you, for your ability to give, to love so freely and generously. You're a good and kind woman. I'm sorry if I hurt you. I never meant to, Polly. Never."

She straightened her shoulders and looked him in the eye. "Maybe what you need to do, McQuade, is think a little less about yourself and a lot more about others.'' With that, she got up from the booth and walked away.

He sat and stared after her, feeling as if his entire world had caved in. The worst part was, he knew he deserved what Polly had just handed him. He sat and brooded over the course his life had taken and knew that any change was better than none. He couldn't go on this way, couldn't let himself slide even deeper into ruin.

What the hell was the matter with him? He felt like he was being pulled along by a runaway train. He was out of control, at the mercy of forces he had no power over. He leaned forward and put his head in his hands, resting his elbows on the table. He sat that way for what could have been minutes or might have been hours, staring at nothing, seeing only the mess he had made of his life.

Finally he got up. Tossing money to cover the bill and tip on the table, he walked out and got in his truck and drove back to his office. He walked in and flicked on the light and in the terrible glare saw the room for the first time in years. With a rush of terrible insight, he realized that his messy office was a metaphor for his entire life. He had wanted someone like a secretary to come in and clean it all up, to make things better, but no one had. He had to finally face the truth: no one was going to. If the mess was ever going to be cleaned up, he had to do it himself.

He stared at his desk, littered with papers and coffee cups and a plant that had died almost a year before. He knew he had to start somewhere, but where? He picked up a bill and saw that it was overdue three months. A stamped warning said his credit would be cut off if he didn't pay within a week. That had been four weeks ago.

Feeling overwhelmed, he began to empty the coffee cups. He threw out the dead plant. Then his eyes fell on a dirty slip of paper. He picked it up. It was the telephone number of the convent in Brockton that Sister Theresa had given him. He stared at it.

When was the last time he'd done anything for anybody? For the past twenty years or more, he couldn't remember doing anything out of the goodness of his heart, perhaps because there was no longer any goodness there.

All his excuses had run out, and he was faced with the truth. Bowing his head, he wept.

Chapter Nine

The plane dropped out of the clouds and glided toward Tan Son Nhut Airport, an enormous silver bird emerging out of the heavy rain that pummeled the land.

"Everything is so green," Tory said, craning her neck past McQuade and peering out the airplane window at the dense jungle vegetation. Here and there roofs emerged from the greenery and there were occasional glimpses of rice paddies and rivers winding peacefully through the countryside.

McQuade didn't respond. His eyes were riveted on his first glance of Vietnam in twenty years.

The pilot's voice came over the public address system: "Ladies and gentlemen, thank you for flying with us today. We will be landing at Tan Son Nhut Airport in Ho Chi Minh City in a matter of minutes. It's raining on the ground and the temperature is a muggy ninety-two degrees. We hope you've enjoyed your flight with us and hope to see you again soon."

The public-address system went silent and the passengers began to fidget in their seats, stretching to peer out the windows. Voices rose and fell in conversations in three or four languages. Somewhere in the back of the plane a baby began to cry. The stewardesses smiled calmly, having collected all the remnants of food and drink and raised the trays.

McQuade stared out the window, seeing everything as if in a dream. During the war, Tan Son Nhut had served as an American air base. From here, masses of soldiers had gone home, some boarding the planes under their own power, too many going home in body bags or metal caskets.

He shivered, not wanting to remember. He had spent twenty years trying not to remember, but the mind plays tricks on you. When you try not to think of something it haunts you, like a phantom in the night.

Now he was back and he couldn't quite believe it. He had thought when he flew home from Tan Son Nhut after his last tour of duty that he'd never return, thought he'd be able to put the past behind him. But life had surprised him, and his past had never been put to rest. Instead it had stayed with him, night and day, dominating his life.

He glanced at Tory in the seat next to him. "Did your father give you directions to Mme Tran?"

She nodded. "Yes, and he gave me a letter for you. He asked me to give it to you when we arrived. Do you want it now?"

He shook his head. "When we get to the hotel will be soon enough." He sighed to himself. He had so damn much to think about. A hidden stash of diamonds was the last thing that mattered. They weren't even real to him. They were like this trip had been until today—dreamlike, a fantasy, something one thought about but knew would never happen.

Tory studied McQuade's face. He looked tired, though he had slept better than she during the flight. "Are you excited about going back?"

"Nervous is more like it." He nodded toward the ground, where the low buildings of Tan Son Nhut were rushing up at them as the plane descended toward the runway. "I left from here twenty years ago. I never thought I'd be back."

Tory touched his hand. "It'll be all right, McQuade."

"Mmm," he said noncommittally, then steeled himself for the smell of Vietnam, the long-remembered stench of death, airplane fuel, rotting vegetation, all mixed in with the faint scent of Vietnamese beer. He had drunk the stuff to numb his senses, breaking open a can the moment he landed in an effort to ward off the other smells. He had never succeeded. At times he would wake in the middle of the night and the odor of Vietnam would be as vivid in his small cottage as it had been during his time in Nam.

Now he clenched his teeth and told himself to stop remembering. Stop thinking. Stop feeling. Just exist. It had worked during the war; perhaps it would work now, as well.

When the plane landed, the human cargo erupted from the seats and a mass of people surged toward the door. Tory picked up her hand luggage and joined the ranks of people descending the metal staircase. McQuade followed more slowly, still trying to prepare himself for what lay ahead.

When he reached the door to the plane, he stopped abruptly, shocked. The smell he had so long associated with Nam was gone. In its place was the familiar odor of airplane fuel and the moist but clean air of the rainy season. He stood in the doorway to the plane and sucked the air into his lungs, hoping it would banish forever the memories of those other smells that had stayed with him so long.

"You okay, McQuade?" Tory asked from the steps beneath him, peering up at him from beneath her umbrella. The rain was letting up, a merciful occurrence in the rainy season.

"What?" Dazed, he looked down at her, then his brain began to function and his vision cleared. "Sure, I'm fine."

A shuttle bus took them to the terminal. Inside, the masses of yelling, crying, sweating, laughing people he had remembered at Tan Son Nhut were gone. A few travelers here and there sat reading books, sleeping, feeding babies. He stepped into line with the others at the customs desk, getting out his passport. As if in a trance, he handed it over, then went toward the baggage inspection table.

Ahead of him Tory was already filling out the customs forms, declaring the exact contents of her baggage. McQuade fixed her with his gaze while the customs clerk checked his passport. If he kept his eyes on Tory, he reasoned, everything would be all right. She was like a lucky charm, someone to hold on to.

He remembered when he was a little boy, about four years old. He had gone shopping with his mother in Boston and had somehow become separated from her. The crowds milling around him seemed to multiply and soon he was truly lost. Alone and afraid, he had begun to bawl. Strange women bent down and looked into his face, trying to cheer him up, make him stop crying, asking him questions: "What's the matter, little boy?"

"Where's your mommy, little fellow?"

"Why are you here alone, little boy?"

"Stop crying..."

"Now, now, now..."

He had been so scared he'd thought he would die. But then a strange woman with a pretty face and yellow hair had knelt beside him and handed him a lollipop. "Here," she said. "Hang on to this while we find your mommy."

He had clung to her with his small hand, clutching the lollipop in the other, huge tears falling down his face as he followed the pretty lady, his head turning right and left, searching for his mother. And like a cloud being parted by sunshine, she had suddenly appeared out of the crowd, his own mother coming toward him, her face filled with fear until she caught sight of him, then relief showing all over her. She ran to him with outstretched arms. Reaching him, she knelt and put her arms around him, hugging him to her.

"Johnny," she'd said. "Are you all right?"

He had nodded, but when he had looked around for the pretty lady with yellow hair, she was gone. Had she truly existed or had he dreamed her up? Looking down, he saw the red lollipop in his hand, and he knew then that she hadn't been a dream.

He had clutched the lollipop all day, and when he got home he put it in his dresser. Years later, a friend had spied it among his belongings and had peeled the cellophane wrapper off and licked it before he could protest. A terrible sense of loss gripped him. He stood and watched his friend eat the lollipop and knew he had lost the pretty woman with yellow hair forever.

At that moment, Tory turned and looked back for him. When she spied him, she broke into a smile. Seeing her, McQuade felt exactly like he had when he looked up as a lost child in Boston and saw the pretty woman smiling at him. Relief flooded him. Tory was here, and somehow he knew everything would be all right.

For weeks now he'd fretted about this trip, unable to sleep because of recurring nightmares, tossing and turning, thoughts of his service in Vietnam mingling with memories of Mai until he had to get up and go outside to stare up at the stars and moon, feel the presence of his beloved surging ocean to begin to relax. Only then, anchored firmly in reality on Cape Cod, was he able to return to bed and get a few hours of rest.

Now McQuade returned Tory's smile and set about filling out his customs declaration form. When he had finished, he turned to find Tory waiting for him.

"This must feel so strange for you," she said.

"You got it," he said, picking up a piece of luggage. "I feel like I'm in the Twilight Zone, complete with that spooky music."

Tory put a hand on his arm. "McQuade, it's going to be all right, you know."

He looked into her eyes, then looked away uneasily. "I hope you're right, Tory, but right now I'd just like to get to the hotel and get settled. Maybe then I'll feel like I'm not walking around inside a dream.''

THE STREETS OF Ho Chi Minh City were filled with noise and the movement of thousands of cycles, scooters and people, tall and short, young and old, some wearing the native Vietnamese dress of black pajamas and conical hats, but many wearing western clothes—blue jeans and T-shirts and baseball caps. Commerce flourished. Various stalls lined the streets, basket makers and woodworkers next to vendors selling lottery tickets, live chickens and ducks, peanuts, fish, vegetables, stalls selling used plumbing parts, auto parts, watches and clocks, silks, woven rugs, shoes.

It was the same, but different. The joyous, raucous Saigon filled with women, liquor and neon lights was gone, replaced by a more sober Ho Chi Minh City that seemed tired even while it teemed with the efforts of human commerce. McQuade stared at the faces, seeing here and there hints of what Mai might have become—old and stooped, with blackened teeth, hunched over fires cooking dumplings, soup or some sort of variation of American barbecue.

He felt a strange sadness well up in him. It was as if American troops had never been here, so completely had Vietnam returned to its original roots.

Then why were we here?

The question echoed in McQuade's head as the taxi drove through the crowded streets. Despite the threat of more rain, the people scurried here and there, heads bowed under their hats, intent on their business.

McQuade stared out at the streets. *Why were we here? What was it all about? Why did my country take me and thousands like me and dump us here, if it wasn't for a reason? What did it all mean, all the killing and death? If even one person died in a meaningless war, that was one death too many. But so many had died. So very, very many...*

The taxi lurched to a stop in front of the hotel. Twenty years earlier this same hotel had been the base for off-duty generals, reporters from newspapers and magazines, television and radio networks. Now it stood like a beautiful woman grown old and poor, looking sadly seedy, mussed, slightly down-at-the-heels.

McQuade sat and stared at the hotel, but it was another hotel he saw, where he and Mai had stayed while he was on R and R.

"The world has gone crazy, Johnny," Mai had said one night when they lay in bed. Outside, Saigon was alive with laughter and music and blinking neon lights. "I wish we could be in my village," she said quietly. "It was so beautiful there before the war. Rice paddies, oxen, chickens..." She had smiled sadly. "Johnny, I was not raised to make love with a man before marriage, but I am here with you now because the world is mad and I may die tomorrow or you may, and what will we have done with our lives? If we could make a baby tonight, perhaps then there would be a reason for all this."

Her dark eyes had looked at him, enormous and gentle in the light that flashed over their bed from a bar across the street.

"In my mind, Johnny, we are wed. You are my husband and I am your wife. And there is no war in my mind, and we are happy and we will have children, Johnny, lots of children, and we will live together in harmony and peace." She had closed her eyes and rested her head on his chest. "In my mind, Johnny, it is beautiful and the world is not crazy and there is no war." A tear had escaped and fallen down her cheek, then trickled onto his chest. "But that is only in my head..."

He sat now in the taxi and felt a huge lump form in his throat. He wanted to reach into the past and grab that moment, to shout to her, "Mai, there is peace now. There is peace." He wanted to defy time, to erase the years that had come after that precious time with Mai. He wanted to go back and change the history of the world, back to the very beginning, so that there would never be any war, never any fighting, never any death. If he could have given Mai anything at all, he would have given her life, but to do that, there would have had to be no war.

He sat in the taxi and felt tears fall down his face. He could not bring her back, could not change the course of history and time. He was hopeless, left alive to curse the fate of the earth, to mourn the passing of the once-loved dead.

He turned his head and looked at Tory. She sat very still, staring at him, her eyes as large and beautiful as Mai's had been. She merely looked into his eyes, but he could not bear to be with her. He opened the door and got out, slammed the door behind him and headed into the crowds.

"McQuade?"

She was coming after him, racing through the crowded streets, frightened and alone, afraid of what was happening because he wouldn't tell her, wouldn't share any of it. Was he leaving her? Would he be back?

"McQuade?"

He stopped and turned to face her. She stopped running and stood looking at him, unsure of what to do or say. Passersby jostled her. The life and motion of the city continued. Bicycles went by, bells rang, people called out all around them. Slowly she reached out a hand. "McQuade?"

He let out a deep breath, looking up the street beyond her to the taxi driver standing by their cab. He had their luggage, so he didn't look very worried at the way they had left him.

It hit him, then, that thinking about the taxi driver was stupid and illogical. Perhaps it was a way to deal with the moment, to keep from having to talk about anything.

"Look," he said, "I'm sorry about leaving like that. It might happen again, it might not. I have no way of knowing. Just give me time, okay? It's all coming back and I don't feel like I can cope with it right now. I needed to get out. Sometimes I get like this. I need to get away.''

"I was afraid, McQuade. I didn't know what had happened, didn't know where you were going. For a minute, I wondered if you were going to leave me here. Just leave…'' She shrugged helplessly, unable to communicate everything she felt, feeling so limited by mere words. "I was afraid you'd go back home and leave me here.''

He felt the pressure of her need for reassurance and wanted to turn and run. Dammit, he couldn't be there for her now. He had his own problems. He couldn't be there for her right now. Couldn't she see that? If she wanted someone to hold her and make things better, then dammit, it wasn't going to be him. He couldn't do it. Not right now. Maybe never. Didn't she see that? Hell, he needed *her* comfort right now.

"Look, I need some space, okay?'' He took out some money and pushed it into her hand. "Here. Pay the driver. He's waiting for you. I'll be back, I just need to get away by myself for a while.''

She curled her hand around the money, feeling the warmth it carried from his body. "Okay,'' she said, knowing she had to trust McQuade. She couldn't expect him to turn to her right away. It would take time. If he needed space, she'd give it to him. "Okay. I…I'm sorry I chased after you like that. I…'' She searched his eyes. "I didn't understand.''

He snorted contemptuously. "Do you think you understand now? You couldn't possibly understand. I made the mistake of trying to confide in people after the war was over, but they either turned away in disgust or listened passively while filing their nails or picking their teeth. I realized, then, my pain only matters to me. No one else cares. No one gives a damn. It was, 'Gee, that's too bad. Could you pass the pickles?' ''

Shocked by his vehemence, Tory backed away. Why was he yelling at her like this? It wasn't reasonable for him to get out of the car and run like that. She'd been frightened. Didn't she have a right to ask him where he was off to?

But hard on those questions came a sudden, stunning insight. She was afraid, and wanted him to make it better for her. But he couldn't. He was too busy trying to make it better for himself. They were like two wounded soldiers, each leaning on the other for support. She saw now that she might need to be far more understanding than she'd ever been in her life, might have to give more than she ever had. Could she do it? She stared at him, feeling him slip away from her, recede into the distance, like a train rushing out of a station.

"I wish I could take away the pain, McQuade."

He nodded, not able to trust himself to speak. He cleared his throat. "Go ahead and check into the hotel. I'll be along in a while. I just need some time. All this has happened so fast..."

"All right," she said, forcing herself to sound cheerful. She clutched the money in her hand. "How much of this should I give him?"

McQuade almost smiled. It was such a trivial matter, yet so important to Tory. Somehow her question seemed to point out the distance between them. She was worried about how much to pay a taxi driver. He was worried that he might not be able to stand the pain he'd been hiding from for over twenty years. If he gave in to it, he might disintegrate, disappear like dust blown off a table. He wanted suddenly to take Tory in his arms and hold her, to protect her so that she would never have to experience the kind of pain he had.

"Give him this," he said, singling out a large bill, "and this for a tip." He smiled at Tory. "You'll be okay if I'm not with you?"

"I'll be fine. I'm not worried about me, McQuade. I'm worried about you." She was lying, of course. She was petrified for herself. "Are you sure you're all right?"

"I'm fine. I just need time. I want to walk around and see things for myself." He smiled humorlessly. "I suppose it's rather like a reorientation. Or decompression. Time to readjust." He inhaled the once-familiar scents of food being cooked over pots in the street. "You'll be all right, won't you?"

"Sure," Tory said. "I'll be fine." She wasn't sure, at all, but she sensed that was what McQuade needed to hear, so she decided to say it and make the best of things.

HE FOUND THE HOTEL where they had stayed. It was empty now, boarded up and crumbling. It looked as if it had taken a direct hit by a mortar attack. He stood in the half-empty street and stared up at the window that had been their room.

In there, for four days, they had been happy. It was such a simple thing, happiness. One took it for granted when one had it, then mourned its passing when it was gone. He saw now, looking back, that happiness consisted of little things—breakfast in the bedroom overlooking the street, a certain slant of morning sunlight, a glass of cheap wine, a shared embrace while walking through the market...

He turned away abruptly, bumping into a passerby. He mumbled an apology and hurried through the streets until he was once more back on the main road. Food stalls surrounded him.

He remembered how Mai had loved the market, the brilliant displays of food, rich and bountiful even in wartime. He saw now that the stalls were just the same, the food even more plentiful. Communism had given way to a sort of personalized capitalism. One sold what one could, to make ends meet. There was a feeling of industry in the air, as if one day these purveyors of food in the various stalls hoped to run their own corporations.

He stopped and looked around, struck by a thought: *Did we help bring it about? Did we somehow, just by being here, make today possible?* One was always tempted to rewrite history, to wish for what might have been rather than accept what was. Perhaps, he thought, we are not meant to question what has happened. Perhaps, like these industrious food purveyors, we are meant only to do the best we can.

Frowning thoughtfully, he began to walk among the stalls.

THE HOTEL HAD BEEN BUILT during the time the French occupied Indochina. The floors and walls were pale pink marble. There were red velvet Louis XIV sofas and chairs that had faded to pale pink and elaborate satin draperies that shut out the noise from the street. The desk was highly polished mahogany, with a brass bell that shone beneath a crystal chandelier.

The desk clerk was solidly built, with short black hair cut in bangs over his eyes. He wore a white jacket and black bow tie. "Welcome," he said. "We are very happy to have you as our guest."

"Mr. McQuade will be along shortly," Tory explained as she filled out the registration card. Her eyes fell on their reservations. Printed were the words "Tory Britton. John McQuade."

She stared at his name. His first name was John. Such a simple, common name.

"We have two nice rooms for you and Mr. McQuade," the clerk said. "We hope you will enjoy your stay."

"I'm sure we will," she murmured politely, then found her way to the ancient elevator, nothing more than a wire cage hidden behind elegant brass doors.

Her room proved to be much more spartan than the lobby had been. There was a double bed, swathed in mosquito netting, a single chair, a small dresser and a lamp on the bedside table. An ancient black phone completed the furnishings. Not the most comfortable room, but it was clean and tidy and the mattress was firm. She noticed the door that led to McQuade's adjoining room, but tried not to think about his being so close.

She checked out the small bathroom. There was a tiny cracked mirror over the sink, a toilet and a hand-held shower nozzle. A drain in the middle of the tiled floor indicated that one stood in the bathroom and hosed oneself off. She thought she might feel rather like a horse, but decided that was a small price to pay for the luxury of cleanliness after almost thirty hours on a plane.

After a quick shower, she put on a robe and decided to lie down. Jet lag had caught up with her. She'd been warned about it, but hadn't been prepared for the utter weariness that overtook her. It was only midafternoon, but she felt as if it were 2:00 a.m.

She lay down and stared up at the mosquito netting suspended above the bed. Its very presence was exotic, hinting at foreign places and unknown customs. She shivered when she remembered that her father had warned her about the geckos. She wished that McQuade hadn't walked off, leaving her to face all this alone. The distance between them suddenly seemed unbridgeable. Filled with doubts, she at last fell into a restless sleep.

She was awakened two hours later by a tap on the door. Startled, she sat up quickly, her heart pounding. Disoriented and frightened, she couldn't remember where she was—then it all came back to her. She was in Vietnam. Alone in Vietnam. McQuade was gone and she didn't know where he was.

The tap sounded on the door again. She got up and secured her robe around her and went to the door. "Who is it?"

"McQuade."

She let out a breath as relief flooded her. She opened the door. He stood with a bunch of flowers in one hand and a bottle of wine in the other. "I thought you'd like something to cheer your room up."

"The heck with my room," she said, breaking into a smile. "It's me I'm worried about."

McQuade followed her into the room and watched as she found a glass and put the flowers in water. "Did I wake you?"

She turned to look at him. "Can you tell?"

He smiled and nodded. "You've got creases on your face where you must have been lying on the pillow."

She smiled. She must look a mess, with her hair mussed and all makeup removed. "I don't know how you've been able to stay up," she said, seeking refuge in chatter. "I was exhausted." She glanced at her watch. "I slept almost two hours."

"I thought we could have dinner in the hotel tonight and then map out what we'll do in the next week," McQuade said.

Tory took out the letter addressed to McQuade. "This is from my father."

McQuade took it, staring down at it. "I suppose it's the information about the diamonds."

"You don't seem to care about them," Tory said curiously. "Why did you come back, McQuade? Wasn't it for the money?"

He glanced up at her from the envelope. "The money was incentive," he admitted, "but I decided I've been running long enough." He looked around the room. "I came back to make peace." He laughed softly. "If that's possible after all this time."

"I hope it is, John McQuade."

He looked at her, startled. "You found out my name."

"It was on the hotel reservation list." Her eyes were warm as she watched him. "Why don't you use it?"

He didn't answer right away. He walked to the window and stood staring down at the street five stories below. "I don't know. I guess Cargo seemed more apt than John," he said. "That's what I did over here—flew cargo planes. Except my cargo was bodies. I'd fly them into Tan Son Nhut, every day, just like clockwork."

He seemed to shiver, his eyes focused on the distant past, seeing once again the steady parade of gruesome cargo produced by the war. "At first, I'd look back over my shoulder, half expecting one of them to move or moan, to cry out for water or a medic. Three tours in Nam, three years of flying bodies out of the jungle into Tan Son Nhut, and not one of those bodies ever moved." Tears sprang into his eyes and his voice lowered to a whisper. "Not one of them."

Tory stared at him, frozen by the horror of what he was telling her. Her hair seemed to stand up on the back of her neck, prickling her as shivers went up and down her spine. She had assumed he'd flown B-52s. Or maybe he had delivered supplies—food, water, ice cream to the troops on hot days. She realized now she hadn't known a thing about him. Certainly his name hadn't meant anything to her. It had simply been a nickname, the kind of catchy name bestowed on a guy by his buddies that had somehow stuck. She saw now why his name had such deadly significance for him, thought she even understood why he refused to use his real name. It was a kind of homage to the dead, a way of bearing witness to the past, a continual daily penance for having lived when so many others had died.

McQuade turned and looked at her. "So now you know how I got my name." His voice was hard, bitter, his gaze cold. It was as if he had to cut off all feeling in order not to go mad.

She looked at him through a haze of tears, understanding so much more now, seeing so much more. There seemed to be nothing she could say. No words were adequate to carry the message she had to send: "I understand. I see. I hear you. I am so very, very sorry.'' She could only stand and look at him. How ironic, she thought, that she should see so much more clearly when her eyes were blinded by tears.

"I'm sorry," she whispered. "I'm so sorry."

He nodded, looking back at the window. "It's hard to talk about."

"Yes," she said. "I can see why now."

"Some things you can't find words for," he said.

She nodded. "They're too terrible."

"Yes." He let out a breath and seemed to relax. It was as if he'd carried the special burden of his name with him all these years and finally he'd let it out. He looked tired, worn, exhausted from the years of hiding his secret.

What did you do in the war, Daddy?

I flew dead bodies out of the jungle, son. I wasn't a hero. I didn't do anything major or terribly important. I just flew the dead, every day for three years. They were my constant companions, my copilots. They listened to me curse and sing and cry. They sat on my shoulder, wailing, asking me why they'd had to die. They were young and they were brave and they were frightened. They were black and they were white. They were rich and poor, blue-eyed and brown. But they had one thing in common—they were all dead.

Chapter Ten

The hotel dining room served excellent Vietnamese food and passable continental dishes. They had a delicious asparagus-and-crab soup, followed by fried rice-paper rolls filled with shrimp and sprouts. They finished with a beef dish, washed down with a very good French wine.

At the end of the meal, McQuade suggested they go outside. There was a walled terrace just off the dining room. It had stopped raining for a while and the world seemed to have been washed clean. Overhead, dark clouds rolled by to reveal a few stars, like points of light on a dark canopy. Somewhere in the bushes, crickets chirped. From behind the terrace walls, the muted sounds of traffic came to them from a distance.

A waiter brought their tea out to them. They were completely alone. No one else ventured out.

McQuade took out the letter from Tory's father. The envelope was thick, as if the general had stuffed a small book inside it. McQuade sat looking at it, then glanced up at Tory. "Looks like it'd take a year to find the diamonds. But even if I found the damn things, I wouldn't be able to get them out of the country. The general never thought of that. There are all kinds of laws about what you can bring back with you, and the Vietnamese government sure wouldn't like it if I tried to smuggle them out." He tossed the letter on the table. "It seems senseless to even think about it."

"Aren't you even going to read it?" Tory asked.

"You read it," he said. "Tell me if there's anything good in it."

"Are you sure?"

"Positive."

Tory slit open the letter with a chopstick. To her surprise, she found three smaller envelopes inside. She took them out.

"There are three envelopes," she said. "One addressed to you, one to me, and one to Mme Tran." She saw a note attached to the third envelope and read its message out loud: "'Please give this letter to Mme Tran. It will explain everything to her.'"

McQuade picked up the envelope addressed to him and smiled humorlessly. "How like the general. He was the kind of commander who never let his troops know everything. He always held something back. Usually it was something they didn't need to know or that might actually harm them if they did know." He chuckled grimly. "I wonder what he's got to say." He pushed the envelope toward Tory. "Go ahead and read it. If anything happened to me, you should know what he had to say."

"McQuade!" she reprimanded softly. "Nothing's going to happen to you!"

"Still, I think it's a good idea that you know what he's got to say. Go ahead and read it out loud. I like the sound of your voice."

She slit the envelope open and took out two closely written pages. She began reading out loud:

"Dear McQuade:

"You must think me a foolish old man, promising you diamonds that might not even exist. I believe they do exist, hidden somewhere in the house that Mme

Tran shared with the Frenchman, but I realize that finding them may be difficult, if not impossible.

"I think, though, that you will be searching for a far more important treasure in Vietnam. I don't think you knew it, but I was aware that you had fallen in love with a Vietnamese girl while you served over there."

Tory faltered and looked at McQuade. "Are you sure you want me to read this?" she asked. "Maybe you should read it yourself. It seems personal."

He shook his head. "You might as well finish it. I imagine you'll find out everything sooner or later, anyway."

Tory hesitated, wondering if she should proceed, but McQuade gestured for her to go on. "Go ahead, Tory," he said gently. "I'd like you to read it."

She took a steadying breath and went on reading in a quiet voice:

"I of course heard how she was killed. I did not see you for a month after it happened, and when I did see you again was too busy to even remember to say anything to comfort you. I saw, though, how you changed. Before her death, you had been a bright kid with shiny ideals.

"Afterward, you were sunk in your grief and guilt. Your decision to stop flying supply missions and fly bodies day and night out of the jungle didn't help matters, either, I'm afraid."

Tory looked up at McQuade. So he had once flown other types of cargo.

McQuade gestured for her to go on. "Save your questions, Tory. There'll be time to talk later."

She went on reluctantly, feeling more and more that she was reading something that had been meant only for McQuade.

"I have kept up with you, even though I never contacted you, because when you served in Vietnam, you struck me as one of the most decent and honorable men I'd ever had the pleasure to know."

Tory's voice caught on the words. She was moved by what her father had written and couldn't keep the emotion out of her voice. She blinked away the threat of tears and went on, her voice slightly choked up.

"It hurt to see you wasting your life, but I did not want to interfere. Do-gooders are not welcomed by most of us, I'm afraid. We like to make our own messes, and usually feel we have to clean them up by ourselves.

"I had hoped you would finally work out your guilt and stop punishing yourself, but it appears you never have. There seems to be an enormous emptiness inside you, and I feel deeply for the pain you must have suffered all these years. I hope that during your short visit to Vietnam with my daughter you will be able to come to terms with what happened.

"That is the real treasure I hope you will find on this trip—peace of mind. I hope you will be able to put the past and its sorrows behind you and get on with your life. You are the best pilot I ever had the privilege to fly with in Vietnam, or anywhere else for that matter. I would like to see you straighten your finances out and start building the kind of life you deserve."

Tory paused. It was difficult to read this letter not only because it was so intensely personal, but also because it was from her father. It showed a compassionate, caring side to him she had never seen in her life. The more she read, the gentler her voice became. It was as if she realized she was in some way her father's messenger.

"The past is a hard taskmaster, John. It reminds us of our failings, our imperfections and mistakes. It holds up a picture of ourselves we seldom wish to see. We run from it, though, at our own peril. I pray that you will take the time to turn and face your past, as painful as it may be.

"Guilt is your prison, and self-hatred, the bars. Only you can release yourself from that prison. The key is forgiveness. You must forgive yourself, for being a boy in a man's war, for being merely human, with all a human being's inherent failings, for making a terrible mistake. You are not the first man to have made a mistake in a war, and you probably will not be the last. You must find a way to live with your guilt and remorse, to take responsibility for it but not blame. You must allow yourself to live, John, or that war will truly have been a waste of life—*your* life.

"In His infinite wisdom, God has seen fit to let you live. Do not make the mistake of thinking you are wiser than God. You are not. Your job now is to find out why you are alive, to find a reason for going on, to take the life He has given you and use it to the best of your ability.

"I pray that you will find the way to do this when you are in Vietnam. You have my prayers and my best wishes. God bless you and speed you home.

Sincerely, Adrian LaPorte"

Quietly Tory put the letter down. Across from her, McQuade sat with his head bowed, his hands clutched into fists, struggling to contain the tears that already were rolling down his face. At last he put a hand to his head and broke into quiet sobs. His shoulders shook and the tears rolled down his face, but he made no noise. They might have been alone on all the earth, so utterly were they cut off from the rest of the world. It was as if a silent, protective God had created an island of quiet, giving McQuade the privacy he needed.

Tory waited. She knew that anything she said right now might disturb more than help. She said nothing, just waited while the accumulated sorrow and pain that had been imprisoned inside John McQuade for more than twenty years at last broke from its confines. Tears welled up in her own eyes as she watched him. She had to keep swallowing to try to remove the lump that had lodged in her throat.

At last McQuade raised his head and looked up at the stars that spangled the dark sky overhead. "The general has always seemed the harshest, most unforgiving person I've ever known, yet he wrote that letter." He looked at Tory. "It's humbling, to find out how wrong I can be about others."

"For me, too," Tory said softly. "My father has always seemed a hard man. It's difficult for me to realize he has so much more understanding than I ever gave him credit for. You're right. Humbling is the word."

McQuade reached out and took the letter. "Perhaps when we look at others and think they're judging us harshly, what we're really doing is judging ourselves. Like looking into a pool and seeing our own reflection but thinking it's someone else."

Tory's eyes were filled with compassion as she studied McQuade. "How did she die, McQuade?" she asked gently. "Can you talk about it yet?"

His brow wrinkled as he stared down at her father's letter that fluttered on the table. Finally he said, "Not yet." It was as if he were picking his way through a mine field. Every word was difficult for him. "I'm sorry, but I'm just not ready to talk about it. I know this must be difficult for you, not knowing what happened, but it's difficult for me, too."

"You don't have to apologize to me," she said. "I'm the one who should be apologizing. It's none of my business what happened. It's just..." She took her time explaining now, knowing that what she had to say was important. "I care about you, McQuade." She lifted her eyes and met his gaze. Her heart was pounding she was so nervous. "I care about you. I can't stand to see you hurting like you are. It's like watching someone hurt in a car accident and not being able to get to them to do anything. I feel so helpless, but I know this is something you have to do yourself. I just want you to know that I'm here. I won't run away, McQuade. I promise you that, no matter how hard it gets. I'll be here for you if you need me."

He bent his head. "The problem is, I haven't wanted anyone, Tory. It feels safer to be by myself. Distance is the only thing that feels right." He looked up at the sky, his face tormented. "I can't believe I cried just now. I must really be coming apart at the seams."

Tory's heart went out to him. "McQuade," she said softly, "there's no shame in honest pain. I would worry about you if you weren't able to cry. That would bother me. I know that something terrible happened to you over here during the war, and I know it's been killing you, a little bit at a time. I wish I could take the pain away from you, but I can't. I only know one thing—you're going to have to feel it. You're going to have to face it. You can't pretend it didn't happen, can't turn a blind eye anymore to whatever it was. You've tried that and it hasn't worked. But don't assume that if you cry I'll think less of you, and don't think that if you're angry or depressed or sad that I'll think you're not a man. They're all just feelings, McQuade. We all have them, men as well as women. Whatever you're feeling is okay."

He sat unyielding, like a statue of stone, his jaw working spasmodically, the only outward sign that he was feeling a turbulence of emotions. He seemed to be engaged in some sort of private inner struggle. He made a move toward Tory, then brought his hand back abruptly. His jaw moved spastically. His eyes contained enormous pain, as if he were suffering in a way that could find no expression. Then, taking an enormous breath, he reached out and took her hand.

He held it as if he were hanging on to a lifeline. He said nothing, just sat clinging to her hand. She reached out gently and placed her other hand on top of his. "McQuade, the greatest torture on this earth is to believe that we are alone, to feel cut off from all others. I know it's hard for you to confide in me, but I'm here just the same."

He seemed to relax a little. Slowly he began rubbing his thumb over the back of her wrist, examining it as if he had never seen a hand before, as if it were some strange, exotic thing that had come into his life without explanation.

"Thanks for what you said," he said, running his thumb and fingers over her palm, massaging the base of each finger. He raised her hand to his lips. "I'm glad you're here." Then, as if he'd said too much, he released her hand. "Your father writes a beautiful letter," he said. "I had no idea the general knew so much about me."

"I didn't either," Tory said. "He certainly didn't tell me anything about you, and I had no idea he'd been keeping informed about you all these years."

"The general was always closemouthed," McQuade said. "He wasn't one for sharing what he felt."

Tory smiled. "That makes two of you, then. And believe it or not, McQuade, I think you've got my father topped by a country mile."

"Maybe he doesn't have as much to hide," McQuade said quietly.

"No," she said slowly, "but he seems to know what happened to you and it hasn't changed his opinion about you, has it? Maybe my father is right. Maybe you've got to forgive yourself for whatever you did. Until you do, it doesn't appear you'll have much of a chance at a fulfilling life."

She was afraid he'd get angry and leave the table, but instead he sat staring at the tabletop, thinking about what she'd said. At last he raised his eyes to her. "Forgiving myself is the one thing I've never been able to do, Tory. I've lived with my guilt all these years and I can't stand it anymore. Sometimes it feels like I'm in some sort of iron vise and it's been squeezed tighter and tighter until I've reached the point where I can't bear it anymore. But somehow I do. That's what's so horrible. Somehow I always bear it, and the pain just keeps getting worse. It doesn't ever go away. I can refuse to think about what happened for a week or a month or three months, but one day I turn around and find it staring at me, unrelenting, like a dog searching out a scent. It just never lets up.''

''Because you won't let it,'' she said softly. ''Because you're the one who won't let up on yourself.''

''Damn it, Tory, I killed her!'' he shouted.

The silence that followed his words seemed to crackle with tension. She sat staring at him, shocked, and he stared back. For a moment neither moved, then he was out of his chair and moving across the terrace to a wooden gate set in the wall.

''McQuade, no!'' she said, getting up to run after him, but he was already out the gate and striding hurriedly down a dark alley toward the street. His footsteps echoed in the damp night air. She wanted to go after him, but hesitated. He obviously wanted to be alone. He'd told her the most damning thing, then had taken off, as if he couldn't bear to see her faith in him disappear. She stood debating whether to follow him when the waiter appeared behind her.

''Is there a problem?'' he asked courteously.

''Oh!'' She turned and forced a smile. ''No, of course not. Dinner was delicious.'' She realized they hadn't paid their bill. ''Could you bring me the check, please?''

The waiter held it out on a small tray.

She smiled and took it from him and went back to the table to get money from her purse.

''The gentleman was a soldier in the war?'' the waiter asked gently.

Startled, Tory looked back at him. "Yes."

The waiter nodded, his old face lined with sorrow. "It is that way many times. Many American soldiers are coming back, and they bring great sadness with them. The war brought much sorrow with it, to your soldiers and to ours." He shook his head. "No one escaped entirely. It is very sad."

Tory looked at the old man, seeing his frail shoulders, the lines in his face, the sorrow in his eyes, and she wondered what losses he had suffered in the war. Had he been a soldier? Had he lost friends in the war, a wife, children, a home? She began to understand dimly what McQuade and every other person who had experienced the war must feel, the sense of complete helplessness at the senselessness of it all. "You are right," she said gently, "no one escaped."

"But we must learn from it," the old man said, "and then go on with our lives. It is the way of the world—that we should learn terrible lessons and then have to live with them."

She pressed the money and tip into his hand. "Thank you for your kindness," she said softly.

The old man smiled and for a moment his eyes were filled with joy. "You are very welcome. Please come again, and bring your friend."

She nodded. "I will, and thank you."

She watched as the old man hurried off, then her eyes fell on the other letters from her father. She reached out slowly and picked them up, looking at her father's shaky handwriting. Her heart twisted with grief. How could she have been so hard on her father? His letter to McQuade had been filled with such compassion and understanding. She wondered if anyone had ever shown the kind of understanding toward him that he was showing toward McQuade.

Regretting her own behavior toward her father, she slipped the letters into her pocket and left the terrace. She would go to her room and read her father's letter. There was little sense in trying to find McQuade now. He had disappeared into the night. She could only hope and pray that he would be all right, and that he would return. Perhaps he would be ready, then, to face the events of his past.

In her room, Tory opened the windows to the night air. A humid breeze blew in, cooling the room and filling it with the scents of the city—food, spices, gasoline, the faint odor of flowers, wood smoke drifting on the air.

She sat down in a chair and pulled her father's letter from her pocket. She almost dreaded opening it. Until now, she had refused to face her feelings about her half brother. She had carefully censored herself, not allowing herself to examine what she felt, instead pushing everything into a small, dark, secret part of herself. In that respect, she suddenly realized, she was a lot like McQuade—running from what she had to face.

Sighing, she slit open the envelope and took out the letter from her father.

Dearest Tory,
Since I had my stroke, you have had to be my arms and my legs, my eyes and my ears, my nurse as well as my daughter. I know it has been difficult for you, but you have never complained. You have been the most loving daughter, and I feel so terrible about what you are going through right now. I know it hasn't been easy, finding out you have a half brother in Vietnam. I had thought I would never have to tell you, that I could keep that secret till I went to the grave. It's strange how life is, Tory. It constantly surprises us, giving us the very things we dread the most.

I found I could not live with the guilt I've felt all these years over having a son in Vietnam and leaving him there, unacknowledged. What had started out as a romantic fling has become the single most painful experience of my life. I ended up having to lie to your mother and thus had to bear by myself what I needed so badly to share with her. She was a wonderful and kind woman, with so much wisdom. She would have known how to forgive and comfort me. Instead I was forced to deal with the guilt on my own, and I botched it horribly.

My secretiveness ultimately ruined our marriage. I believe she guessed that something had happened in Vietnam, but of course I couldn't tell her about it. I was afraid I'd hurt her too much. At least that's what I told myself while she was alive. I have come to see, though, that I was merely protecting myself. I didn't tell your mother about it because I couldn't stand for her to find out what I had done. I wanted to be a perfect husband. I ended up being an abysmal failure, as a husband, a father and ultimately as a man.

Because of my pride, I sacrificed my marriage. While the doctors say she died of cancer, I believe she died of a broken heart. Not because I had an affair, but because I broke our marriage vows in a more profound and fundamental way—I turned away from her. I stopped sharing everything with her. In a marriage, total sharing and honest communication are essential. They are the bedrock upon which a stable marriage is built. I destroyed our marriage by undermining its very foundation.

And now I have asked you to right my wrongs. I know, of course, that it will be almost impossible for you to do that. The boy will have grown into a man never knowing me. He will probably not welcome my advances now, nor will his mother, Mme Tran. Do not be surprised, therefore, if they reject my request for him to come see me in the United States.

Why then did I ask you to go? Truly, I cannot answer that. I only know that something in me said that you must go to Vietnam. What you do with this trip is entirely up to you. You have complained so much that I am bossy, domineering, an interfering father who's always trying to run your life. I suppose, dear Tory, that I sent you to Vietnam to discover something about yourself. Perhaps I thought that if you could see the forces that shaped me and McQuade, you might understand men better. I hope that from that clearer understanding of men, you would come to a greater understanding of yourself.

Tory stopped reading. Her throat had a lump in it. She was finding out so much about her father, so much she had never suspected. Guilt shimmered inside her. How could she have been so blind, so self-centered, not to see what her father had been suffering? She wished that it could all be different, but saw now that life offers few choices, then insists that we live with the choices we make. She picked up the letter and resumed reading.

In a strange country, away from all that is familiar to us, we often see with a clarity we have never before had. This is what I wish from you, my dearest daughter, that you try to see me as just a man—human, prone to mistakes—and that you find it in your heart to forgive me for all the pain I have caused, to both you and your dear mother.

I love you with all my heart, and wish for you all things beautiful, all things good, all things bounteous and joyful. May God bless you and bring you an abundance of love.

Your loving Dad

She raised tear-filled eyes. Her whole world seemed to be toppling upside down. Ever since she was a child she'd seen her father as strict, authoritarian, unyielding. He was like a god, unsmiling, hard, fashioned from a great slab of granite. She smiled sadly. Then she had read his letters.

Suddenly things were no longer black-and-white. Nothing was simple now. She couldn't just categorize him as a hard man, a harsh father, an unloving husband. It had been comforting to do that. It had made everything simple. It had helped her feel superior and righteous and she'd been able to judge him easily.

But now she saw that things had happened that she'd known nothing about. It was like opening a secret door in her father's room and finding an entire assortment of personal articles she'd never known existed. Everything changed with new knowledge. It was like turning on lamps in a dim room. She could see more clearly now. She was no longer in the dark.

She felt sadness well up inside her. She wished suddenly she wasn't half a world away from him. If she had been in Boston, she would have gotten in her car and driven to see him. She would have put her arms around him and just held him. She would have poured out her love for him, telling him she understood. But she wasn't in Boston. She was in Vietnam, and he was half a world away.

She lifted tear-misted eyes and gazed out the window at the clouds that were beginning to drift like black gauze over the moon.

"My father is going to die one day," she thought, "and I've never told him I love him."

She dropped her head into her hands. Why do we wait until it's too late? What are we waiting for? Do we think we'll live forever, that it will never end? That someday we'll be able to say all the things we've held inside and never said? She shivered, as if her father had already died and she'd never get the chance to tell him she loved him.

How horrible to lose someone you love and not have told them how much they mean to you. How horrible to know you can never say it to them, that they will never hear it. She wished she were back home. She wanted to tell her father all this before it was too late.

She sat alone, with tears streaming down her face, and in the midst of her grief, she remembered McQuade. Was this what he had suffered all these years, this searing pain, this terrible regret?

Lifting her eyes, she saw that the clouds were rolling in, that the moon was almost covered now. The breeze was picking up, whipping the curtains back, stirring the mosquito netting around her bed, filling the room with a damp chill that made her shiver.

"Dear God," she whispered, tears glittering her eyes, "please take care of both of us—me and McQuade. Please help us find our way through this mess."

She realized, then, that they were both indeed in a foreign country—not Vietnam, but a land of unexplored emotions and frightening prospects. McQuade had to face his past. She was pulled along almost against her will, forced to face changes in her life because of things her father had done over twenty years ago.

The sins of the fathers are visited upon the children.

The words echoed in the room, like the hushed specter of an unwelcome ghost. She sat in the chair and watched as the clouds moved over the moon until it was finally obscured completely. The rain began again, slowly at first, a few large drops splashing onto the window sill and tapping against the glass, then the heavens opened and the rain came down in torrents, whipped across the rooftops by winds that grabbed the outdoor shutters and banged them shut.

She waited until her eyes grew heavy, then she closed the windows and went to bed. When she at last fell asleep, McQuade had still not returned.

THREE BLOCKS AWAY McQuade stood in a doorway, his collar turned up, his shoulders hunched as he stared at the rain that pummeled the streets. He remembered nights like this in his hooch, when rain had pounded against the tin roof like a horde of furies trying to get in. The roof had leaked, so he would set out tin buckets to catch the drips. He remembered listening to the rain ping into the bucket until the bottom was filled, then watching the water level slowly rise until he'd have to get up and empty it, then set the bucket down to begin all over again.

It had always seemed endless, the rain. Yet somehow it had always ended, and then the dry season came and it was so hot you prayed for the rains to come again. It was a land of extremes. Perhaps that was why it had been so easy to behave in extreme ways.

Sighing, he pulled his collar up around his throat. He would return to the hotel and try to get some sleep. Tomorrow they would try to locate Mme Tran and the general's son. And then, sooner or later, he'd have to face his past. Wasn't that why he'd come?

Ducking his head, he dashed into the rain. When he reached the hotel, he was soaked, and no lights shone in Tory's bedroom. He wished she was awake. He would have liked to talk to her tonight. He wished he hadn't run off like that, but that seemed to be the way he coped lately—by running away.

Exhausted, he went to bed and fell into an uneasy sleep.

Chapter Eleven

Sometime in the night the winds picked up and the heavens opened, pouring out a torrential downpour. Rain pounded the rooftops, clattered down the gutters, attacked the windows like fearful children trying frantically to get in. Outside Tory's bedroom the wind tore at the shutters and banged them against the side of the hotel. It grabbed the windows and flung them open. They crashed back into her bedroom and one pane shattered, breaking the quiet of her sleep.

She awoke with a start, her heart pounding. She saw the shattered glass, heard the wind howling and the outside shutters banging furiously against the side of the hotel. Lightning cracked open the night sky. Thunder rolled through the heavens, like heavy caissons carrying cannons through dark and menacing streets.

Suddenly she was a child again, trembling in her bed, fearing some terrible catastrophe she could only marginally imagine—the house might be swept away by the high winds and drenching rain, she might be parted from her parents, they might die...

She sat up in bed, shaking. She didn't want to be alone. She had to stop the numbing fear that threatened to overwhelm her, had to find someplace to hide, someone to shelter her. Then she remembered McQuade. Suddenly there

seemed to be nothing more important than taking refuge in
his arms. If she could get to him, she'd be all right. He
would take care of her. He'd wrap her in his strong arms and
she would be safe.

Thunder cracked the sky and lightning lit it up and Tory
bolted from her bed, racing to the door and pounding on it.

"McQuade! Open up!"

In his room, McQuade stirred. Mai was calling to him.
She was somewhere in the night, calling his name, screaming for his help. He couldn't bear it any longer, couldn't
stand the visits from the ghosts one more night.

Tory pounded on the door. "McQuade!"

He sat up, startled, and realized it was Tory. He got out
of bed and went to the connecting door. Turning the lock,
he opened the door. Tory flew into his arms.

"Oh, McQuade," she whispered shakily, "thank God."

"What's the matter?" he asked, not knowing where to
put his hands. Finally he put his arms around her. He was
immediately aware of the way her breasts pressed against his
bare chest, of the clean rose-tinted scent that surrounded
her, the softness of her skin. He suppressed a groan and
lifted her chin with his finger. "Tory? What's the matter?"

"It's the storm," she whispered, not meeting his eyes. She
looked utterly miserable, as if she wanted to slink away and
crawl under a rock. "I know it's silly, McQuade, but I can't
help it. Ever since I was a kid, I've been this way and—"

She was interrupted by thunder that shook the floor. She
jumped as if she'd been shot, then buried her head in his
chest. He felt her entire body shivering and wrapped his
arms around her protectively.

"It's all right, Tory," he crooned to her, rubbing her back
as he held her. "It's all right. Nothing's going to hurt you."

She put her arms around him and clung to him, feeling as
if a great burden had been lifted. He wasn't chiding her or
making her feel silly or stupid. He was simply holding her.
That's all she had ever wanted, ever since she was a child—

someone to hold her, to make her feel safe. Was that so silly, so foolish? Then why hadn't anyone until now ever given her this simple, basic thing she had craved so badly?

Despite the booming thunder, the rain that lashed against the windows, the streaks of lightning that seemed to part the sky, slowly her shivering began to subside.

"There, now," McQuade murmured. "You see? You're fine."

She shook her head, still clinging to him. "Only because you're holding me."

He smiled at that and tried to get her to look up at him. "Nonsense," he murmured. "How could my holding you make things so much better?"

"Because I feel safe," she said, her voice quivering slightly. "I know it's foolish to be so afraid, but I've always been afraid of storms and everyone has always kidded me or told me how silly I am, but no one's ever just held me and that's all I need, for someone just to hold me." She lifted her head at last and looked at McQuade with pleading eyes. "Please, just hold me," she whispered. "Please."

He could no more refuse her than he could walk to the moon. He held her as if she were the only woman in the world and he were the only man, as if there were no other chances. He wrapped his arms around her shivering body, and closed his eyes and felt warmth seep into his bones. Vaguely he wondered why holding her should make him feel so warm, but then he stopped thinking, stopped questioning. He picked her up and carried her to his bed. He sat down and held her in his lap and she clung to him, her arms around his neck. He rocked her, crooned to her, kissed her hair and eyes and cheeks.

"It's all right, Tory," he whispered.

"Oh, McQuade." She burrowed her forehead into his, touched his nose with hers, left her lips poised hesitantly over his. "McQuade."

She raised her head and looked into his eyes and found a thousand questions staring back at her. Slowly she reached up and touched his cheek. Her eyes were filled with wonder. "I'm not afraid anymore."

"Then I suppose you want to go back to your own bed."

She shivered slightly at the suggestion. "My window blew open and broke. The wind and rain are blowing in . . ."

"Well, you can't stay here."

She moved her hand over his bare chest, shivering with delight at the feel of his smooth skin and the wiry hairs that covered it. "Why can't I?" she whispered, her lips close to his.

He felt something let go inside his head and suddenly he didn't care if he was doing the right thing, he only wanted her. He ran a strong hand down her back, stopping at the swelling curve of her hip. His breathing became unsteady as long-denied desires surfaced like dolphins bursting from the sea. He lowered his head to the curve of her neck and inhaled the sweet smell of her. He felt dizzy, devoured by a need to touch her, hold her, learn the soft and secret places of her body.

She lay back on the bed and drew him down to her, running her hand up his chest and down his muscled arm, soaking up the sensual delight that coursed through her.

"McQuade," she whispered. "I want you inside me."

He groaned and lowered his lips to hers. A whirlwind seemed to take him, transporting him into a new world. He couldn't get enough of her, couldn't taste her enough, smell her enough, couldn't kiss her deeply enough. He shook inside, as if he had never kissed a woman, had never made love. He ran his hand up her arm, his mouth on hers, as his tongue dipped into her mouth and tangled with hers.

Ecstasy filled him, so sharp and sweet he thought he might faint. He held her face and plunged his tongue deeper into her mouth, delighting when she answered him, responded so readily, as if her need for him equaled his for her.

Her breathing grew hard and her hands were all over him. She writhed beneath him, moaning softly as his lips caressed her neck and throat. She cried out when he pulled down her gown and found her breasts. Her nipples stood up firm with arousal and he drew them into his mouth, laved them with his tongue. He buried his head between her breasts and ran his hand down her body. Her skin was smooth as satin, soft and creamy under his hands. He shook inside as he gently pulled her gown from her hips, then down the long, silky length of her legs.

She arched beneath him, pressing her breasts into his chest, moving her hips in sensuous circles. She sighed and ran her fingers through his hair, down his back, then slid her hands into the waistband of his shorts. He gasped when she found him, hard and throbbing with strength.

They rolled upon the wrinkled sheets, writhing as if in some sort of mortal combat, the air filled with their sighs and panting breath, the storm outside forgotten as this inner storm enveloped them. They couldn't get enough of each other, couldn't kiss enough, touch enough, explore enough. Always there was this inner need, urging them further until their desire mushroomed and there was only one way out, only one way to end the sweet torment that held them in its grip.

He entered her slowly, making her groan in ecstasy as she felt the length of him glide inside her. Her only aim was to pull him closer, deeper, to have him bury himself so deep inside her that he was one with her, a part of her, no longer separate.

Some primordial rhythm took over, urging him first to press further, then retreat. The friction was delicious. He gloried in the softness of her, the sweet dampness that enveloped him, urging him on, drawing him ever deeper into her depths. He wanted only to merge and merge again, to go so deeply into her that he would become lost in the hollow of her soul.

At the end it became necessity, as air and water are necessary for life. He could not bear it, could not stand the sweet pain that seemed to rip him apart. Swifter, harder, the need for her became insatiable, implacable. Frantic, he pressed and pushed and buried himself inside her, over and over, repeatedly, torn with anguish, going forward toward the light, the light, the light—

It burst around them like an explosion, shattering their souls, merging them completely with its heat. Throbbing, pulsing, he emptied into her, then collapsed, his body covered with a fine sheen of sweat, his lungs gasping for air, his body exhausted.

Beneath him, she wept, soft and gentle tears of joy. She held him as she had never held a man, with love and gratitude and deep rejoicing. "McQuade," she whispered. "John McQuade."

He raised himself up and looked down at her, his face transfigured. "Are you all right?" he asked, so gently his words were like an absolution, a blessing, a sanctifying oath.

She smiled and nodded, lifting her hand to his face as a tear rolled down her face. "It was wonderful, more beautiful than anything I've ever felt or known before."

He shifted his weight off her and took her in his arms, turning her to face him, her head cradled on his arm. "Yes," he murmured, completely satisfied. "Yes."

They held each other, and this time the holding was gentle, filled with satisfaction and fulfillment, no longer seeking and urgent. Tory lifted her gaze and watched the storm outside recede. The thunder had moved away and was only a distant rumble now. The lightning no longer split the sky, but fluttered occasionally outside like a butterfly hovering over a flower. The rain fell steadily, enveloping the world in a hushed atmosphere broken only by its steady drumming and gurgling through the gutters, rolling off into empty streets and splashing in the storm drains.

"They made me feel so stupid," Tory said. "My father and Daniel. They told me I was silly and foolish, that storms couldn't hurt me, and I knew they were probably right, but that didn't seem to matter. I just wanted to be held. And tonight when you held me, I knew I'd been right—that it wasn't foolish or silly or stupid of me to need someone to hold me. Perhaps if my father had held me when I was a little girl, this terrible fear would never have grown inside me." She looked at McQuade, her face filled with questions. "How could he have been so wrong? If he loved me, why didn't he know that holding me was what I needed? Why was it so hard for him, and then for Daniel?" she studied McQuade. "And why was it so easy for you?"

He smoothed his hand over her hair, letting a long, silken strand slide through his fingers. "Perhaps it's because I know what it's like to be afraid."

"But surely they've been afraid..."

He shook his head. "Maybe not in the same way. I think a person has to have suffered to understand another person's suffering. That's when your heart goes out to them, because you know what they're feeling. You've experienced it. Maybe not the exact same fear, or under the exact circumstances, but you understand. You've been there."

Tory watched him with compassionate eyes. "Yet you never talk about your own fears."

He rolled onto his back and stared up at the ceiling. "Some things maybe you shouldn't talk about."

"You give so much to me, yet you refuse me the same opportunity to give to you. What makes you think I wouldn't understand?"

He pondered her question, filled with uncertainty and foreboding. How could he ever talk with Tory? She had never been to war, had never seen ugly death up close, had never carried in her heart the kind of terrible guilt that burdened him. There was a chasm between them, a gulf composed of his experience and her lack of it. He doubted it could ever be bridged. It would require more of her than she was probably capable of giving.

But perhaps he wasn't being fair. Maybe he didn't want to tell her for fear of what she might think of him. She could lie with him now in the afterglow of lovemaking, simply because she didn't know him. What would happen if she did? Would she recoil with distaste? Would the empathy she promised now disappear, leaving her revolted by the story he had to tell?

"McQuade," she said softly, "why won't you answer me?"

He kissed the curve between her neck and shoulder. "When you pounded on the door, I thought it was someone else calling me. I thought it was Mai."

"Mai?"

"She was the woman I fell in love with over here."

Tory lifted a hand and touched his cheek. "What happened to her, McQuade? You said you killed her."

He gritted his teeth. The past was always present, no matter how he tried to elude it. It always caught up to him. He felt as if he'd been running all his life, yet he couldn't seem to stop. he had to tell her sometime, he'd known that from the start, and yet he couldn't bring himself to do it. He felt as if he might disintegrate if he opened up that wound. He was held together now by a patchwork of barbed wire and bobby pins. If he ever started talking about it, he might not be able to stand it. He thought he might go crazy if he ever looked squarely at the past. Better to keep it tamped down, contained, letting it leak out slowly, a drop at a time.

"Don't ask, Tory," he said quietly. "Just don't ask."

She rested her head against his chest. Disappointment filled her, yet she knew she had to abide by his wishes. She couldn't force him to trust her. She simply had to wait, hoping that someday, at some time, he would turn to her and open up his heart.

"I love you, John McQuade," she whispered silently. "I love you." She closed her eyes and smoothed her hand over his chest, her heart suddenly heavy. How strange love was. Sometimes it was more like pain than joy, more sorrow than happiness.

Chapter Twelve

Rain was drumming against the windows when Tory woke up the next morning. It rattled in the tin gutters outside and splashed in the street five floors below. She lay in bed and listened to it, feeling safe and warm, protected from the elements. She reached out to touch McQuade, but he wasn't there.

She sat up swiftly, looking around the room. Disappointment flooded her. He was gone. Why couldn't he have stayed to wake up with her? Why had he had to run off, like a thief in the night?

Noises from her room next door caught her attention. Vietnamese voices, the sound of broken glass being swept up, and hammering told her that McQuade had already reported the damage the storm had done last night. The connecting door to her room opened and McQuade stepped in, shutting the door quietly and locking it.

"They're fixing your window," he explained, but his eyes were fastened on her, sitting up in the middle of the bed, the sheet held to her breasts, her shoulders bare, her tousled hair falling magnificently around her face and shoulders. She was the picture of sensuality, a woman made for lovemaking, her mouth wide and voluptuous, her eyes filled with the sleepy heat of desire. Slowly she let the sheet drop and all he could do was gaze at her breasts, so white and full, tipped with rosy-beige nipples that hardened even as he looked at them.

He felt himself respond, even though he told himself he shouldn't. Last night had been a mistake. He didn't want to repeat it.

He dropped some clothing on the bed. "I took the liberty of finding some clothes for you," he said. "I've already taken my shower, so you're welcome to use my bathroom."

Tory lay back against the pillows, her eyes following him as he walked toward the window. "I'd rather that you came over here," she said softly.

He stood with his back to her, staring out the window. "It's getting late," he said, ignoring her invitation. "We have a lot to do today."

"It can wait," she said.

"I'm afraid it can't," he answered. "I don't want to be here any longer than I have to." He glanced at her and said sharply, "Get dressed, Tory."

She stared at him, sitting up slowly. "What about last night?"

"What about it?" he said, staring resolutely out the window. He refused to look at her. Even the merest glance could be his undoing.

"Are you sorry it happened?" she asked quietly.

He frowned at the rain. "No."

"Neither am I," she said. "And I'd like it to happen again. Right now."

He turned to warn her off. "Tory..." he said, but she was out of the bed, splendid in her nakedness, coming slowly toward him, refusing to listen.

She stopped in front of him and reached out and began to unbutton his shirt. She pulled it from his trousers and slid her hands over his chest. "I want to touch you so much," she said. "Don't you want to touch me?"

He put his hands out to push her away, but somehow they went to her sides, sliding up the silky smooth skin, his thumbs finding her nipples.

She sighed and went up on tiptoe, kissing his lips, pressing her breasts into his chest and moving her hips against him. "Please," she whispered. "I'm shaking inside." She took his hand and led him toward the bed. "Make love to me, John."

She had called him John last night and in the heat of the moment it hadn't mattered, but now he realized he hadn't heard his name on a woman's lips for over twenty years. He stood staring down at her, seeing the desire in her eyes, the way her auburn hair flared out around her, and suddenly she was another woman, in another hotel, at another time. He whirled around and strode toward the door.

"I'll see you downstairs in the dining room. I'll order breakfast. Don't be too long. I'm starved."

Then he slammed the door shut and she was alone, filled with frustrated heat, angry enough to wish she could strike him. "Damn you, John McQuade," she said out loud. "Damn you for being so stubborn."

"I READ THE LETTER from my father last night," she said over breakfast in the dining room.

"Did you?" McQuade said. He thought of her father's letter to him which she had read out loud last night. He remembered what her father had said, that he hoped McQuade would find something infinitely more valuable than diamonds. It didn't seem possible, he thought now, his mood dark and somber. He wasn't able to walk away from the past. His conscience wouldn't let him.

"Yes," Tory said, watching McQuade as she sipped her tea. She was determined to break through the barrier he'd erected against her. The only way she knew to do that was to share her own feelings, to let herself be as vulnerable as McQuade was afraid of being. "I realized last night that I've been living in a kind of dream. I've never known my father. I always thought I did, but I didn't.''

McQuade looked up from his eggs. "Why do you say that?"

"There's an entire side to him I never knew existed, a compassionate side, filled with remorse and guilt. I realized it after reading your letter, but it was reinforced after I read his letter to me." She looked around. A few other hotel guests were scattered around the dining room and there was the pleasant undertone of idle chatter, the reassuring rustling of the morning paper, the clatter of dishes in the kitchen. She found to her surprise that she wanted to share her feelings with McQuade, not to show him how to do it, but because she needed someone to talk to and she found him a surprisingly good listener.

"It's strange how hard it is to love someone who always seems to control events," she continued. "That's how my father always seemed to me—in charge, with no irrational thoughts, no emotions, just this juggernaut of a man, this fierce force who strode through life without any doubts. He always seemed so certain, as if he never had any second thoughts."

"And his letter showed he did?" McQuade asked.

Suddenly she was filled with sadness. "Yes," she said slowly. "I keep wondering how so much escaped me. Was he putting on an act, or was I just blind? If I'd looked harder, been more responsive to him, could I have seen what he was suffering?" She frowned as she tried to gather her thoughts. "But worst of all is knowing that I've been hiding from my own feelings. I've been pretending this half brother doesn't exist. But he does exist, and how am I going to feel when I see him? That's what worries me. I love my father, and I've come over here to do what he asked me to do, but..."

"But?" McQuade prompted.

She sat back, feeling restless. "I haven't wanted to face it, McQuade, but I was jealous when I found out about him. I was my father's only child, the darling. At least that's what I always told myself. It made it easier to bear when he ignored me or was gone or wouldn't talk to me. I could always tell myself I was his only child and he had to love me, even if he didn't show it. But now..." She felt woebegone, as if the last of her illusions were being stripped away. "Now I know there's another child, and it's been killing me, McQuade. It has hurt so much to know my father's obsessed with this boy. He has practically ignored me. But then I read his letter..."

Without even knowing what he meant to do, McQuade reached out and put a hand on hers to comfort her. She looked at him gratefully. "I'm scared, McQuade. My father wants to see his son so much, but I'm afraid if he does he'll forget me completely. I want him to see his son, but I dread it at the same time." She forced a self-deprecating laugh. "Aren't I the wonderful, loving daughter?" She rubbed her arms and looked away. "Sometimes I hate myself so much. And what's so terrible is knowing how rotten I'm being, how selfish and jealous and small. And realizing how I've been whistling Dixie the past couple months, pretending that everything was all just fine. I broke up with Daniel and met you and the whole time I wasn't even facing what I was feeling about the bomb my father dropped when he told me he had a son."

"Now you sound like me," McQuade said. "Beating on myself."

She half smiled. "I know. I saw that last night, too—how alike we are. I hoped you'd see it, too. To accept ourselves, I think we need to look at others. It's easier to feel compassion for others than it is for ourselves. We're so hard on ourselves."

He frowned at his plate. What was she telling him? Was she saying she would comfort him if he shared what had happened during the war with her? But she didn't know what had happened, so it was easy to think she'd understand. He decided to ignore the whole matter and change the subject. "Have you spoken to Mme Tran yet?"

Tory shook her head. "She still runs a restaurant," she said. "My father gave me the address."

"I suppose you could just show up and ask to speak with her," McQuade said.

"No, I'd rather see her in her home, but tourists aren't allowed in private Vietnamese homes and Vietnamese aren't allowed to visit tourists in their hotels." She sighed. "I suppose we'll have to send a note and hope she responds."

"All right, then write a note. Have it delivered to her restaurant. See if she responds. If she doesn't, then you'll have to think of some other way of seeing her."

"But that could take days."

"We don't have a rigid time schedule, Tory. We can sign up for one of those tours the new Vietnamese government likes to have tourists go on. You can take pictures." He smiled ironically. "I could start trying to make sense out of my life."

"But what about the diamonds?" Tory asked, lowering her voice so no one could overhear them. "We'll have to talk to Mme Tran, if you're ever going to get the chance to get inside her house and look for them."

"Diamonds," he said, chuckling. "I'm sorry, Tory, but I don't think they exist. I don't think your father does, either. I think he used that old legend as a lure to get me to agree to go with you."

"What are you saying? That you don't even care about them?"

He shrugged. "Your father was right—I have more important treasure to find over here."

"Do you think you'll find it?" Tory asked, studying him.

He looked away. Her gaze was too direct, her eyes too honest. A frisson of anxiety shot up his spine. "I'm not sure I can," he said.

"Don't do this to yourself, McQuade," she said quietly. "You've been running long enough. Maybe it's time to face what you've been running from."

He studied the table. "Sometimes it's not that easy, Tory. Sometimes it's easier to run."

"But the cost is higher," she said quietly, her eyes filled with compassion.

He nodded. "Yes, the cost is very high."

"I can't tell you what to do, McQuade. I don't know what's right or wrong, but it seems to me that when you're in so much pain, trying another approach couldn't be any worse."

He sat and stared into space. "You're right," he said at last. "Maybe I should go back."

For a minute, Tory was puzzled. Hadn't he already come back? Then she realized he was talking about a specific place. She sat and waited, watching as he seemed to fight silently with himself. At last he looked up at her.

"Do you know anything about travel outside Saigo—" He caught himself. "I mean Ho Chi Minh City?"

"Only that the government can arrange tours to specific places within the country. They require a government guide to go with tourists."

"Do you think we could arrange for a car and a guide? The village was destroyed during the war, and I'm not even sure it would be there, but we could try."

"I'll call them right now," Tory said. "And then I'll send a note to Mme Tran. I read in the guidebook that pedicab drivers will often deliver notes, especially when you want to be discreet."

But McQuade wasn't listening. He was hearing instead the rhythmic whoosh of helicopter blades cutting the air. To this day he couldn't hear one overhead without being back in another one, lifting up into the brilliant blue Vietnamese sky and looking back one last time at a burned-out village, seeing sprawled on the ground the lifeless body of the woman he loved.

"McQuade?"

Tory's voice called him back. For a second he wasn't even sure where he was, then he saw Tory's worried face. "I'm sorry," he said. "Sometimes I remember things."

Her eyes were filled with pain as she studied him. "I wish I could do something," she said. "I wish I could help you. I feel so..." she gestured vaguely "...so inept, like this incompetent fool, just incapable of doing anything to—" She broke off, aware that she was going on about herself just when McQuade needed her the most.

"There's nothing you could do for me, Tory."

"Of course there is!" she cried softly. "I could be here for you, listen to you, hold you, offer you comfort, but you're not letting me! You insist on keeping everything to yourself. You won't share, won't talk, won't even make love to me."

Aghast at her quiet outburst, she sat back, her face growing red. "I'm sorry," she said, pushing back her chair. "I'm terribly sorry."

She hurried out of the dining room, making a beeline for the ornate elevator, heading for the only privacy she had— the little room upstairs. She could only hope that the repairs were finished on her window so she could be alone for a while and regain her composure.

She dashed through the lobby, not caring that the few people stared at her. She made it to the elevator and was about to close the door when McQuade appeared. His large hand came out and stopped the elevator door from closing. She could only stand and look at him, her face a picture of misery.

McQuade stepped in and the elevator door slid shut. They were encased in silence, broken only by the protesting squeal and squeak of the ancient mechanism that hoisted the elevator upward.

"I'm sorry, Tory. I didn't realize you felt so strongly about all this."

"Please don't apologize," she said, unable to look at him. "It's I who should apologize. I suppose I have this picture of myself as the Healer, Lady Bountiful, all goodness and understanding, listening to you reveal the depths of your agony so I can 'cure' you." She snorted at herself contemptuously. "God, how I hate myself sometimes."

"Tory, don't."

She lifted miserable eyes to him. "It's only because I care about you so much," she said, her voice trembling. "I can't stand to see what you're doing to yourself. The past is the past, dammit. I don't care what you did, it isn't worth destroying your own life over!"

Unwanted tears spilled from her eyes and she dashed them away, uncertain if she was angrier at McQuade or herself.

"You really mean that, don't you?" McQuade said.

"Of course I mean it!" she barked. "God, I'd like to stomp my foot and beat on you till you finally listen to me. What does it take, McQuade? What gets through your colossal ego? Do you think you're the only person in the world who's had terrible things happen to him? The only one who's made mistakes? We all make mistakes! All of us—" She broke off and burst into tears.

"Dammit," she said through her sobbing. "I don't even have a handkerchief."

"Here," he said gently, "take mine."

She managed a garbled "thank you," then escaped as the elevator doors opened. She raced toward her bedroom, not wanting to have to face McQuade anymore, but just as she opened her door he came up behind her.

"I think we need to talk," he said, and gently guided her into her room and closed the door behind them.

"Do you really care this much?" he asked, leaning back against the door and watching her intently.

She took a deep breath. "More than I even knew," she said and turned her back on him to go stand at the window.

Outside the rain came down steadily, like a shadowy curtain obstructing the view, turning the street below into a blurred impressionist landscape. Even at mid-morning, street lights were on and neon lights reflected in the wet streets. Pedestrians in conical hats raced back and forth and umbrellas peppered the avenue.

He dropped his gaze and studied the floor. He had made a lot of fool mistakes in his life, and none worse than hurting the women who had cared for him. Maybe he owed Tory the truth. He had come this far with her.

"Tory," he said. "Come sit here on the bed with me. I have some things I want to tell you."

Startled, she turned and looked at him, then obeyed without question. She sat down at the head of the bed, turning to face him as he sat on the end.

He sat gazing at the bedspread, then lifted pain-filled eyes to her. "I don't know why it's so hard to talk about it," he said at last, "but it is. It's like a terrible lump inside my soul, sitting there, black as night. I've carried it so long that I don't even know where to begin." He lifted his gaze and looked around the room. "I had never thought I'd come back here. It was a miracle I survived, or perhaps an ironic quirk of fate. I had hoped I'd die over here, but I didn't, and so I went home hoping my life would improve." He sighed heavily. "It never has."

"That doesn't mean it can't," Tory said gently.

He shook his head. "Maybe it could have when I first came back, if I'd gotten help, but in those days no one wanted to talk to Vietnam vets. We were outcasts, pariahs in our own country. They hadn't figured out there was any such thing as post-traumatic stress syndrome, and even if they had, the VA sure didn't seem to care about us. We've spent over twenty years fighting for our rights, and only now is something being done about us, grudgingly.''

"You sound angry," Tory said quietly, nonaccusingly.

He nodded. "Angry, bitter, and more."

"Maybe that's why you have such a hard time talking about it," Tory suggested. "Maybe you feel like you were used..."

"I *was* used, damn it! We were all used. It was a lousy war, but at least we had each other. We found out what friendship was in that war. The men we fought with became closer than our families. But when we came home no one wanted to be seen with us. Friends would walk down the street and look the other way when I got home. People burned the very flag we had fought for, they spat on us and jeered at us." His eyes burned fiercely as he remembered the past. "And we'd just been doing what our government asked us to do."

"It was a no-win situation," Tory said quietly.

"You bet," McQuade spat. "Big time."

"So are you going to keep punishing yourself just because your country let you down?"

He looked at her, frowning, as if he'd never looked at it that way before. "You think that's all it is," he asked at last, belligerence echoing in his voice. "You think I'm just acting like a spoiled brat, having a tantrum because things didn't go the way I wanted them to?"

"No, I didn't mean that at all. I'm just wondering if your anger at the entire situation is keeping you from being able to resolve it. I mean, you were terribly wounded by what happened in the war, and then doubly hurt when no one back home seemed to care. That's like two blows. It wouldn't be so bad if you'd been able to come home and find someone who'd listen to you, care for you, hold your hand while you cursed your fate, but you didn't go home to that. You went home to people who didn't give a damn about what you'd experienced. I guess that'd make me pretty darned bitter."

He sat on the bed, nodding, his eyes filling with tears that he struggled to contain. "Yeah," he said at last, his voice strangled by his efforts to contain the emotions that threatened to overflow. "Yeah," he said again, but this time his voice carried relief, for at last, after more than twenty years, someone had finally understood him.

Watching him, Tory felt a building sense of compassion and love and understanding, all piled together in a great tangle, filling her with actual physical warmth. Her eyes misted with tears as she watched the emotions cross McQuade's face. She wanted to reach out and take his hand but held herself back. She didn't want anything to destroy what was happening, and something in her sensed that at this point McQuade needed someone to just listen.

He let out a sigh and looked around the room, seeing not this hotel room but that other one, where he and Mai had stayed for four perfect days. He felt as if he were going back in time, being transported to that other Vietnam, the one when war ravaged the land and violent death was a daily occurrence. He could almost hear the sounds—the mingled shouts and laughter of his command post, the high scream of mortars coming in at night, the tracers in the night sky, lighting up the world like fireworks on the Fourth of July. He saw again the dense jungle vegetation, the red dust covering everything, the tropical trees blowing in the wind, the rice paddies slumbering in their watery fields.

He saw the Vietnamese hurrying by in their conical hats and black pajamas, their heads ducked down, their eyes averted, heard the jabber of their voices in the marketplace, smelled the rich, intoxicating aroma of fried meats on sidewalk stoves, heard the laughter bursting from the bars, the angry shouts, the bottles breaking, glass smashing, the strange, exotic music in the night.

And then he saw her. Mai, standing as he'd first seen her in the marketplace, a piece of lavender silk in her hands.

"I'd only been over here about a week when I first saw her," he said out loud, talking more to himself than to Tory. "She was in the market here in Saigon. I spoke to her, asked her her name. The Vietnamese don't usually look into a person's eyes when they are talking, I learned that right away. But that first day in the market, Mai lifted her eyes to me and I fell in love with her. She was very young, just sixteen, and extraordinarily beautiful. There was an innocence about her, a goodness that shone inside her like a lamp lighting up a room. Her eyes met mine and I felt the love in her eyes like a warm flame, looking into my eyes, warming me."

Tory sat quietly. The rain fell steadily outside, but otherwise the room was wrapped in silence. All her attention was on McQuade. He was the only thing that mattered now. She watched him with eyes filled with compassion. She knew he had finally crossed the bridge he'd avoided all these years. They were together in a strange country and he was at last talking. It was as if everything in both their lives had led them to this place, to this moment in the city that had once been called Saigon.

Chapter Thirteen

"I didn't think I'd ever see her again," McQuade continued, "but the next day she was at the market again, and I followed her home. She had left her village and was living in Saigon with a sister. Her mother had been visiting, but had returned to her village that morning. Mai was looking for work. About a month after I met her, she finally found a job as a housekeeper in a rich man's house. One night he tried to force himself on her. She escaped by screaming. She gathered up her few belongings and came to me in my hooch..."

McQuade looked back into the past and saw the young, frightened Mai, saw himself take her in his arms and hold her, comfort her, and realized that what had happened between them had been, at once, terribly beautiful and impossibly sad.

"There was no hope for us, but I didn't know that then. I was young—just turned eighteen. I already knew how to fly both planes and choppers, so I'd gone through the army's flight-training school in record time and been shipped over here before I even knew what was happening. I was a kid, but I thought I was a man."

He paused, remembering his youth, gone now, never to be retrieved. It was lost in the carnage of war, destroyed by a brutal reality that no person should have to witness. He felt sorrow rise up in him for that lost youth, that innocence, for all the dreams that might have been but were gone now, forever unattainable.

"That night," he continued heavily, "both Mai and I lost our virginity. We were both awkward, but it wasn't just sex. There was a gentleness to it, so it seemed almost holy. Afterward we lay in my cot and listened to the mortars coming in. They lit up the sky and the ground shook under us, and I guess we should have known it couldn't last, but we didn't. We had that blindness that belongs to the young, that certainty that the war would never touch us."

He stared at those young lovers, grieving for himself as much as for Mai. "We were so young," he said, "and so very innocent."

Tory sat listening, unmoving. She knew she didn't have to say anything. McQuade was talking now, and he wouldn't stop until he'd told her everything.

"I was flying choppers then, dropping supplies—food for the troops, medicine, bandages, ammunition. Flying over the jungle, you're not actually part of what's going on below. You're above it all, both literally and symbolically. I'd get shot at, but it was like a game to me. The gunners would let go with a burst of fire and I'd dodge the bullets and feel invincible. It was like playing chicken on Saturday night on a dark road outside of town. You'd get this rush every time you were shot at. Once my chopper was hit and we stumbled into Long Binh with a smoking engine. I felt like a hero. Long Binh had swimming pools and golf courses. It didn't *feel* like a war there, but you got to thinking it was romantic and dangerous and I had this beautiful young girlfriend who loved me. I thought I had it all, and in a way I guess I did. It's only when the dream ends that we wake up and discover reality."

"How did it end?" Tory asked quietly.

He sat staring into the past. He hadn't realized until this moment exactly how much he needed to talk about it. It was as if the very words he'd needed to say had been pressing in on him like a pillow held to his face. He'd been suffocating from the weight of the words he'd held inside all these years.

"Our time together lasted a little over six months. I'd taken my R and R and spent it with her here in Saigon. Most guys went to Thailand or Australia or Japan, but I stayed here with Mai. It was perfect. I didn't realize then that we were living in never-never land. It wasn't real. It was a stupid dream." He took a deep breath and opened the last door. He'd kept this door shut all these years, too afraid to open it. Now, he saw it all again, felt the terrible knowledge of what was to come and knew he couldn't ever do anything to change it.

"I'd been living with blinders on," he said at last. "I hadn't lost any close buddies. A few pilots died, but I hadn't known them very well and I just went on, thinking I was invincible. Death has to touch you before you understand it. You have to feel its breath on your cheek. Then the blinders get torn off and you wake up." He bowed his head. "At least, that's how it was with me."

He shook his head. "I don't know. Maybe I was just pretending I wasn't afraid. You know, flying all those supply missions, lowering the rations to the troops, then taking off, flying away, not having to participate in the war on the ground. But something in me must have known it was dangerous, that I could die. Maybe I was like the kid who whistles real loud and swaggers down the street, trying to prove he's not afraid."

Looking back now, he felt a strange compassion for that boy who had thought he was a man. A terrible sorrow welled up in him. Youth and trust and innocence should be lost gradually, eroded over time, the way rain erodes a field. They shouldn't be devastated abruptly by the ugliness of war. Age mellows. War embitters.

"So," he said. He took a deep breath. "On this particular day, Mai and I were together, horsing around with a

buddy of mine, Ted Simpson.'' He smiled at the memory of
Ted, perhaps for the first time in twenty years. ''He was a
great guy. He was short, and no matter how hard the army
had tried in boot camp, it hadn't been able to make him
thin. He was a chunky guy, with an amiable disposition.
You just couldn't get Ted angry, you couldn't upset him. He
was the nicest guy you'd ever want to meet. Everyone called
him Teddy Bear. He was cuddly like one. Mai loved him.
Hell, everyone did. He was the kind of guy you'd die for...''

McQuade rubbed his face. The pain was shimmering inside him now, like a throbbing tooth, nagging, persistent,
impossible to ignore.

''Mai was homesick for her mother and father. She
wanted to go back to her village and see them. We knew
there'd been action in that area and told her it wasn't safe,
but she kept insisting. Mai had a way about her. She looked
at you with those big eyes and said 'please,' and there was
no way you could refuse her.''

He rubbed his forehead, the pain pulsing inside him.
Normally he'd get up and leave, walk or run or take up his
plane, anything to distract himself from it, but today there
was no way out. He'd tried running for twenty years and it
hadn't worked. Today he had to walk right into the pain, go
right through it. He couldn't turn away any longer.

''She begged me to take her up in my chopper, but I
wasn't flying that day. Ted was.'' He ground his teeth, as if
actual physical pain might drown out this other, more terrible pain. He dropped his head and fought the urge of
anxiety that welled up inside him. He told himself he
wouldn't die if he talked about it, but it felt as if he might.
Something close to panic pulsed inside him, raced along his
nerve endings, radiated warnings. His breathing grew la-
bored and he felt sweat break out on his forehead. His palms
were wet with fear. He could actually smell it. It rose off him
like the stink of garbage in a dump.

He wished he could say that Mai had asked Ted, wished he didn't have to take responsibility. He wanted to lie about it, to skip this part, to forever absolve himself from his guilt. But something in him wouldn't let him. Some inner voice, scalding in its quest for honesty, forced him to tell her exactly what had happened. He let out a shaky breath.

"I knew Ted was flying reconnaissance in the vicinity of Mai's village. I wanted to be the guy who answered all Mai's dreams..."

He bent his head and closed his eyes. The guilt he'd stored away all these years was hammering at him.

Seeing his anguish, Tory put a gentle hand on his arm. "It's all right, McQuade," she murmured softly. "It's all right."

He almost laughed, cynicism and bitterness and hatred of himself all clamoring to scream at her, to tell her it wasn't all right. It never would be.

"No," he said coldly, "it's not all right. I asked Ted to sneak Mai and me on his chopper, to do us a favor and fly us to Mai's village." He looked away, tears pricking his eyes. He blinked them away, hating himself so much he wouldn't even allow himself the comfort of tears.

"And Ted," he said softly, his voice now filled with tenderness. "Ted was so great, such a true friend. I knew he wanted to refuse. He kicked a couple stones around and looked away, like he was struggling with himself over what to say, then he looked back at me and shrugged and just grinned. 'Sure, why not?' he said. 'There's no danger out there now.'"

Watching McQuade, Tory felt a terrible premonition of what was to come. She had the sudden urge to stop him, to get up and walk away. She didn't want to hear it, didn't want to know what was going to happen. In that instant, she knew a little of the agony McQuade had felt all these years. She realized now what he had long ago known—that something terrible had happened, and even if she got up and walked away, nothing would change. She closed her eyes, sick with the realization that she wasn't as brave as she wished she was. It was this realization that saved her, for she suddenly saw that she was no different from McQuade, no different from anyone who tried to escape the deadly burden of the past.

"It was a lark," McQuade said slowly. "It was as if there was no war, no killing, no death. We were just three kids, taking a helicopter out on a joyride." He smiled at the memory, seeing that day again so ripe with promise, so filled with adolescent glee. "It was a beautiful day, just magnificent. It was just after the rainy season and the intense heat of summer hadn't yet burned the land and covered it with red dust. Everything was so green it almost hurt your eyes. And the sky—so blue you had to blink at it, with puffy little clouds like boats on the sea, just floating up there, so tranquil. I remember thinking that I had never been so happy in my life. There we were up there together—me and Mai and my best friend, Ted—and I remember thinking that there could never be a more perfect day..." He bowed his head. "And there never has been," he added quietly.

Tory swallowed awkwardly, feeling a lump in her throat. McQuade was so quiet now. All his anger seemed to have dissipated. He sounded almost impassive, as if nothing else could ever hurt him. He recited his story as if he were recounting an uneventful trip to the grocery store.

"As we approached the village," he said, "we knew something was wrong. Wisps of smoke were rising up through the trees. We got close and then we saw it. The village had been burned. Everything was destroyed. Bodies were scattered around the ground.

"Mai got hysterical. She began to scream, calling out for her mother and father and her baby brother. I told Ted to take us back, but she went crazy. She beat on me with her fists, crying and screaming. She tried to throw herself out of the chopper. It was stupid what we did. We should have turned back. I still don't know why we didn't. To this day—" He broke off, shaking his head as if to shake out the memory. He took a shaky breath and continued.

"Ted set the chopper down in an open field near the village. Mai scrambled out of the chopper and raced toward the burned-out hut that had been her home. I followed her. And we found her father, her mother and her little baby brother.

"I remember just staring down at the bodies, then lifting my gaze and seeing it all expand, like a movie camera panning out, going from a close-up to a long shot." He stared at the carnage, seeing it again as he had seen it then, smelling the foul stench of it.

"Then—" He frowned, as if he still couldn't make sense of what happened next. "Someone started shooting. Guns were firing all around us. I remember standing there and watching little spikes of dirt explode in front of me, and for a minute I didn't know what they were. It took me a while to connect them to the sound of the gunfire. Then it hit me—they were the bullets sending up little sprays of dirt when they hit the ground around me.

"It was so crazy, surreal almost, like a dream. I was disoriented and bullets were spattering the ground around me and Mai was screaming. She kept yelling over and over, 'No. No. No.' Everything was crazy—the noise and the bodies and the smell, and Mai screaming, and I just wanted to put my hands up to my ears and make it stop, make it all go away, but it didn't go away, and then I saw an American rifle on the ground near me and I dived at it and got it, rolled over and over in the cooling ashes and came up firing, screaming at Mai to take cover. I was firing into the jungle and kept calling Mai to come with me, but she was lying on the ground, sobbing over her family's bodies. I remember scrambling to my feet and running toward her and grabbing her hand and trying to pull her up, but she fought me, screaming at me, her face distorted with so much hate. 'You bastards,' she screamed at me. 'You killed them!'

"A bullet hit me in the arm but I didn't even realize it until a couple hours later. Bullets were spewing all over the place, and then I heard Ted shouting at me to leave her and get to the chopper. But I couldn't leave her there. I just couldn't..."

He swallowed thickly, staring at the past, his eyes wide with fear. "And all of this happened in maybe thirty seconds, but it felt like hours. And then Ted was running toward us, firing his rifle into the jungle and he kept shouting at me, and Mai was screaming, and the bullets were rattling, and somehow I got it together enough to take cover. I was finally able to tune out Mai's screams and focus on what was happening. There were about five or six snipers in the jungle. Ted focused on the ones to the right and I took the ones to the left.

"And we kept falling back because they had us in their sights and we needed to find better cover. Me, I dived behind a dead cow and used it as a shield. Ted was behind a hut that was still standing. I shouted at Mai to stay where she was, not to move until it was safe. We got two of them, then Ted was shot."

He paused, remembering the moment as it had seemed then. Everything had changed to slow-motion. The world became incredibly focused. He'd been lying on the ground peering over the cow and suddenly every blade of grass seemed a mile high. An ant became the size of a dog. Every granule of dirt seemed magnified, as if he were seeing each speck under a microscope. And incredibly the sky was radiantly blue and the jungle phosphorescently green and the world seemed so sweet, so beautiful. Then he saw Ted.

He zigzagged toward Ted, coming to a stop and placing his hand on the wound in Ted's neck, cursing, hyperventilating, trying to hold back the blood.

"Live, damn it," he'd shouted. "Live!"

If only he could hold the blood in Ted's body, Ted might live. McQuade's hands were sticky. He looked down and saw they were covered with blood. He began to whimper, to sob, yelling at Ted to live.

But Ted did not obey. He lay and looked up at the sky, his eyes empty, staring into eternity. McQuade shuddered at how empty those eyes were, how dead and lifeless. Where was Ted? Where was the spirit that had moved his body? He'd been there only a moment ago, shouting at him to take cover, firing his rifle to protect McQuade so he could get to safety. But where was Ted now? Where had he gone in the instant his blood began to empty onto the ground?

Please, God, let him be with you. Please, God, let him be safe, let him be where there is no pain, no war, no death. Let him be free and filled with laughter. Let him know only love and joy, not sorrow or pain, nor agony nor cruelty. Let the sky there be as blue as the one above us now. But let there be peace. Please, God, let there be peace.

McQuade sat staring into the past, seeing it all again, feeling it. Silent tears filled his eyes and he felt sorrow well up inside him like a great crescendo of music, sweet and pure and shining, and he wept for Ted, for himself, for the entire world, yoked as it was to the unending pain of death.

Slowly the tears subsided and he rubbed his face. He felt as if he'd climbed a mountain and sat now, just beneath the peak, staring down at everything that had brought him to this place, this precise moment in his life. He knew he had one more slope to climb, one final gradient which would take him to the peak. His voice was weary but he continued:

"They were still firing. A bullet came so close I could hear it whiz by my ear. I did the only thing I knew how to do. I turned around, already firing." He sat and stared into the past, dazed by what he saw. "But Mai was running toward me. As soon as I turned and saw her, I knew what was going to happen, but I couldn't stop it."

The bullets were already gone, flying in a terrible path, bringing McQuade and Mai to their appointed destinies.

Tory sat and stared at him, her throat closed up, her mind refusing to accept what he was telling her. "Please, God," she prayed silently, her lips trembling as she tried to stop from crying. "Please don't let it be true. Don't let it happen. Stop it somehow. *Please.*" But she knew what McQuade was going to tell her, knew because he had already told her last night. But it was so much more terrible now, so much more real, so sad, so terribly sad...

McQuade closed his eyes and bowed his head, letting the memory wash over him, bringing with it the inevitable feelings of inadequacy and helplessness, blame and guilt, of seeing a split second before it happened what was to come, yet not being able to stop it. Why had he been firing the gun before he even had a target? Why had Mai run toward him at that exact moment? Why had it had to happen? The questions had tortured him for twenty years.

He lifted his head and his eyes were filled with anguish. Pain shimmered inside him. If he could do one thing, he would reach out and grab the bullets, fling them harmlessly to the ground. He would reach out and change the history of the world. He would even direct the bullets at himself if he could. Anything not to have to face the terrible results of his impulsive act.

"I don't remember anyone shooting at me," he said at last. "I don't remember anything but seeing Mai there on the ground, crumpled up and bleeding. I ran to her. Just ran. When I got to her, she was barely alive. I took her in my arms, begging her to be okay, to talk to me. She looked up at me—"

His voice broke and tears began to roll down his face. "Oh, God, she was so beautiful. And all I could do was hold her. I guess I was in shock. I couldn't believe what I had done. And she reached out to me—" His face crumpled. "And she said she was sorry," he whispered. "My God! That *she* was sorry!"

He raised his head and howled with pain, all the torment spilling out of him in a grief-stricken cry that was swallowed by the steady rain outside. He felt alone on all the earth, isolated from all others by his anguish and his grief.

"But, Mai," he whispered, his voice harsh and broken. "It's *me* who's sorry. Can't you see that? It's *me!*"

Tory stared at him, her heart filled with anguish for McQuade. She was overpowered by helplessness. What could she say to him? What could she do? Why had a loving God created such a world? Why had he given us so much pain and so few ways to ease it? If she ruled the world, there would be no pain like his. All sin and guilt and remorse would be abolished. Love would stamp out hatred and division and wars. But she didn't rule the world, and pain abounded.

"McQuade," she whispered. "McQuade."

He raised his head and looked at her and then he was in her arms, and she was holding him, holding him so hard that it was as if she thought she might be able to banish all his pain with just her strength.

"I left her there," he said in a choked voice.

Tory sat back and looked into his eyes, her own eyes filled with anguish. She touched his face, took his hands in hers, not saying anything because she didn't know what she could say. "There, there, everything's all right," as if he were a child waking up from a bad dream? "There, there, it's not so bad. You'll be better soon"?

But he hadn't gotten better soon. It was twenty years later, and the pain was just as bad. What platitudes could she parrot back at him, what nonsense phrases designed to appease him? She could only sit and look into his eyes, her own eyes filled with enormous compassion, her hands holding his as she silently urged him to go on, to at last purge the ugliness from his soul.

"I did the only thing I could think of," he said at last. "I picked up Ted's body and ran back to the chopper. A few bullets zipped past me, hit the chopper, clanged against the metal, punctured it, ricocheted off. I felt like the world had gone insane. Moments earlier, I'd been just a kid with his girl, laughing at the world, and somehow we had stumbled into hell. Nothing has ever been the same since. Everything changed in that Vietnamese village."

He sat and looked back at the past, knowing that it was almost over. He had just a few more things to say. "I don't remember flying back to Long Binh, but I did. I guess I flew on sheer instinct. I did what I had to do. I brought Ted's body back."

He sat quietly then, feeling the calm that comes from knowing he'd emptied himself of nearly all he'd had to say.

"I was reprimanded, but by the grace of God, I wasn't court-martialed. I have your father to thank for that. They told me later that the Viet Cong were hidden in the jungle. They went back and wiped them out, then burned the dead villagers. Mai was one of them. Then they flew the bodies of the American soldiers out in body bags. And that's when I knew what I was made for. I asked them to take me off supply missions. I volunteered to fly the choppers that took dead bodies out of the jungle. Then I'd fly the C-130 transports to Tan Son Nhut, where we'd put the bodies on a plane for home. I guess I thought it would somehow make amends for what I'd done, but it never did."

He sat brooding over the past, seeing Mai's body as he'd last seen it, twisted and crumpled like a rag doll on the ground. "Sometimes I think about her spirit," he said. "I wonder if she's with God, and able to see and understand all. I wonder if she's forgiven me."

He took a deep breath. "Everything that happened, right from the beginning, was my fault. If I hadn't been so damned stupid, if I hadn't been living in a dream world, if I'd known how serious everything was, I wouldn't have asked Ted to take us to Mai's village. If I'd used my head, none of it would have happened.''

He dropped his head into his hands. He would never come to terms with it. It would last forever, the responsibility, the guilt, the wishing he could go back and rewrite the past.

Tory's heart went out to him. Every part of her felt his anguish, shared his pain. Tears glittered in her eyes, but she didn't feel them. Everything now was for McQuade.

''John McQuade,'' she said gently, ''it wasn't your fault. You can't blame yourself. Ted could have refused to take you. When you turned to shoot at the snipers, you had no intention of killing Mai. You thought she was still by the hut. It was an accident, McQuade.''

He shook his head. ''But I can't live with myself. I hate myself, as much as Mai must have hated me when she died.''

''Mai understood,'' Tory said softly. ''She forgave you before she died, when she said she was sorry.''

''Maybe, but I can't forgive myself.''

''Perhaps in time you'll be able to,'' Tory said softly.

He shook his head. ''Never,'' he said, ''because it's not just Mai's forgiveness I need, it's Ted's also. I killed them both and I can never forgive myself.''

Watching him, Tory thought she'd never seen so much despair. ''No God in heaven could ever punish us as much as we punish ourselves,'' she said. ''Sometimes I think this thing we call life is really hell, and when we die, we'll all go to heaven, because we've suffered so much here on earth.''

He turned his head and saw Tory, saw her anguish at his pain, and something in him stirred, some deep realization that when we punish ourselves we also punish the people who care for us.

''Tory...'' he said.

She looked at him, her eyes brimming with pain for him. ''I am so sorry,'' she whispered. ''So very, very sorry.''

Reaching out, he put his arm around her. They sat on the bed like that for a long time, two wounded people drawing sustenance from each other. There were no words or tears, just the sure knowledge that they were together, and the hope that somehow, in some way, all things would one day be understood.

Chapter Fourteen

"I sent the letter to Mme Tran," Tory said over lunch. But she wasn't really thinking about Mme Tran. She was more concerned with McQuade, who was still sunk in thought. Since leaving the room after sharing his story with her, McQuade had been remote and uncommunicative. Things were suddenly awkward between them, and she didn't know how to regain the intimacy they had shared in her room.

"Mmm," he said absently. "That's good."

Tory sipped her mineral water, studying McQuade from under lowered lashes. "Are you all right?" she finally asked softly.

At that, McQuade looked up. "Of course. Why wouldn't I be?"

She shrugged. "It's just that you're not saying much. I don't know whether you'd like me to be quiet or chatter on and on endlessly, just to fill the air."

"What do you want to do?" he asked, sitting back and studying her.

She shrugged. "Talk to you, I guess, but if you'd rather I be quiet..."

"Why? Do you think I'm some sort of emotional cripple you have to tiptoe around now? Quiet, so you don't disturb the killer?"

His angry questions startled Tory and for a moment she was tempted to retort the same way, then she realized that McQuade was worried about how she had reacted to his story about the deaths of Ted and Mai.

"No," she answered carefully, "I'm not worried about that at all. I'm just feeling a little unsure of myself. I don't know what you're thinking or feeling right now. Maybe if you told me it would make it easier to know what to say or not say."

Her quiet words seemed to ease his defensiveness. "I'm sorry," he said, "I shouldn't have snapped at you like that."

She smiled. "That's okay. I don't bruise all that easily."

One corner of his mouth turned up reluctantly. "I suppose that comes from being the daughter of Old Iron Ass."

"I suppose it does," she said, smiling. Then she sobered. "Army brats get lots of practice hearing war stories, McQuade," she said gently. "None of them is easy to hear and all of them are terrible in their own way, but one thing is certain, I've never heard a soldier talk about his experiences that my heart didn't go out to."

"So you're saying you pity me," he said belligerently.

She sighed, her patience and understanding nearing an end. "No, I'm saying you don't have to worry that I think you're some sort of emotional cripple or killer."

He stared at the table, then raised his eyes to hers. "Then what do you think?"

She gazed at him evenly. "I think you're a human being, like everybody else." She picked up the menu. It was time to start thinking about more practical things. "I also think we should order. If we're going to traipse all over the country trying to locate Mai's burned-out village, we'll need all the sustenance we can get."

"We?"

"Of course. Did you think I wouldn't want to go?"

"Oh, no," he said, shaking his head. "If I do go on some sort of pilgrimage, I'm going alone."

She studied him, then dropped her gaze to her menu. If that's what he wanted, that's the way it would be. She was oddly disappointed that he didn't want to share this with her, yet realized that McQuade had a right to time alone in memory of Mai.

"Well?" he said. "Aren't you going to argue with me?"

She glanced up at him, then went back to reading the menu. "No."

He gazed at her, nonplussed. "It's not that I wouldn't want you to come..." he finally said.

She pretended absorption in the menu. "Oh?"

He had the uncivilized urge to rip that damn menu right out of her hands. His fingers were itching to do it. If she wasn't such a lady, sitting over there looking so damned proper and dignified, he would.

Tory looked up and met his stormy gaze. "Is something wrong, McQuade?"

He glared at her. "All right, you can come with me."

"What do you really want?" she asked, tired of his vacillating. "Do you want me to go with you or don't you?"

That was the hell of it. He didn't know *what* he wanted. His first impulse was to push Tory away. That's how he'd managed all these years—pushing people away, distancing himself, playing it cool and safe. But another part of him was remembering the way Tory had listened to him. He saw again the compassion that had glowed in her eloquent eyes, felt her caring and concern, and he was drawn to that caring, the way a cowering puppy is drawn to a gentle hand.

"I don't know what I want," he finally admitted.

She put down her menu. "McQuade, if you want me to be with you, I want to be. If you'd prefer to be alone, I'll understand."

Poised on the brink of indecision, not knowing what he wanted, he felt cornered, anxious, filled with conflict. Dammit, he should just tell her he wanted to go alone, but something in him held him back, made him hesitate. He frowned, confused, disoriented, temporarily lost in a place he'd never been before.

What was the matter with him? He looked at Tory and the memory of last night came back to him, flooding him with images of their lovemaking. He felt again the softness of her skin, inhaled her perfume, ran his fingers through the thickness of her hair, remembered the utter peace of fulfillment, saw again her sleeping face and felt the same sweet wave of tenderness that had washed over him last night as he lay watching her return once more.

But all this was too new, too disquieting to comprehend. He only knew that something in him preferred being with Tory to being alone. So take it for what it was, some sort of atavistic need for companionship surfacing in him after years of being alone.

"Sure, why don't you come along?" he said, feigning disinterest. "You could bring your camera. The countryside outside Saigon is beautiful."

"What an enthusiastic invitation," she said dryly, going back to reading her menu. "It almost overwhelms me."

He felt the corner of his mouth turn up. He had to hand it to her—she had a way of keeping him on his toes, making it exciting to be with her. She didn't simper and fawn and bat her damn lashes like most women. She was dead honest and straightforward, with a wit that could cut him in two if he let it. He liked that in her, liked her sarcasm and spirit, liked the way she didn't back down but stood toe-to-toe with him, ready for battle. He figured if he was lucky, he might meet another woman like her just once the rest of his life. But, then, he'd never counted on luck, had never had much to count on.

Sitting back, he found himself smiling at her. Not only was she plucky, she was damned attractive. Better than attractive. She was beautiful. And classy and smart as a proverbial whip. He'd be a fool to let her go. But then he'd always been a fool, especially when it came to women.

By A STROKE of good fortune, they were able to arrange for a government guide to take them on a tour of the countryside surrounding Ho Chi Minh City that afternoon. The guide turned out to be a pretty young woman, dressed in jeans and cowboy boots, her long, dark hair swinging halfway down her back. Her name, she told them in excellent English, was Vo Thi Anh, but they could call her Miss Anh.

She herded them expertly into a tiny car and gave the driver quick instructions in Vietnamese, then settled back in the front seat, while Tory and McQuade shared the backseat. She chattered on and on, filling them with the official version of the new Vietnam. They drove through streets cluttered with bicycles and pedicabs until the city slowly gave way to the countryside.

Here, all was serene and peaceful. Palm trees and banana trees flourished and the paved roads gave way to muddy tracks filled with watery potholes, but the little car refused to bog down and they trekked farther and farther from Ho Chi Minh City, passing by miles of rice fields that idled under inches of water, the rice sprouts just beginning to peek above the water's surface.

Exotic birds flew in and out of the thick vegetation and small villages appeared here and there on the roadside. Cattle strolled peacefully along the roads and small children ran alongside the car and waved. Here and there they passed wagons drawn by oxen, the drivers perched precariously on top, conical hats their only protection from the threat of rain.

"It's like stepping back in time," said Tory, enchanted by the utter peacefulness of the scenery.

"It's better than that," McQuade answered. "Twenty years ago they were being bombed. It must seem like heaven to the villagers."

"Are we close to Mai's village?"

"Getting near it, anyway. It all looks different now." He let his gaze run over the rich deep green vegetation that grew rampant under the threatening skies and felt a strange feeling of kinship with this place. He had dreamed of it for twenty years, remembered it with pain and guilt and remorse, but now he saw that it slumbered peacefully under the sky. It had returned to itself, had perhaps been able to forget the past more easily than he.

"It's as if we were never here," he mused. "Almost as if it never happened."

Tory pointed to a rusted-out hulk of a plane lying on the edge of the road, partially covered by encroaching plant life. "Not quite."

He gazed at the wreck and wondered if he'd known the pilot, yet he couldn't get over the feeling that Vietnam had shaken off the oppression of war and returned to its roots, almost untouched by what had happened two decades earlier. Perhaps it was just the people who bore the scars. The land recovered more easily.

"We are getting very close to a village I used to know," he said to their guide, Miss Anh. "I wonder if it would be possible to stop the car and get out?"

Miss Anh turned to look at McQuade. "You were here in the war, then?"

His face was grave. "Yes, Miss Anh, I was here."

She nodded. "My father was in the war. It is possible he fought against you."

"Is he well?" McQuade asked.

Her face was quietly sad. "He lost his brother in the war, and his parents died and my mother left him for another man. Most of his comrades were killed. My father was very lucky to escape, but he remembers it all. He dreams of it almost every night. His eyes are sad and filled with ghosts." She tilted her head and studied McQuade. "I see your eyes, too, carry much sadness."

McQuade touched his chest. "And here, too," he said.

Miss Anh seemed to consider, then nodded. "We will stop the car. It is not policy to do this, but it cannot hurt, I think, not after so many years. Perhaps you have come here to exorcise the ghosts.''

"Yes," McQuade said, and turned to look out at the countryside, his eyes suddenly filled with tears. He had not been alone in that terrible war, had not been the only one to suffer. Lives had been destroyed, yet the world went on. He felt such sadness well up in him that he was afraid he'd break down and sob, but he contained the feelings, kept them inside, fettered in his heart.

And then they rounded a curve and he knew they had arrived. There was no village, no thatch-roofed huts, no small children running alongside the car, no old men and women toting buckets over their shoulders, no family altars, no Mai, but he knew this place. He had carried it in his heart for over twenty years.

"Please," he said, his voice strangled with emotion. "Stop the car."

Miss Anh spoke to the driver and the car glided to a stop. For a moment McQuade sat there, then he opened his door and got out. He stood looking over the place where once a village had stood, then looked back at Miss Anh.

"Could Miss Britton and I take a walk alone?"

Miss Anh nodded. "Take as much time as you need."

Gratitude filled him. "Thank you."

He took Tory's hand and helped her out of the car, then set out toward the spot where the village had been.

"It was over there," he said, gesturing toward a clearing near some trees. "The snipers were in those trees. The huts were just in front of the trees."

They stood and looked around and felt only peace, stillness, silence. Somewhere in the distance birds sang and a monkey called to its mate. They walked through the tall elephant grass and at last reached the spot where Mai's village had stood .

McQuade turned and let his gaze sweep over the entire clearing, and then he saw it, a simple post erected in the ground, with Vietnamese writing on it. He walked toward it, knowing what it was. Someone, probably a relative of those who had died, had returned to the spot where the village had stood and erected a grave marker.

He stopped in front of it and stared down at the writing, tears once more misting his eyes. He didn't know what it said, couldn't read the words that were already corroding from the elements, but he knew what it meant: ''Here lie the people of a small Vietnamese village, wiped out during a battle in 1969. Here lie the women and children, the old men and young boys, taken forever by the terrible carnage of war.''

And here, he knew, lay Mai, slumbering under the giant sky, forever lost to life but living in his memory. He bowed his head and closed his eyes and gave himself up to sorrow—for all they had been, those two starry-eyed youngsters who had been foolish enough to fall in love in war, for Mai, gone now, forever gone, for his youth, his innocence, his joy, all lost, too, on the battlefield of war.

He knelt and opened his heart to God: ''I wish it had been different, God,'' he said in silent prayer. ''I wish Mai hadn't died. I wish I hadn't killed her. I wish we'd never taken the chopper up that day. Maybe now Ted would be alive and Mai, too. Maybe my entire life would have been different. Please, God, forgive me for my mistakes. Please hear my prayer. Listen to me. Help me. I have spent twenty years wandering in a desert, alone and filled with pain. Help me to live again. Help me to find a way to want to live. Help me, today, to bury my dead.''

And then the words of his youth came back to him, words he'd learned as a child in church, listening to the gospel read every Sunday morning. He remembered the story of the disciple who was asked to follow Christ: ''Lord, let me first go and bury my father,'' he had said.

And Jesus had replied: ''Follow me, and let the dead bury their own dead.''

And suddenly he saw that he must let the dead go, must walk into the future and leave the past behind. And he knew that he'd been mourning the dead for over twenty years and that he had to stop now, had to live the life that God had given him. *We are not meant to grieve forever,* he realized. *We are meant to live.*

He saw now that the past was a siren, as deadly as the sea nymphs that had once lured sailors to their death in ancient Greece. He realized that life is for the living, not the dead, that we turn our backs on life at great peril, for we are put here to find our destiny.

And he saw that the general had been right—we are not smarter than God. If God had let him live, it was because something more was expected of him. To refuse to live was blasphemy, for it was refusing God's will.

He felt a tangle of emotions rise up in him—sorrow and pain and guilt and remorse and joy and beauty and love, all piled together on a pyre that burned inside him, and he felt a great burst of light inside him, a shocking confrontation with God, and he knew then the past would one day die, wiped out forever by the necessities of today.

Bowing his head, he prayed, humble at last.

"YOU FOUND what you wanted?" Miss Anh said when they returned to the car about an hour later.

McQuade nodded. "We found it."

"But there is nothing here," Miss Anh protested.

"There used to be a village here," he explained. "I was in love with a young girl who lived here." He looked at Miss Anh. "She was very much like you—young and very pretty."

Miss Anh smiled. "She is gone now?"

"Yes," he said, taking Tory's hand. "She is gone."

"And that is sad for you," Miss Anh said quietly.

"Not so much as it used to be," McQuade said. "It's better now."

"Then it was well that you came back to Vietnam," Miss Anh said quietly. "It was good to exorcise the ghosts."

McQuade looked at Tory. "Yes," he said. "It was very good. We can turn around now. It's time to go back to Saigon." He gestured. "I'm sorry, I can't get used to calling it Ho Chi Minh City."

"That's okay," Miss Anh said, smiling. "Many southerners still call it Saigon."

She turned around and began talking to the driver, who started the car with a lurch and turned around toward Ho Chi Minh City.

WHEN THEY RETURNED to the hotel, they found a letter waiting from Mme Tran. Tory held it in her hand and stared down at the elegant handwriting on thick ivory parchment.

She had dreaded this moment, had tried to block it from her consciousness, but it was here now and to her surprise she felt herself tremble. She lifted her gaze to McQuade. "It's a letter from Mme Tran."

He nodded. "Are you going to open it?"

She slid it in her pocket and walked toward the elevator. "I suppose I'll have to, won't I?" They entered the elevator and Tory glanced at McQuade. "It's odd. We came over here ostensibly to find my father's son, but we've spent more time with your concerns."

"Are you angry about that?"

"No, not at all. It's just that I see that I've been hiding from my own problems by concentrating on yours."

"And now mine are more settled and you can't escape any longer," McQuade said gently.

"Exactly," she said, her voice trembling. She glanced at McQuade. "I'm a fine one, aren't I?"

He put an arm around her and drew her against his side. "I happen to think so," he said.

She lifted her eyes to his, her own eyes filled with worry. "I'm afraid, McQuade. I don't know what's going to happen. Maybe she won't see me. Maybe—".

"Hold on a minute. There's no sense getting yourself worked up. When you get to your room, you'll read the letter. Then we'll just have to go from there."

"We?"

He hesitated, then said slowly, "You've shared my problems. I suppose the least I can do is share yours."

She smiled, gratitude blossoming inside her. Though she could see that McQuade was still reluctant he hadn't turned away from her. "Thank you," she said. "I need someone to lean on about now."

They stood looking at each other, oblivious to the elevator that creaked its way toward their floor, and then he drew her into his arms and kissed her, feeling a glorious burst of promise, holding her as he'd never held a woman in his life, without thought of what the future would bring, feeling only this moment, this incredible joy of feeling her body in his arms.

"Thank God you're with me," she murmured, her eyes closed as he dropped feather-soft kisses on her upturned face. Her fingers curled into the lapels of his jacket. "Oh, McQuade, where have you been all my life?"

He smiled and stepped back a step, looking down at the happiness that shone in her face. "Are you trying to tell me you like me, Tory Britton?"

She smiled, her eyes filled with quiet pleasure. "Perhaps a little bit, John McQuade."

"Enough to put up with me for the next few nights?"

She tilted her head. "Nights?"

His face grew serious. "I want to sleep with you tonight. I don't want last night to be all there is."

"I don't, either," she said.

He drew her into his arms and was about to kiss her again when the elevator lurched to a stop and the ornate gilded doors glided open.

"Ah," he said, disappointment ringing in his voice, "we're here."

Tory slid her hand in her pocket and felt the letter. Her heart began to pound uncomfortably. "Yes," she said. "So we are."

"You're worried," McQuade said as he watched her fumble with her key.

She nodded. "Very worried. It's getting real now. It's not just talk anymore." She unlocked the door to her room and stepped inside.

McQuade stood in the hall looking at her. "Do you want me to come in?"

"Please," she said. "I need all the moral support I can get."

He closed the door and watched as she walked toward the window. It had begun to rain again. She stared out at it, her hand still in her pocket holding the letter from Mme Tran.

She drew the letter from her pocket and stared down at it. "The past couple months have been so strange. When Dad told me about this son of his, I didn't believe him at first. I just sat there in the den and stared at him, wondering for a moment if he had lost his mind. It was so unbelievable, like finding out his whole life had been a lie, that my father wasn't who I thought he'd been after all. He was a stranger, with another life in another part of the world that had never touched me till that moment." She lifted worried eyes to McQuade. "But it's touching me now," she whispered, tears misting her eyes. "And I don't feel ready, McQuade. I'm scared."

He was across the room in a minute, taking her in his arms while she gave herself to the tears she'd held back for over two months.

"What are you scared of?" he murmured, stroking her hair gently.

"Oh, just that things are changing, that my comfortable life will never be quite the same. This new person has entered it now, or he may..." She reached for a tissue on her dresser and blew her nose. "I feel so foolish. You must think I'm such a child."

He ran his fingers gently across her cheek. "I think you're a very beautiful woman," he murmured. "Not a child at all."

She smiled and wiped her eyes and squared her shoulders. "I suppose I have to read it, don't I?"

"I suppose," he said, smiling gently.

She hesitated, then ripped open the envelope. She drew out a single piece of thick parchment, her heart beating fast.

Dear Tory,
It was a pleasure receiving your note requesting that we meet. Your father was a dear friend during the war, and I am sure we will have much to discuss. While it is difficult for westerners to visit Vietnamese homes, it is not impossible. Please make reservations at my restaurant for eight o'clock tonight and we will be able to meet in my private quarters to talk and get to know each other.
                     With warm regards, Nguyen Thi Tran

Tory looked up from the letter. It's happening, she thought. It's finally happening. She gazed out the window, her heart beating fast, the letter held tight in her hand.

"I'll make the reservations for you, if you like," McQuade said quietly.

She looked at him. "You'll come with me, won't you?"

He hesitated, then said, "If you want me to, I will."

"Yes, please."

"You'll be all right, you know, Tory," he said quietly. "You'll be just fine."

She smiled, looking as if she didn't quite believe him. "Well, at least I'm going to meet with her. Maybe Dad's wish will come true or maybe it won't, but at least I'm trying."

"You're a good daughter."

She smiled and watched as he turned and walked away. The door closed behind him. A good daughter. Strange how those words meant nothing when McQuade said them, but would have meant everything if her father had. She turned and looked out at the rain, wondering why she had ended up here in this city halfway round the world. It felt as if her entire world was stretching past its usual boundaries, expanding to take in so much more than she had previously understood or even known.

Standing there, she thought: How strange it is that our lives are often touched by events from the past over which we had no control. Someone in a far-off land did something and it slumbers for years, like a bear in a cave, until one day the bear wakes up and we find ourselves confronting the rubble from that long-ago event.

And in the process, she thought, we are changed forever.

Or at least that was how it seemed to her, standing there staring out at the rain. She felt as if she would never be the same, that her life had changed irrevocably. She thought back to the time she had spent with Daniel and it all seemed a dream. This was her real life, she realized, this grasping for understanding, the fear and anxiety at all that was happening so unexpectedly.

And the most unexpected thing of all, falling in love with Cargo McQuade.

Chapter Fifteen

Mme Tran's restaurant was located in an impressive house on a broad, tree-lined boulevard near the botanical gardens in the city's northeast sector. Here, presumably, the Frenchman had lived while serving in the legionnaires.

McQuade paid the taxi driver and took Tory's arm. "Well, here we are. Are you nervous?"

"Petrified," Tory said, taking a calming breath. She carried a shopping bag filled with gifts for Mme Tran and her son. The general had advised her to bring gifts when she visited Mme Tran. The Vietnamese, he had told her, loved presents, and in this respect, at least, Mme Tran was very much a Vietnamese.

McQuade took the shopping bag from her. "You'll do fine," he said encouragingly, but Tory wasn't so sure about that. She felt unsure of herself and wondered what she would even say to Mme Tran now that she was here.

"Just stay close to me," she said under her breath as they ascended the steps to the front door. The house was made of stucco, with a wide porch across the front supported by thick pillars. Comfortable wicker chairs sat around in pleasant groupings. The roof was red tile. The house might have been on an avenue in southern France, but for the tropical vegetation that surrounded it.

Now, at night, soft lighting glowed among the foliage and the windows were aglow with welcoming light. Tory stopped on the sidewalk approaching the house and took another deep breath. Butterflies filled her stomach, making her feel as if even the sight of food would be too much to take.

McQuade turned to her. "Tory, it will be all right."

She forced a smile and smoothed her hand over her dress. She had chosen to wear a simple black silk skirt and blouse with pearls. Now she wondered if she was dressed properly. All kinds of doubts assailed her. Would Mme Tran be friendly? Would she be cool to the general's wish? Would her son be here? Would Tory meet him tonight? What would he look like? Would he even care that he had a father halfway around the world who wanted to see him after all these years?

"I suppose the worst that could happen is that she'll ignore my wish to meet my half brother."

"Exactly," McQuade said. "And if she does, you'll simply have to tell your father that you tried but she wouldn't cooperate."

She thought of having to go back and tell her father that, and she felt an enormous surge of regret and self-recrimination. She had promised him she'd bring his son back. How terrible if she failed. She wanted only to please her father. If she brought his son back to him, perhaps he would at last give her the love she so desperately needed from him. But if she didn't...

Tory couldn't think about that. It was too painful and made her approach toward the steps that led to the restaurant even harder.

They were early. A maître d' showed them into a formal dining room furnished with impressive French antiques. He smiled and said, "Your waiter will be with you in a moment. Please make yourselves comfortable. May I get you some tea or a cocktail?"

They refused drinks and took their seats at the secluded table located in a corner of the elegant dining room. Large potted floor plants were placed so as to nearly hide them from the rest of the room. They noticed that a door was nearby. It seemed as clandestine as a silly war movie from the 1940s, but perhaps that door would be the one they'd take to Mme Tran's private quarters.

She had no sooner thought this than a young man appeared in black pants and a white top and asked them to follow him. Indeed they went through the door and followed him down a corridor past the kitchen, through another door and into an impressive hall tiled in black-and-white squares of marble. A crystal chandelier hung from an ornate plaster ceiling, illuminating a magnificent red-carpeted curving staircase that led upstairs.

The boy opened two double doors and showed them into a private sitting room. "You will wait here, please, and Mme Tran will be with you in a moment."

They took seats on a red velvet couch and the boy left them, quietly closing the doors after them. Tory glanced nervously at McQuade who was examining a wooden box inlaid with ivory. He opened the lid and found two silver pistols inside, with carved ivory-and-wood handles.

"They were dueling pistols," a woman said from the doorway. "They are very beautiful to be so lethal, are they not?"

Tory stared at the woman. She was much taller than most of the Vietnamese Tory had met so far, with an unlined face, jet black hair fashioned into a chignon, and almond-shaped eyes. She wore a pair of black silk trousers, a white silk blouse, and a red-and-gold embroidered jacket. On her fingers were half a dozen gold rings set with large winking diamonds.

"I am Mme Tran," she said, extending her hand to Tory graciously. "And you must be Adrian's daughter."

Tory rose and took Mme Tran's hand. "I am so pleased to meet you, Ba Tran," she said, almost stumbling over the polite form of address that McQuade had suggested she use. "I am Tory Britton, Adrian LaPorte's daughter, and this is Mr. McQuade."

Mme Tran turned to McQuade. "You like shooting, Mr. McQuade?"

"Not in the least, Ba Tran," he answered.

"But you find those dueling pistols interesting."

"Actually I was more interested in the box."

"Yes, it is very lovely." Mme Tran smoothed her hand over it. "It belonged to a French soldier who was killed at Dien Bien Phu. I lived here with him." She gestured for them to take their seats. "I am very honored that you came so far to see me."

Tory held tightly to her father's letter to Mme Tran. "Thank you for seeing us so promptly," she said. "I have a letter for you from my father."

Mme Tran made no move to take the letter. She sat with regal posture on the edge of a straight-backed chair. "I wonder what could be so important that he would send his lovely daughter to bring me this letter? He has written me before, you know."

"Yes," Tory said, "I realize that."

"He sent me money," Mme Tran explained. "For our son." She met Tory's even gaze. "You knew we had a child?"

"Yes, he told me recently."

"It must have been for you—how do you say it? A surprise?"

"Very much so," Tory said quietly.

"Yet you are here."

"My father isn't well. He had a stroke a couple years ago. In the past few months, he began to speak of the son he'd left over here. He asked me to come and find him."

"To simply find him?" Mme Tran asked.

Tory hesitated. She knew she had to speak truthfully with Mme Tran. "He asked me to find him and bring him home to see him, if that is possible."

"I see," Mme Tran said slowly, then gestured with her beautiful hands. "But why should this surprise me? I have always known that one day he would want to claim his son."

Tory sat forward. "But you understand why, don't you, Ba Tran? He is old now and perhaps doesn't have much time to live. He wants to set things right now, before it is too late."

Mme Tran looked past Tory, toward the windows overlooking the broad, tree-shaded avenue. "Yes," she said quietly. "Of course he would like to see him, he is his only son."

"Is he here?" Tory asked.

"My son no longer lives with me."

"Could you tell me where to find him?"

Mme Tran looked at Tory. "I could tell you where he is, yes."

"I'd be very grateful," Tory said. "It's very important to my father."

"I wish it had been important when my son was born," Mme Tran said. "To wait so long…" She sighed and looked at McQuade, who was running his hand over the smooth surface of the inlaid box. "You like that box."

"Very much," he said.

"But not the contents?"

McQuade opened the lid and stared at the pistols. "Not particularly. Much harm in my life has come from guns."

"I hate guns," Mme Tran said quietly. "They have caused much pain in this country." She cocked her head and looked at McQuade. "Were you here in the war?"

"Yes," he said. "I was here."

"Then you perhaps know what I mean."

He nodded. "I know."

"And you came back with Miss Britton to try to put it behind you."

"Yes."

Mme Tran leaned back at last. "Yes, that is good, to come to terms with the past. But it is very difficult." She smiled sadly. "Everything I have ever loved in my life, I have lost to guns. My mother and father, my sisters, a brother, the Frenchman..." She took a breath. "Everyone."

Watching her, Tory realized that Mme Tran was older than she had first appeared. There were tiny lines around her eyes and mouth, and her eyes were filled with shadows. A deep sorrow seemed to sit on her shoulders, weighing her down.

Tory held out the letter from her father. "My father wanted me to give you this, Ba Tran."

"Please, you must call me Mme Tran. I have long used the French title rather than my native Vietnamese." She took the letter Tory held out to her and gazed down at the handwriting. "He has grown much older. His handwriting is no longer firm." She gazed at the envelope for a long time, then said, "I have never answered any of his letters. There is so much to tell him. There is so much he doesn't know."

"Perhaps you could tell us," Tory suggested softly, "or write him and we can bring the letter back with us."

"Perhaps," Mme Tran said.

Tory took out a beautifully wrapped box. "I hope you like this. It was made in America by a native American craftsman."

Mme Tran smiled, taking the box and unwrapping it. With a low sigh of pleasure, she took out a sterling silver bracelet, inlaid with turquoise stones. "It is lovely," she said, smiling in delight as she slipped it over her hand and admired it on her wrist.

"And here's something else I hope you like, a gift from me to you."

Mme Tran took the flat package. She opened it and drew out a photograph. Taken by Tory, it was a picture of the Nantucket moors, overlooking the rolling surf.

"It's a picture I took of the place where I live in Massachusetts. I wanted to give you something personal."

"It is lovely," Mme Tran said, gazing at it intently. "I have seen pictures of England. It reminds me of those."

She looked at McQuade. "You like that box so much, Mr. McQuade, you must have it. A gift from me to you."

He stared at her. He knew that Vietnamese had very diferent ideas about gifts than Americans, but he felt he couldn't take such a lovely gift. "Mme Tran, that is too kind of you. I couldn't take it."

"But you must," she said, smiling warmly. "Please, Mr. McQuade, take it as a gift from me to you. I would like it to belong to someone who admires it. I do not." She smiled. "Even if it contained the famous diamonds, I would want you to have it. Its very presence weighs on me, but the Frenchman always kept it there. Until now, I have not been able to move it."

"Diamonds?" Tory asked.

Mme Tran smiled. "The Frenchman smuggled diamonds out of Germany after the second World War. Quite a legend grew up about them and most people thought it was mere fiction. I know differently, of course." She displayed the diamond rings on her fingers. "These are part of them. The Frenchman hid the rest somewhere in this house." She looked at her hands, her face suddenly sad. "You are welcome to them," she said quietly. "When I was young, I thought that money would bring me happiness. I know now that happiness is a fleeting bird. One can try to catch it, but it flies away. Only when one leaves the bird to sing in the branches of the tree, does she find her happiness. You see, happiness is listening to the bird, not owning it."

"Why do you suddenly want to give this box away now, Mme Tran?" McQuade asked.

Mme Tran's eyes were filled with sadness. "Perhaps because I know that the time has come when changes will take place in my life once again. For twenty years I have had my son to myself. Now his father has once again entered my life. He could take my son from me." She gestured again, the magnificent diamonds winking on her elegant hands. "I have learned the wisdom of embracing change rather than fighting it. So I will give you the beautiful box and all it contains. It is yours now, and gone from my life. Perhaps it will bring you more happiness than it has brought me."

"Thank you very much," McQuade said, bowing slightly. "It is very beautiful."

But somehow mere thanks seemed insignificant. Something about her nagged at him. He felt as if she was telling him something he wasn't able to understand. It was as if she were speaking in a language she knew fluently, while he only understood a few words. He stared down at the box and wondered what its significance was to her, that she would keep it for twenty years, then suddenly give it to a complete stranger.

And why him? Why not a relative, a close friend, even an acquaintance? He frowned thoughtfully, running his hand over the wood, feeling its satiny finish, the many coats of lacquer that covered the inlaid wood.

Mme Tran smiled. "You remind me of my Frenchman," she said, watching him. "He, too, was a handsome man, as you are. Big and tall and filled with a quiet strength. I sense that strength in you, Mr. McQuade. I sense in you deep compassion and deep suffering. You are the only man I have met who deserves to own that box, I think."

Again McQuade bowed. "I am very honored, Ba Tran."

Mme Tran inclined her head, then smiled at Tory. "And for you, I have some wonderful gifts. Pardon me while I get them for you."

When Mme Tran left the room, Tory looked at Mc-Quade. "She's very generous. Her home is impressive, isn't it?"

McQuade nodded, looking around. "The French were in Indochina for years. They did most of the colonizing. This kind of house is fairly common." He looked back at her. "You're right. It's very impressive."

"Most people are impressed with my mother's house," a voice said from the doorway. "But you are the first Americans to visit here."

They looked up to find a tall young man standing in the door, smiling as he lit a cigarette. He was probably somewhere in his twenties and was at least six feet tall. He wore a suit that looked like it had come from the best tailor in London, but it was hard to tell what nationality he was. He had the high cheekbones of an oriental and his hair was dark brown, but something about him seemed different than the other Vietnamese they had seen. Perhaps it was his manner. He was extraordinarily handsome, and so sophisticated and urbane he looked as if he'd be completely comfortable in Paris at the poshest social event of the year.

"I am Nguyen Van Dinh," the young man said as he entered the room. "Mme Tran's son."

Something like an electric shock ran through Tory. She could only stare, stunned by the sudden appearance of the man who might be her half brother. She wondered if Mme Tran had other children. Or was this the boy her father had sent her halfway around the world to find, this handsome young man who seemed so at ease and sophisticated. He made her feel like a child, a stammering, foolish child.

She hurried to her feet. "I am Tory Britton," she said, searching his face. "Tory LaPorte Britton." Her father's name didn't seem to mean anything to him. He took her hand and bowed gallantly over it, then held out his hand to McQuade.

"My name's McQuade," he said, shaking Dinh's hand. "Ms. Britton and I are here to see your mother."

"And to see you," Mme Tran said quietly from the doorway.

"Mother," Dinh said, going to her and kissing her right cheek and then her left. "You are looking beautiful as usual."

"Thank you, my son," she said, resting her palm on his cheek and looking up at him with adoring eyes. She turned then to Tory and McQuade. "This is my son, Dinh." She hesitated, then said, "And this is your half sister, Dinh, Miss Britton."

Dinh's urbane sophistication fell away, leaving shock in its place. He stared at Tory. "What do you mean? You had a daughter I did not know about?"

"No, my son," Mme Tran said gently. "Your father has a daughter."

"My—" Fire seemed to leap into his eyes. "My father does not exist," he said, his voice choked with passion, his cheeks turning to flame.

Tory's hopes fell. She stared at Dinh, seeing the anger and hostility burning in his eyes. "He does exist, Dinh," she said softly. "And he sent me to find you."

Dinh's face closed up. "It is too bad he waited so long to think of me," he said sharply. "It would have been nice to know I had a father who cared when I was young."

"My son," Mme Tran said disapprovingly.

Tory thought she understood. She, too, had been angry when her father had finally told her about Dinh. "It must have been very difficult for you," she said softly, "not having a father as you grew up."

Dinh's jaw worked methodically. He glanced at his mother. "It was difficult for my mother. For me, my father did not exist. He still does not."

"But he's ill," Tory said. "He had a stroke a couple years ago. He speaks of you all the time now. He is getting old, Dinh, and he wishes to see you. That's why I came."

Dinh's eyes contained fire. "Old men must learn to live with the regrets of their youth. I have no pity for him, nor any love. He deserted my mother when I was born. He never cared for her. He used her, like a dog uses another dog, for ugly furtive coupling in the night."

"Dinh!" Mme Tran said, her cheeks filling with heat. "You must remember, I lay with your father for my pleasure. He did not use me. We cared for each other."

"He left you with his bastard son!" Dinh spat, eyes blazing. "He did not care enough to take his responsibility to you and his child seriously."

"He was from another land, my son," Mme Tran said gently. "Another country, where he had a wife already."

"Then all the more reason for his shame and yours. I will not be a partner in that shame."

Mme Tran closed her eyes, her face shimmering with pain. "My son, in war we do things we might not do at other times. You are too young to understand that, too young to see that rigid rules snap in two, like the stout young branches of a tree. In war, the gods give us supple rules that bend but do not break. It is their gift to us to make up for the pain we must suffer."

"You are saying that circumstances change what is right and wrong," Dinh said, his head held high, his eyes still blazing with righteousness. "I love you, my mother, with all my heart, and I forgive you, but I cannot forgive the man who fathered me."

"Your father would like to see you now. It is up to you, of course, if you choose not to go to America."

Dinh lit up another cigarette. He was recovering his aplomb quickly. He looked at Tory. "You came here just to tell me this?"

"That's right," she said, holding out a gift to him from her father. "My father regrets so much that he never acknowledged you as a child. He has been eaten away by guilt and remorse. He wants to see you now, before he dies."

"I want nothing from him," Dinh said. "He would not give me his name, so I do not want his possessions."

Tory felt her heart go out to him. "I'm not sure what he wants to give you," she said gently, "except perhaps his love."

"Love?" Dinh said scornfully. "Was it love he felt when he abandoned my mother and me? Was it love he felt when he sent those checks? I think not. Guilt, perhaps, but not love." He stared at her through the haze of cigarette smoke. "He wants to buy peace of mind now. You see, I understand people very well. It is not love he wants to give, but forgiveness he wishes to receive."

"But doesn't the need for forgiveness imply love?" Tory asked softly. "If we didn't care for someone, what we've done to them wouldn't bother us and we wouldn't have to seek their forgiveness when we hurt them."

"I will not go," Dinh said sharply. "If he loved me, he would have come before, a long time ago."

"He was a soldier, Dinh," Tory said quietly. "He couldn't come back then. And when he retired, he had a stroke. He told me just a while ago how he had intended all along coming back here when he retired. The stroke stopped him from coming."

"He could have made time when he was still a soldier." He sneered at Tory. "The U.S. was not in a war plundering a foreign country *all* these past twenty years."

"Dinh," his mother said reprovingly, "the Americans were here to help us."

"But they succeeded only in hurting us," he said. "They were the imperialist army, interfering in a civil war. The business of foreign countries is not their business. They think they are giants, that because of their military strength they can go anywhere and impose their will." He blew out a stream of smoke. "They would do well to heed the lessons the Vietnamese taught them—that they must leave other nations to fight their own wars."

"Dinh," Mme Tran said, "no one escaped free from that war. Not the people nor the soldiers, on any side. The war memorials in both our countries show that."

"Are you taking his side, then?" Dinh demanded of his mother irately.

"I am not taking sides," his mother said gently. "I am asking only that you open your heart. It is time for forgiveness, Dinh, not hatred."

"But hatred is what I feel!" Dinh said, stabbing out his cigarette. "I will not go to see the old man, even if he is my father. You tell him that," he said to Tory. "You tell him," he said again, then turned and left the room.

Everyone was silent, then Mme Tran spoke: "My son is still very young. He carries in his heart much pain. I would ask that you try to understand what he feels, and not condemn him. He will learn as he gets older, but now..." She shrugged lightly. "He is too young, too filled with bitterness and pain. Give him time."

"But time may be just what my father doesn't have," Tory said, stricken by Dinh's harsh words.

Mme Tran met her gaze evenly. "In life, we all make choices, and then we must live with them. Your father came to realize very late that his son meant something to him. It is sad, but perhaps he must bear this pain. We all bear pain, after all. It is the way of life. Each of us is put here on earth to learn lessons. Sometimes the lessons are very hard."

McQuade nodded to himself, acknowledging that sometimes the lessons were very hard indeed. He wished he could get up and find the boy and bring him back, reason with him, but he knew that wouldn't work. The boy had to work things out for himself. It seemed that life was a series of tragic events that wove in and out of the tapestry that made up each succeeding generation's experience. Mme Tran had her tragedies, the general his, and McQuade had had his. Even Tory was touched by the events of the past. No one was untouched by these tragedies of life. Perhaps the only resolution lay in learning to accept them and get on with life.

He reached out and took Tory's hand. "Mme Tran is right. Give the boy time. Let him work it out for himself. Perhaps in time he'll understand and agree to visit your father."

"But it may be too late then," Tory said.

"Yes," McQuade said, nodding. "It may be."

She sat and digested his words, pain radiating inside her. Why did it have to be like this? She had wanted only to please her father and now she would fail. She would have to go home without his son, and she didn't think she could bear the pain that would cause her father. She wanted to scream at the God who had done this to her, to rage at the moon. She had wanted only good, and instead there was only more pain. Why was the world filled with nothing but frustrated hopes and dashed dreams? She felt impotent. She couldn't even give to her father the one thing he wanted most in all the world.

Tears glittered in her eyes as she contemplated the failure of her mission. "My father will be devastated," she said, forcing herself not to cry. "I came over here wanting only to bring back my father's son because that's the only thing Dad wants in life. But I can't do it for him. I can't give him the one thing he truly wants."

"Life is very painful," Mme Tran said gently. "All of us find out at some time that we cannot make the world the way we want it to be. Some of us fight that knowledge all our lives, struggling to change things, fighting the world, fighting everyone, angry and bitter and filled with discontent. But some of us learn to accept. We let go of the struggle and let the world be the way it is. There is a pattern here, a strangely beautiful pattern that we are too close to see, too close to appreciate. As we grow older, if we are lucky, we can look back and begin to discern the pattern over which we had no control, but which is so very, very beautiful, since it is the work of the gods." Mme Tran smiled gently. "My son is doing the hard work now, just as we all have to do. I can only pray that with time he will be able to forgive his father. I can only hope it will not be too late. But that is not up to me or you or even your father. It is ultimately up to the gods. And Dinh, of course."

"You seem so accepting," Tory said.

"I have struggled," Mme Tran said, smiling, "so I know what you are feeling. But I have been lucky; I have learned to let go."

Tory looked at McQuade, understanding even better now what he had been feeling. "It seems we all have to learn that."

McQuade shook her hand. "I think it's the hardest lesson in the world," he said. "The one we struggle most with."

"Tory," Mme Tran said, "may I call you that?"

"Of course," Tory said. She was surprised how much she liked this woman. She had thought she would hate her out of sheer loyalty to her mother, but she didn't hate her at all.

"You must go home to your father and tell him what happened. It will be painful for both you and for him, but that is the way of life. The person who runs from pain runs from life itself. Now," she said, holding out two slender boxes. "I have these presents for you. You must open them and forget what has happened with Dinh. In the midst of pain, the only recourse is joy."

Tory took the boxes reluctantly. How could Mme Tran speak of joy when she felt as if everything in her life had fallen apart? She glanced at the woman, wishing she could give back the presents, but Mme Tran gestured for her to open them.

She stared down at the first box, then forced herself to open it. Inside was a magnificent silk scarf. She looked up at Mme Tran, enchanted. "It's beautiful," she breathed. "Simply beautiful."

"The other present is perhaps even nicer," she said, nodding to the other box.

She opened the box and sat staring down at the contents. It was a photograph of Dinh, standing by the fireplace, looking handsome in a dark tuxedo.

"Please give it to your father," Mme Tran said. "And tell him that I hope he is well."

"Thank you," Tory said, tears shimmering in her eyes. "Thank you so much."

"Perhaps some day he will see his son in person. We will pray for that, both of us, yes?"

Tory nodded, feeling her heart open completely to this marvelous woman. "Yes."

She stood up and extended her hand, but Mme Tran opened her arms and embraced Tory. "My child, I am so very happy that we have met. Perhaps some day we will meet again, eh?"

"Perhaps," whispered Tory, tears shimmering in her eyes. "I would like that very much."

But she had the sudden intuition that she would never see this woman again, and she felt a sweeping sense of loss, as if she had seen for the first time that life requires faith and trust and hope, yet offers little to support any of those feelings. Indeed, it suddenly seemed that life was a process of finding something only to lose it, often in the space of a single day.

Chapter Sixteen

They flew back to Massachusetts the next day, Friday, leaving Ho Chi Minh City at noon in a downpour. When they landed in Boston, it was midnight on Thursday, and hot and humid, a typical muggy New England night, though a breeze blew in off Boston harbor, cooling the airport somewhat.

"Are you awake enough to fly back?" Tory asked McQuade as they stepped outside the almost deserted terminal.

"I'll manage," he said. "Can you get a cab home at this hour?"

She searched his face. Was this goodbye, then? Would he leave her here at Logan Airport and fly out of her life forever? She didn't think she could bear that, but didn't know how she could stop him. "I was hoping you'd want me to go back with you," she said.

His eyes flickered away. He looked around, appearing suddenly uncomfortable. "I've got things to do, Tory."

She stared at him, angry at the way he was trying to sneak away. "Don't do this, McQuade," she said. "Don't run away again."

His jaw worked as he seemed to fight with himself. At last he said, "Look, I can't make any promises, Tory."

"I didn't say I wanted promises," she said, anger vibrating in her words. "I just want a chance. That's all, that's all any of us get, a chance to try to make things work."

"Look, I'm a poor risk, Tory. What happened in Vietnam was wonderful. I'll never forget you. You're a very special woman, but we're back home now and things are different."

"They're only different because you think they are," she said, her voice shaking. "Damn you, why won't you take the risk and *try?*"

"Because the stakes are higher for me, Tory," he said, his voice taut with suppressed anger. "What did you think would happen? That I'd go to Vietnam and have some sort of epiphany and come back with everything all tied up in a neat pink bow? Dammit, it doesn't work that way, Tory. Life isn't neat, okay? It isn't even pretty. It's damn hard, and right now I don't know who the hell I am, much less who you want me to be."

"I don't want you to be anyone but yourself!" she said, her voice filled with urgency. Damn him, she had to make him understand. Couldn't he see that she cared about him? Cared? Dammit, she loved him! Couldn't he see that? Didn't it matter to him?

"Then let me be who I am," he almost shouted, a muscle working spasmodically in his jaw. "Don't expect anything from me, okay? Don't ask for anything from me. Just let me *be.*"

She felt tears threaten and she willed them away, blinking them back, her gaze fastened on McQuade. "I love you," she said, and her voice contained all the feeling and need and pain that filled her. "I *love* you, John McQuade."

He looked away, as if she'd said the exact opposite of what he'd wanted to hear. "I'm sorry, but I can't say that. I don't even know what I feel. I need time, Tory. I need to be by myself and figure things out."

The tears wouldn't stay inside any longer; they fell from her eyes, trailing down her cheeks, but she didn't even feel them. She felt as if her heart was growing inside her, swelling with pain until it seemed as if her chest would burst and she would die from everything she felt.

Damn him, she had been there for him in Vietnam, and now when she needed him so desperately he was turning his back on her.

"Fine," she said, her voice strangled on her tears. "Just walk away. Run if you have to. I don't care. I don't care, do you hear me?" She scrubbed the tears from her face and turned away, running back into the bright lights of the terminal, her footsteps echoing in its deserted halls.

McQuade watched her go and felt a sinking sensation in his chest, as if he'd just pushed away the only person who had ever really understood him, but he couldn't stop himself. He needed time to be alone, time to sort out everything that had happened. What had she expected? That he'd take her in his arms and they'd fly off into the night with all problems resolved to live happily ever after? He'd never lived happily in his life. How did she expect him to start now?

Feeling utterly dejected, his shoulders sagging tiredly, he turned and walked toward the hangar where he'd left his plane.

THE NEXT MORNING McQuade lay in bed in his cottage, listening to the surf rolling up on the beach. Gulls squawked cheerfully and the wind blew the wind chimes that Tory had bought McQuade in Vietnam. He had unpacked them last night and hung them in the open window and now they tinkled merrily in the gentle breeze which carried the salty scent of ocean air.

Instead of feeling at home, he felt strangely ill-at-ease. For the past three nights, he and Tory had slept together. He remembered now, with a rush, the feel of her body next to his, the way she smelled, the delicious touch of her, the strength of her long legs as she wrapped them around him, arching her hips under him, begging him to empty himself inside her.

Groaning, he sat up and looked around. Nothing had changed, yet everything had. The cottage that had been his home so long seemed bare, unfriendly, like a cheap motel room rented for a night.

He got up and began to dress and his eyes fell on the inlaid box Mme Tran had given him. He ran a hand over it lightly, admiring the gleam of the wood. He did a little woodworking himself, so the box appealed to him. It had obviously been made by a craftsman.

Taking it back to the bed, he sat down and opened it. He took out one of the dueling pistols and held it in his hand, hefting it to feel the weight, looking down the sights. He put it down and took out the other pistol and bent to examine the box.

He held it up and ran his fingers over it, admiring the workmanship, then he frowned. Why did the box seem so much deeper on the outside than in the gun compartment? Idly he ran his hands over the velvet-covered bottom inside the box. It was interesting to see how it was put together. The sides were dovetailed. To his amazement, when he pushed on one of the legs the velvet-covered bottom in the gun compartment suddenly sprang open.

"Hey," he said out loud. "What the . . . ?"

He carefully lifted the velvet bottom, then stared. A small velvet bag with a golden cord sat in the bottom, nestled in faded tissue paper. He drew out the bag and opened it. "Good God," he said, dumbstruck. "It's the diamonds."

They sat in the bag, a couple dozen of them, winking in the morning light, gleaming like a million prisms.

"Lord," he whispered. "They were in here all along." He picked up a handful of diamonds and let them sift through his fingers, then lifted his head. It came to him suddenly, like a sudden shot heard in the night: Mme Tran had known all along. This was what she'd been hinting at when she gave him the box. She had wanted him to have the diamonds, hoping he would have a better life with them than she had.

He emptied the diamonds out of the bag into the velvet-lined box and stared down at them. He had no idea what they were worth but knew it was probably a small fortune.

He sat on his bed and slowly felt the impact of his discovery all the way through his body. He wouldn't have to worry anymore about making ends meet. He'd have no more financial troubles. He could buy another plane and hire another pilot. He could expand. Why, he could even hire a secretary and bookkeeper...

Then he remembered Mme Tran's words: *"Happiness is listening to the bird, not owning it...."*

He looked around his cottage and knew he could now afford almost anything, but would financial security and money in the bank bring him the happiness he longed for, any more than it had for Mme Tran?

Empty. That's what his life was. And would it be any less empty if he filled it with possessions? Would a new plane and another pilot bring him what he longed for? Would they ease the emptiness in his soul?

He sat and pondered the fate that had brought him the promise of material comfort but left his soul friendless. Even with money he was a wreck of a man, too afraid to reach out and take the one thing he truly wanted.

He thought of Tory and his heart ached with pain. Would she even want him if he went to her now? Hadn't she raced off into the night in tears, claiming she didn't care about him?

He bowed his head and wondered why he had even gone to Vietnam. It seemed now he had just exchanged one source of pain for another. He had said goodbye to Mai only to come home and lose Tory. Or had he lost her?

He lifted his head and remembered her words: "I didn't say I wanted promises! I just want a chance."

And he had turned away from her, left her exactly the way he'd left Mai...

The realization struck him like a blow. He reeled under the shock of it, feeling sick in his soul.

"God," he begged, "just give me another chance. Please, give me a chance."

He began to dress, pulling on his clothes with shaking hands. Please, he prayed, don't let me be too late.

TORY DROVE THE YELLOW Jaguar without thinking. She had made this drive to her father's home so often, she felt as if she could put the car in drive and it would automatically head for her father's place without her doing another thing.

She had a monster of a headache. Jet lag was part of it, but she knew most of it was the realization that she had to tell her father that his son refused to see him. She didn't even want to think about McQuade. Her heart felt heavy as a stone in her breast. There was no joy in her as she relentlessly pressed the accelerator to the floor, only a dead, gray feeling of failure. She had failed on her quest for her father, and she had failed to win the man she'd fallen in love with. McQuade had simply turned and walked out of her life last night. She didn't even know if she'd see him again.

Her temples thudded with pain as she tried to push all thoughts of McQuade out of her mind. She needed to figure out what she'd say to her father, needed to prepare for the harsh criticisms he'd heap on her when he found out she had failed.

When the wrought-iron gates of her father's estate loomed up ahead of her, she still hadn't prepared a speech. Tears glistened in her eyes as she spied a thin line of smoke curling up from the central chimney. It was July and still her father needed the warmth of a fire. How much colder and older would he feel when he found out she hadn't brought him his son?

She pulled the car to a stop and sat looking at the impressive front door, unable to confront her father yet. She needed time to gather her wits, to steel herself against the inevitable wrath that would greet her news.

She probably should be used to her father's incessant harping on her failures, but she wasn't. Every fresh assault was as bad as the first, when she was still a child and he had pounced on her every mistake, no matter now infinitesimal. He had berated her for every *B* she had ever made in school, for not becoming a National Merit Scholar, for not being chosen by her college's best sorority. He had belittled her choice of husband, so that eventually Barry Britton had left, unable to stand the constant criticism and sniping by her father.

Yet she loved him. Every criticism, every disparagement, every time he belittled her attempts to learn a new sport or try out a new hobby, all only made her need his love even more. She yearned for his acceptance and approval, longed for him to say, just once, "You have done well, my child." But the praise and approval she thirsted for had never been forthcoming.

And now, at the end of his life, when age and illness had debilitated him, when he longed for only one thing, she had failed yet again. She sat in the car and felt hot tears fall down her face. She felt as if she had never done anything right in her life, had always failed, would always fail. Hurt radiated inside her like pain from a toothache, filling her with an agony she thought she wouldn't be able to stand.

But she had to stand it. She had to dry her eyes and get out of the car and face her father yet again, empty-handed. But if her hands were empty, her heart was full. If only he could see the love that filled her, if only he could understand that she would do anything for him, even if he never praised her, never once told her he loved her. Her heart was bursting with pain as she got out of the car.

Then she faltered. Up above, a silver plane was circling, swooping out of the blue summer sky and heading for the open field adjacent to the manicured grounds of her father's estate. Suddenly her heart rose. She shaded her eyes and strained to read the writing on the side of the plane. While the writing was too small to make out, she recognized the target painted on the side. Only one plane carried that target—Tough Luck Airlines.

She felt her hopes soar and then she was running, racing across the velvet-green lawn toward the field where the small plane was bumping to a stop, flinging off her pocketbook and cares, running, stumbling, laughing, tears falling down her face. It was McQuade. Nothing else mattered. It was McQuade.

She ran into his arms and buried her head in his chest, holding him as if she'd never let him go, crying, laughing, sobbing out his name.

He stroked her hair back from her face and covered her with kisses. "It's all right," he crooned. "It's all right."

She lifted her head and gazed into his eyes. "Why did you come?"

He seemed unable to answer. He stood and searched her face, and said, "I just wanted to be with you, that's all."

It was enough. It was all she needed, to have him with her, to know he hadn't walked out on her, to know he was here for her when she needed him most.

"Have you talked to your father yet?" he asked.

She shook her head. "Not yet. I've been sitting in my car, trying to gather my courage."

McQuade looked down at her, his face filled with regret. "I'm sorry I left you like that last night. You were there for me every minute in Vietnam, and I repaid you by walking out on you."

"It's okay," she breathed. "You're here now. That's all that matters."

"Then it does matter that I'm here for you," he said.

"More than anything," she said. "I need you so much, McQuade. I'm afraid what my father will say, how he'll react. I feel like such a failure..."

"No," he said, cupping her cheek in his palm. "Never. You did everything you could and more. Your father will understand."

"He may not," she said, wishing he would, hoping he would, but afraid to believe he would. Experience had taught her that her father was a hard taskmaster, an unforgiving man who expected perfection but never rewarded it even when she achieved it.

McQuade drew her into his arms and cradled her against his chest. "This time I think he'll understand," he said. "If he doesn't, we'll make him."

Tory laughed uneasily. "I thought you knew my father, Cargo McQuade. I thought you worked for him awhile."

"But that was the man he used to be. Remember the letter he sent you, Tory. When you talk to him, talk to that man, the one you never knew before."

"Yes," she breathed, "the letter..."

And suddenly she felt her hopes rise. Perhaps she couldn't give her father his only son, but she could give him her love. Perhaps if she understood her father more, he would understand her, too. Perhaps to be received, love has to be offered first. Perhaps she had spent all her life wanting her father's love, but not truly loving him without thought for herself, freely, asking nothing in return.

She squared her shoulders and remembered the letter her father had sent and then she felt it break inside her, a great rush of compassion for her father. She had been so busy worrying that she had failed to do what her father wanted, that she'd forgotten how her father would feel. And then she knew that he needed her love and compassion as he had never needed it before.

She looked up at McQuade, gratitude shining in her eyes. "Thanks for being here. You put things in perspective for me."

"Do you want to talk to your father alone? I could wait out here for you."

"No, please, come in. You make me feel stronger just by being with me."

He put an arm around her shoulders and they walked back toward the house.

INSIDE THE HOUSE the general sat in his wheelchair at the window of his study, his eyes filled with tears as he watched them walk together toward him. Maybe not everything had gone as he had hoped, but at least things looked promising between his daughter and McQuade. Perhaps he'd sent Tory to Vietnam with McQuade not so much to bring back his son, whom he supposed he'd lost a long time ago, but rather for her sake and McQuade's.

He had made a lot of mistakes in his life, not the least of which had been his apparent harshness to his daughter. He supposed she'd have a hard time believing it, but he'd done everything for her because he loved her so much and wanted her to learn to go for the best, to achieve more than she even thought she ever could, to reach for the stars and not settle for dust on the ground.

But he had used techniques more properly used in the army, been more a drill sergeant, he supposed, than a loving, supportive father. He wondered if he could ever undo the damage he might have done. He sighed and lifted a trembling hand to his eyes, dashing the tears away. It wouldn't do to let them find him looking weak. It wouldn't do at all.

TORY SMILED AT THE NURSE who cared for her father and inquired how he was.

"He's fine, Miss Britton," the woman said. "A little on the down side, but I expect he'll be feeling much better now that you're here."

Tory felt a flutter of apprehension. If her father had been feeling depressed, how would he feel now that she'd come back with bad news? She glanced at McQuade, as if by just looking at him her spirits would be revived, then opened the door to her father's study.

He was bent over a book in front of the fireplace, seemingly oblivious that she and McQuade were here.

"Dad?"

He looked up, startled, and then he smiled, his face suddenly filled with expectation. "Tory! You're back." He held out his hands to her and she rushed to him and enfolded him in her arms.

"Oh, Daddy, it's so good to see you."

He patted her back awkwardly. "It's good to see you, too, child." His eyes went to McQuade, who stood in the background, near the door. "Come in, McQuade. Come in, don't be shy, man."

"General," McQuade said, shaking the general's hand. "It's good to see you looking so well."

"Yes, well, it's that damned nurse. She feeds me night and day. Trying to put weight on me, she says." He harrumphed and turned his wheelchair so he faced away from the fire. "So tell me, how was the trip?"

"It was extraordinary, really," Tory said gently, sinking into a chair facing her father. "We were able to meet Mme Tran and Dinh..."

"Dinh, yes, that's his name. How was he? And Mme Tran, is she well?"

"She's fine. She's the most amazing woman and still so very beautiful. She was just so nice to us, so gentle and welcoming."

The general smiled and nodded. "She was quite a woman even twenty years ago. I imagine now she's stunning. Experience, you know. It makes some women and breaks others. Her, I'd expect it would only make her stronger." He gazed into space, then looked at Tory. "And the boy? How is he?"

"He's tall and strong and very handsome," Tory said, drawing something from her pocketbook. "I have a picture of him for you. Mme Tran wanted you to have it."

With trembling hands, the general reached out and took the photograph, then sat staring down at it, eyes filled with tears, feeling pride burst inside him. "My God, he's a fine-looking man," he said, his voice shaking. "Just fine-looking."

Tory's eyes misted with tears. "You can be very proud of him, Daddy."

"Yes," he said, nodding once, still staring down at the photo, his hands trembling, his lips moving with emotion. "Yes." He nodded again, once, a sharp movement of his head, looking like a tiny bird, querulous and surprised.

"Yes," he said again, his eyes still on the photograph. At last he looked up. "Well, is he coming to see me?"

Tory's heart went out to him. Never had she seen her father so vulnerable. He was old and weak and she wished she could put her arms around him and give him everything he had ever wanted in his life. "It may take time, Daddy," she said gently.

He nodded again, that same sharp movement of the head, then he fumbled with the photograph, holding it up to the light. "Stubborn like me, eh?"

Tory smiled softly. "Yes. He's very much your son."

His fingers fluttered on the photograph frame and he nodded. "Wouldn't have wanted a son who was a namby-pamby. No, sir. I'm glad he's got some spunk to him."

She had never loved her father more than she did at that moment, had never been more proud of him, of his courage and pride. Her eyes filled with tears and she couldn't sit there any longer. She got up and went to him, knelt by his chair, and put her arms around him.

"I love you so much, Daddy," she said, tears running down her cheeks. "I've loved you all my life, but I have never loved you more than I do right now, at this very moment. I'm so very proud of you. I wish I could have brought Dinh back to you more than anything on earth, but I couldn't, Daddy. I hope you understand."

Her father released the photograph and put his arm around her, bending to place his cheek on the top of her head. "I love you too, honey. Always have. Never showed it much, but I've always been so proud of you. You're everything a father could ever want in a daughter. I'm sorry Dinh wouldn't come see me, but maybe in time he will, eh?"

She nodded, her face shining as she looked up into her father's face, at last hearing the words she'd waited all her life to hear. "Oh, Daddy," she said, tears falling down her face. "I'm so glad you're all right. When I was in Vietnam and read your letter I wanted to come right home and just put my arms around you and hold you. It was such a beautiful letter, Daddy. I'll always treasure it, the way I treasure you."

The old man fought to contain his tears but they escaped his control and ran down his face. He patted Tory's back a couple times, then sat back. "Ha! Look at me! Crying like a pup." He wiped his eyes and made a fuss over placing the photograph on the mantel.

"You put it up there, Tory, next to your picture. Then get me my cane. I want to show you something."

When she had placed the photograph on the mantel, she looked around and discovered her father's cane.

He took it from her and pounded it on the floor a couple of times. "Help me up, damn it," he ordered.

She looked at him, her heart swelling with love. "Do you mean to say you're going to try to walk?"

"Hell, I've been walking the whole time you were gone, running all over that damn fool Vietnam. I'll show you. Just help me up."

Watching them, McQuade felt his throat close up with emotion. He'd never known a loving family, had left home as soon as he could and gone to war and there had lost everything that had ever mattered to him. For twenty years he'd lived in his own personal hell, isolated and alone, drifting on the fringes of life. He wished more than anything he could join in the joyful time that Tory was having with her father, but he couldn't. He'd lived too long alone. Maybe in time he'd learn to be easy in company, but for now he just itched to get up in the sky again, soaring over it all. The sky was his only home, his plane his only comfort. Even while he longed for Tory, he couldn't reach out to her. The habit of solitude was still too comfortable. Hope was too new, too tentative.

"Told you I could walk," the general growled. "Now pour me a drink, McQuade, and something for yourself and Tory. Stay for dinner."

"I'm sorry, but I can't stay," McQuade said, rising from his chair and trying not to see the disappointment that flooded Tory's expressive face.

"But—" She looked at him, her eyes filled with pleading. "Please, stay. I want you to."

He looked away from her, unable to bear the disappointment in her eyes. "I'm sorry, but I can't. I have some things I need to do." He glanced at her hurriedly. "Maybe you could walk to the plane with me."

"Of course," she said, her voice quiet, her eyes serious. "Dad, I'll be right back."

They walked together across the lawn toward McQuade's plane. The sun was beginning to lower in the afternoon sky and a breeze blew Tory's hair back and whipped her skirt around her legs. At the plane, McQuade looked at her, frown lines deep in his forehead.

"I'm sorry I'm disappointing you. I don't want to, but I have some things I need to do."

"When will I see you again?"

He rubbed his chin. "I'm not sure."

She looked straight into his eyes, not letting him look away. "When will you call me?"

He hesitated. "I don't know."

She felt her heart begin to ache. "Don't you care for me at all?" she whispered, her eyes pleading with him.

He looked at her and couldn't stand it. With a hoarse cry, he took her in his arms and kissed her, kissed her as if she was the last woman on earth and he the last man, kissed her with desperation and despair, afraid to let her go, yet equally afraid to stay.

"I care so much I ache inside," he said at last when he was able to take his mouth from hers. "It's just that I have to take it slow, Tory. I can't rush into anything. So much has happened. Things I haven't even told you about. Give me some time. That's all I need, just a little time to sort things out."

She felt love blossom inside her, rising up like a dove, radiant in celestial light. "I'd give you anything you wanted if I could," she whispered. "If time is what you want, I'll give you that. Just please don't leave me. I love you, John. My life would be empty without you. It would have no meaning."

He put his arms around her and hugged her to him, this dear, wonderful woman he'd stumbled on by some amazing quirk of fate. "I love you, too," he said, feeling hope rise inside him—shaky, fearful hope, too new to be sure about. "I love you so much I'm scared. Maybe the things that happened to me will leave scars forever. Maybe I'll never be able to have the kind of life other people have."

She looked at him and heard Mme Tran's words echoing in the quiet air: *"Happiness is listening to the bird, not owning it . . ."*

She loved him enough, she realized, to give him his freedom, to give him time. "Then go," she said. "But every day I'll pray that you come back to me."

He stared at her, confusion in his face. "See, I have to call this nun . . ."

She frowned. "A nun?"

"Yes, she called a while back, needing some help, but I refused her. I have to call her. Sister Theresa her name is. She and the other nuns have an island off Woods Hole. They need someone to fly some kids out there on weekends. This is very important to me, Tory. I have to help her. I don't know if you can understand, but it means so much to me to be able to help her."

Little by little, Tory's face changed. Joy came quietly, slowly, until her face was shining and she was smiling up at him. "Then call her. Just don't forget to call me."

He looked at her and he knew he couldn't leave her, couldn't fly away. He put his arm around her. "Come on," he said, walking with her toward her father's house. "Maybe I can call Sister Theresa from here. And I suppose we'll have to break it to your father."

"Break what to my father?" she asked, so filled with joy she could hardly think.

"About us," he answered, beginning to grin. "If he disapproved of Daniel Sullivan, what's he going to say about me?"

Laughing, she went up on tiptoe and threw her arms around him. "I don't care what he says. I don't give a dimpled damn. I love you, John McQuade. I love you."

From his window the general began to smile. Thank goodness. Things were finally beginning to turn out right.

This October, Harlequin offers you a second
two-in-one collection of romances

A SPECIAL
SOMETHING

THE FOREVER
INSTINCT

by the award-winning author,

Barbara Delinsky

Now, two of Barbara Delinsky's most loved books are
available together in this special edition that new and
longtime fans will want to add to their bookshelves.

Let Barbara Delinsky double your reading pleasure with
her memorable love stories, A SPECIAL SOMETHING and
THE FOREVER INSTINCT.

Available wherever Harlequin books are sold. TWO-D

H A R L E Q U I N

Romance

**This October,
travel to England with
Harlequin Romance
FIRST CLASS title #3155
TRAPPED
by Margaret Mayo**

"I'm my own boss now and I intend to stay that way."

Candra Drake loved her life of freedom on her narrow-boat
home and was determined to pursue her career as a company
secretary free from the influence of any domineering man.
Then enigmatic, arrogant Simeon Sterne breezed into her life,
forcing her to move and threatening a complete takeover of her
territory and her heart....

MILLION DOLLAR JACKPOT
SWEEPSTAKES RULES & REGULATIONS
NO PURCHASE NECESSARY TO ENTER OR RECEIVE A PRIZE

1. Alternate means of entry: Print your name and address on a 3" ×5" piece of plain paper and send to the appropriate address below.

In the U.S.	In Canada
MILLION DOLLAR JACKPOT	MILLION DOLLAR JACKPOT
P.O. Box 1867	P.O. Box 609
3010 Walden Avenue	Fort Erie, Ontario
Buffalo, NY 14269-1867	L2A 5X3

2. To enter the Sweepstakes and join the Reader Service, check off the "YES" box on your Sweepstakes Entry Form and return. If you do not wish to join the Reader Service but wish to enter the Sweepstakes only, check off the "NO" box on your Sweepstakes Entry Form. To qualify for the Extra Bonus prize, scratch off the silver on your Lucky Keys. If the registration numbers match, you are eligible for the Extra Bonus Prize offering. Incomplete entries are ineligible. Torstar Corp. and its affiliates are not responsible for mutilated or unreadable entries or inadvertent printing errors. Mechanically reproduced entries are null and void.

3. Whether you take advantage of this offer or not, on or about April 30, 1992, at the offices of D.L. Blair, Inc., Blair, NE, your sweepstakes numbers will be compared against the list of winning numbers generated at random by the computer. However, prizes will only be awarded to individuals who have entered the Sweepstakes. In the event that all prizes are not claimed, a random drawing will be held from all qualified entries received from March 30, 1990 to March 31, 1992, to award all unclaimed prizes. All cash prizes (Grand to Sixth) will be mailed to winners and are payable by check in U.S. funds. Seventh Prize will be shipped to winners via third-class mail. These prizes are in addition to any free, surprise or mystery gifts that might be offered. Versions of this Sweepstakes with different prizes of approximate equal value may appear at retail outlets or in other mailings by Torstar Corp. and its affiliates.

4. PRIZES: (1) *Grand Prize $1,000,000.00 Annuity; (1) First Prize $25,000.00; (1) Second Prize $10,000.00; (5) Third Prize $5,000.00; (10) Fourth Prize $1,000.00; (100) Fifth Prize $250.00; (2,500) Sixth Prize $10.00; (6,000) **Seventh Prize $12.95 ARV.

   *This presentation offers a Grand Prize of a $1,000,000.00 annuity. Winner will receive $33,333.33 a year for 30 years without interest totalling $1,000,000.00.

   **Seventh Prize: A fully illustrated hardcover book, published by Torstar Corp. Approximate Retail Value of the book is $12.95.

   Entrants may cancel the Reader Service at any time without cost or obligation (see details in Center Insert Card).

5. Extra Bonus! This presentation offers an Extra Bonus Prize valued at $33,000.00 to be awarded in a random drawing from all qualified entries received by March 31, 1992. No purchase necessary to enter or receive a prize. To qualify, see instructions in Center Insert Card. Winner will have the choice of any of the merchandise offered or a $33,000.00 check payable in U.S. funds. All other published rules and regulations apply.

6. This Sweepstakes is being conducted under the supervision of D.L. Blair, Inc. By entering the Sweepstakes, each entrant accepts and agrees to be bound by these rules and the decisions of the judges, which shall be final and binding. Odds of winning the random drawing are dependent upon the number of entries received. Taxes, if any, are the sole responsibility of the winners. Prizes are nontransferable. All entries must be received at the address on the detachable Business Reply Card and must be postmarked no later than 12:00 MIDNIGHT on March 31, 1992. The drawing for all unclaimed Sweepstakes prizes and for the Extra Bonus Prize will take place on May 30, 1992, at 12:00 NOON at the offices of D.L. Blair, Inc., Blair, NE.

7. This offer is open to residents of the U.S., United Kingdom, France and Canada, 18 years or older, except employees and immediate family members of Torstar Corp., its affiliates, subsidiaries and all other agencies, entities and persons connected with the use, marketing or conduct of this Sweepstakes. All Federal, State, Provincial, Municipal and local laws apply. Void wherever prohibited or restricted by law. Any litigation within the Province of Quebec respecting the conduct and awarding of a prize in this publicity contest must be submitted to the Régie des Loteries et Courses du Québec.

8. Winners will be notified by mail and may be required to execute an affidavit of eligibility and release, which must be returned within 14 days after notification or an alternate winner may be selected. Canadian winners will be required to correctly answer an arithmetical, skill-testing question administered by mail, which must be returned within a limited time. Winners consent to the use of their name, photograph and/or likeness for advertising and publicity in conjunction with this and similar promotions without additional compensation.

9. For a list of our major prize winners, send a stamped, self-addressed envelope to: MILLION DOLLAR WINNERS LIST, P.O. Box 4510, Blair, NE 68009. Winners Lists will be supplied after the May 30, 1992 drawing date.

Offer limited to one per household.

LTY-H891